BOOK ONE OF THE
REMNANT OF CHAOS SERIES

REMNANT
OF CHAOS

B. STORM

CONTENTS

PROLOGUE

In a place that exists between time and space, there is a floating island over a sinister nothingness. It serves as more of a large platform than a proper island. The structure is battered and broken. Pillars attempted to sprout from its surface, but the overpowering presence of the Void tore them apart. Rubble swirls in the air even though no wind is present. This isle calls the deepest reaches of the Void its home. Very few would be lucky enough to reach this place with their lives still intact.

It is not a land of death, nor is it a land of life. It is a place where nothingness has managed to take root. Just the mere graze of any foreign object and it will be erased from reality. The Void is most unforgiving.

At the center of this island over nothingness is a single demon. She is sitting cross- legged with her eyes closed tight. She is calm, almost in a state of meditation. She is an elderly, feminine demon. Her skin is crackly gray, her hair hanging limply from her head. Despite her hair being a mess, she shows little concern for it. Her horns reach upwards, barely containing her wild gray hair. She sensed that a man was entering her realm, and her calm state felt threatened as she realized who it was.

He appeared in a burst of shadow. He is a tall, burly man, cloaked in black armor. He is bald with fiery red eyes. Beneath his bottom lip, there is a goatee that forms a simple line. He wore a ragged cloak around his neck, and spikes were protruding from his shoulder pieces. Once he struck fear into all manner of creatures across this very universe. But now he is just a husk of what he once was. His power still far surpasses most creatures he would come across, but the demon sitting in front of him is an exception. He sensed no fear from her, a scary thought for sure.

The feminine demon opened her eyes and gazed up at him with yellow eyes that seemed to be withering away. Being trapped in a place like this was a cruel consequence.

"Chaosbringer," she stated. "Why are you here?"

"I think you know why I am here," the Chaosbringer said.

"You wish for another prophecy?"

"I don't wish for one. But I have seen just how real your prophecies can be. I need to know what is to come."

"You see what happens when you don't trust me?" she asked. "You're scared. I can hear the fear in your voice."

The armored man cleared his throat before balling his hands into fists.

"Listen, Seer," he growled. "Remember who you're talking to. I'm not here for your judgment. However, if the information from your next prophecy proves to be fruitful, then maybe I will consider freeing you from this place."

She chuckled. "There is always just **one** more prophecy."

"What does that even mean?" he asked.

"Don't worry your simple mind over it."

The Chaosbringer could feel it. His anger was beginning to spike. Still, he needed to keep his cool. He needed the information that she possessed. That only she could provide.

"Just tell me what you have seen, Seer," he demanded. "I only hope that for your sake it is a fate that can be avoided. Your last prediction brought about the end of the great demon deity. The only one fit to rule this universe."

"You truly think Chaos was the greatest being in this world?" she asked.

"Enough of your fucking riddles!" he shouted. "Don't forget the Void always hungers for more! Maybe I will give it another snack to appease its appetite!"

"I know very well the ways of the Void, Chaosbringer," she responded, unfazed. "Very well. Before you threaten me again, however, remember you are just a small part of what you once were. If I wished it, even **I** could destroy you."

"You speak too much, old bitch."

She chuckled and placed her hands neatly onto the cold, cracked ground next to her. "Let us begin."

Her back arched forward into what looked like quite an uncomfortable position, and her eyes rolled into the back of her head. Then she released a shriek that pierced the very air as the spirits engulfed her body. All the swirling rubble stopped moving in place. It seemed as if time itself had stopped all around them. The old demon rocked wildly in front of him. He wasn't sure if he should shake her awake, but then she spoke.

"Our Lord Barbatos will fall." She proclaimed. She spoke as if the many spirits all tried to speak at once. "All by the hand of one bearing the title of Darsetts. The spirits have spoken."

Then she slunk back down into her cross-legged position. This seemed to be her place of comfort. Then all the rubble seemed to come back to life and continued swirling in the air around them.

"That's it?" the Chaosbringer asked. "That's the great prophecy that I came all the way down to this shithole for?"

She looked up at him unblinking and unconcerned. "You wanted a prophecy. I gave you one."

"So, you're telling me that Michael hasn't had enough. After killing the great deity, Chaos, will he kill our king as well?"

"Maybe it could be the other one," she suggested.

"**Other** one? You mean there's more than one of them?"

"In this world maybe," she chuckled.

"Enough of your games," he snarled. "Give me a straight fucking answer!"

"Look for the one named Roy Darsetts," she advised. "Then you will have the answers that you seek."

The Chaosbringer bent down and picked up a stone off the ground. In this place it gave off a vibrant purple glow. He knew that the glow would be dull once he left the Void, but the magic would still endure. This is a Void Stone. He could use his mind to have it display images. He knew that it would prove its usefulness soon enough. He knew it to be so based on how things were beginning to unfold.

"Anything else you need from me, servant of Chaos?" she asked him.

"Not from you," he replied. "It seems that your prophecy will keep me quite busy."

4

"Glad to help. I can only hope that my prophecy will help prevent another great tragedy. Maybe it could even help free me from this bleak prison."

"Your freedom will depend upon how reliable this prophecy of yours is," he declared. "If it's nothing more than pretty words, I can guarantee you will **never** leave this place."

"Only time will tell, it seems."

"I wouldn't rely on time as your ally, Seer," he warned. "Nothing will be able to save you from your fate."

"It matters not. I know of everyone's intertwining fates. Mine isn't any different."

"Of course you do," the Chaosbringer grumbled. Then he vanished in a puff of darkness, as if he had never even been there.

The elderly demon sighed. "I should probably let **him** know what is coming."

***

In an office on Earth, hidden away from prying eyes, a bald man in a suit sat behind a desk. His cellphone came to life in front of him. The face of an aged demon projected itself from the screen of his phone. The man wouldn't have believed it if not for seeing it for himself. Her face had twisted into a bright pixelated image floating in front of him.

He slid back from the desk, startled. He knew this was not a part of his current phone plan. Clearly something strange was happening. Something that couldn't be explained by technology.

"Who are you and why were you **in** my phone?" he asked, still in disbelief.

"You haven't heard of me?" she asked, clearly disappointed. "I'm pretty well known over here."

"I know at least you're some sort of demon," he noted. "Although I don't know how it is you were in my phone. Stranger yet, all the demons were supposed to be wiped out in the battle with Chaos."

"You really think that I would fight in that madness with a physical form? Are you insane?"

"I don't even know who you are," he said. "Who am I to judge your character?"

"I have had many names," the demon said, mulling over his question. "Being alive for centuries I have met all sorts of companions. Each of them decided to call me by different names. I will allow you to call me the Dark Messiah. Seems simple enough for a human to understand. I once served as Chaos' right hand. I find it surprising that you haven't heard of me. I am a demon that can see all the outcomes."

"So, what do you want?" the man asked her.

"I have used my magic to project myself from this device to warn you," she explained. "The one who calls himself Roy Darsetts will soon be in a great deal of danger. I need you and your organization to protect him. I know you pride yourselves on protecting mortals who know nothing of the supernatural threat. You hide yourselves in the shadows to keep the average human safe, and I must say you do excellent work.

"Just know that this Roy Darsetts is part of an important prophecy that involves the death of the Demon King, Barbatos. Tell anyone that you have left, that if you do this, it will help you all in your fight against your newest enemy. The Chaosbringer."

"How do you even know all of this?" he asked.

"I inhabit a place between time and space, mortal. I see all."

"Right," he said, still doubting her. "Of course. A place between time and space. Why didn't I think of that?"

"Do not jest, human. I have news that I will need you to relay to Michael."

"Now you want to help Roy's brother as well," he replied, growing increasingly suspicious of her. "Just what are you trying to accomplish here?"

"Enough of your trivial questions!" she demanded. It seemed that she was losing her patience. "You will need to look into a demon that calls itself the Tomekeeper. He is the one from Chaos' ranks that still lives. Michael will be quite grateful for the chance to track him down. I know that much to be true."

"And where would I even find this Tomekeeper?"

"You will use your technology on a newly formed planet that will come to be known as Khais. It is there that you will find him."

"Why are you going so far to help us?" the man asked. "We haven't exactly done much to help you."

"The Chaosbringer wishes for you to fail. This is all the reason I need to offer my assistance. For I know whatever he believes in the most is the opposite of how things should be. It will become necessary to bring about his inevitable downfall."

"Your kind of scary, you know that, right?"

"My magic has run its course," the demon responded, sidestepping his question. "As long as I can rely upon you to do everything that I have told you, then your next greatest foe will eventually be shown his end."

The Dark Messiah's face blinked out of his sight and the man let out a sigh of relief. But then it popped right back in front of him.

"Jesus!" the man shouted, jumping in his seat.

"I forgot to tell you," she said. "Warn Michael of the Tomekeeper's chains. Once he is ensnared by them, he won't be able to escape. Not without an incredible amount of magical power."

"Got it. I'll tell him." He was breathing heavily as he recovered from this demon constantly startling him.

"Very well," she said. "Good luck."

Then her face vanished again, but he stared at the air for a couple of minutes just to be sure. From the outside, he was sure he looked insane. Nothing happened. He must be in the clear. He wasn't sure what to think of all the things that the Dark Messiah had told him. He knew of the Tomekeeper from the battle with Chaos. However, he **didn't** realize that he was the only demon that had survived. But the Chaosbringer was new to him. Whoever he was, he had not heard of him until today, at this very moment. He plopped his face into his hands and took a deep breath.

"Well, at least this job is never boring," he sighed.

CHAPTER 1

LAST REMNANT OF CHAOS

The night is bleak on a planet like Earth, but at the same time, it's so different. A storm raged across the landscape. This planet is a place known as Khais. It is a place that seems harmless but is in fact full of many dangers. Lightning crackled throughout the land, while thunder boomed in the distance. A single man drove a motorcycle across the muddied ground. A large, ominous castle stood out in the distance. He squinted through the heavy rain. He would reach that place; nothing on this planet would get in his way.

The never-ending pouring rain has left his clothes drenched. They were already in miserable condition, torn in at least four places. His flimsy hood did little against the power of the storm's fury. Still, he continued, fighting the wet weather. Only one thing was on his mind. A monster lurked within the castle in the distance, demanding his attention. If he succeeded in stopping the monster, then there was a chance that his little brother would never remain blissfully unaware of the supernatural world of which he was so oblivious.

He is known to his friends as Michael Darsetts. For the demons, such as the one he was currently hunting, he is a demon slayer. However, he's no ordinary demon slayer. He has already made a reputation for himself as a legendary demon slayer. Most demons would fear his very name. His thoughts drifted as the storm echoed around him. He remembered that day approximately three years ago. The demon deity known as Chaos had just been defeated by his hand. The war against his armies had ended. He had gone into the office of the director of a powerful organization. This was the same organization that had helped him defeat Chaos. Without them it would never have happened.

The Director sat behind his desk in a comfortable chair and peered up at Michael. He was bald and neatly dressed in a button-up shirt. The way he was built, his shirt seemed to have a hard time containing him. He had a sense of power on the outside as well as on the inside. Michael looked to be in an unbearable state. He had been through a lot at this point. Fresh cuts spread out across his battered and bruised face.

"Feel free to take a seat," the director offered.

"I'll stand," Michael grunted.

Despite feeling pain throughout his body, he refused to relax. He needed to know what the Director would be able to tell him. He was sure it was information that he would need to know.

"Suit yourself," he said disappointedly. "I really hate seeing you like this, Michael. Just know that we are here for you."

"Just tell me," Michael said lividly.

"You were right, Michael. There is one demon that survived. A remnant of Chaos if you will. A demon that is known as the Tomekeeper."

"I remember him."

He clenched his hands into fists just at the thought. The Tomekeeper had caused this organization a great deal of headaches. If he could just kill this demon, then his brother would never have to deal with any of this supernatural bullshit. There was only one problem.

"Don't get too excited yet, Michael," the director said.

"What aren't you telling me?" Michael asked, frustratedly.

"We haven't actually found him yet."

"Are you serious?! What the hell have you been doing?!"

"We are doing our best, Michael. We will let you know when we have found him."

***

Two years passed as Michael waited for the organization to find the demon. In that time, he gained a rather impressive physique. He was no longer the boy that had a hard time doing what needed to be done. No one would hold him back anymore. His phone rang, and the Director that he had spoken to two years previously was on the line. "We need to talk, Michael."

In no time at all, a man knocked on his door. He walked over to the door and swung it open. The man at his doorway wore tactical gear and had short brown hair. An earpiece was placed snugly in his ear. His T-shirt showed off his bulging biceps. A vest was draped over his shirt. Each of his pockets was holding a different device.

"Michael," the man said.

"Let's get going," Michael replied, not wanting to strike up any sort of conversation.

"Of course."

He led Michael out into the hallway, and Michael followed him out the door, closing it behind him as he went. He got into the man's SUV parked outside, and after a long drive, he was back in that office nestled in the walls of the powerful organization he once worked for. Now the Director that he had grown accustomed to sat behind the desk. It was as if nothing had changed at all. The Director now had a gray beard, but other than that he looked the same as he had before.

"We have found him, Michael," the director said, looking up at him with tired eyes.

"Took you long enough," Michael scoffed. "It's been two fucking years."

"I know. We had to scour an entire planet. It has only existed for a couple years. But finally, we found him."

"A planet?" Michael asked. "What the hell does that have to do with anything?"

"We believe the planet was formed when all the malevolence within Chaos was released. It didn't appear until after Chaos' death. It is on this planet that the Tomekeeper is hiding. We have deemed this planet to be called Khais."

"This whole thing sounds ridiculous to me. But if you need me to go to another planet to kill the bastard, then that is exactly what I'll do. No distance will keep him safe from my wrath."

"I figured you'd say as much," the Director remarked. His face remained emotionless, hiding his true feelings. "I know I can't stop you; just remember to be careful."

He slid open a drawer at the top of his desk and grabbed a small silver orb from within. He fidgeted with the orb, revealing the red button in its center. This is a device known as a Portoball. It is used to teleport to places that would seem impossible. Such as another planet across the galaxy.

"Just one piece of advice, Michael," he remarked. "Don't get caught up in the demon's chains. If you do, we cannot help you."

"Just hand it over," Michael demanded impatiently.

He tossed the orb towards Michael, who caught it in the palm of his hand.

"Here's hoping that this supernatural shit will be done when I get back."

He pushed the button and vanished from the room.

"I really hope you're right," the Director sighed. "I really do."

Michael appeared on the surface of Khais in a puddle of mud. He pushed himself up and spat out the filthy water onto the muddy ground. He seemed to be in a valley of some sort that stretched on for miles. The deafening roar of thunder burst through the air, lightning crackling all around him. Michael pulled the hood up over his head, he couldn't help but wonder what the hell kind of place this was. At least he didn't need to become an astronaut to get here. So that was a bonus.

He spotted an overturned motorcycle nearby and made his way over to it. He fought against the fierce downpour of rain to reach it. Once he did, he brought the motorcycle up and climbed onto the seat. It started easily enough with a twist of the throttle, and he drove down the slimy wasteland.

***

Now at present, he has been driving the motorcycle down the grimy ground. He kept closing in on the castle in the distance. He noticed that the muddy ground was coming to an end. He approached a cliffside that looked down at the castle. It seemed to be more of a ramp than an actual cliff. A rather convenient setup. He veered the motorcycle towards the face of the cliff and accelerated as he drove up its surface. He reached the edge, and he flew. He seemed to glide down towards the castle. The motorcycle fell towards the castle and smashed through a window.

He had done it. He had made it inside. But now the thought came to focus. What is he supposed to do now? He continued down the halls, noticing the rather ornate feeling that the castle gave off. Old, faded paintings adorned the walls with torches of blue flame situated just far enough to not bother one another. Michael could hear footsteps approaching from around the corner. He braced himself for what could possibly be coming for him next.

It seemed that all the commotion he had made drew some unwanted attention. A man in dark clothes had appeared from around the corner. He could tell almost immediately that Michael didn't belong there. Michael lifted his bike into a wheelie and pushed it towards the man who was approaching him. The motorcycle slid across the hall and pushed him through the window that lay in wait behind him. There was a loud crash as both the man and bike busted through the window and fell down the cliffside. The bike threw Michael onto his back, but he managed to get back on his feet. He continued down the hall, unknowing of what this place would throw at him next.

He stopped at the broken window and glanced down below. If the man had been lucky enough to survive that, then he would be quite miserable.

"Damn," he said whistling. "That is a long way down."

Now he knew that would **not** be his escape from the castle. Just something helpful for him to keep in mind. He needed to keep going. He wandered around the corner that the man had come from and made his way down the hall. The corner had led him to a flight of stairs. As he ascended the stairs, he couldn't help but wonder what else this place would try and hide from him. The stairway led him up into a large and open room. Ancient-looking pillars were lined down the room's center. More torches were placed upon the walls, ablaze with an eerie blue flame. The eerie blue flames create a foreboding atmosphere.

Two more men in the same dark clothes from before seemed to be waiting for him in the center of the room. It gave him the sense that all this had been set up for him. He would have to be on guard going forward. The two of them began advancing towards him.

"Who the hell are you?" the man on the right asked.

Michael pulled forth a pistol from his jacket and fired several rounds into him. He stumbled back against a pillar and slowly slid to the floor. The blood had smeared onto the stone as he had made his descent. Peculiarly, the blood wasn't red but black. These people were not human, for sure. He wasn't sure what they were exactly.

"Not important," Michael said.

15

He turned his gun towards the other one. The man had rushed at Michael and tackled him, knocking the gun out of his hand. It was incredible how strong he was. He looked like an ordinary man, but it was like being plowed by a bull. It didn't make any sense. He hurled a fist at Michael's face, but he ducked under it. His fist smashed through the concrete of the pillar. Michael could feel the bits of rubble rain down on him. He would need to do something and do it fast.

He reached into his jacket and found the curious contraption that he had been searching for. He was relieved by the strange gadgets he had picked up from his time in that secret organization. It appeared to be a small crossbow of sorts. He pulled back on the notch, firing a chain out towards his enemy. The chain was stitched through the innards of his jacket. It seemed to hone on the man in front of him and bound his opponent's hands together before he could make another strike. He hadn't been expecting that, but he still tried to break free of the enchanted chain.

Michael headbutted him in the face, and the man staggered back. He kicked the man in the stomach, and he fell over backwards. He brought another trinket from his jacket. It appeared to be the hilt of a sword. He pushed against the sigil in its center, springing a blade forth from the device. He stepped on the unsuspecting man's chest and held the blade at the ready.

"This means nothing," the man wheezed, sounding out of breath. "You have already been caught in our trap. You just don't know it yet."

Michael grunted as he jabbed the sword into his chest. He pressed along the sigil to retract the blade and sheathed it back in the confines of his jacket. He leaned down and grabbed his pistol. He tucked it back into the safety of his jacket and made his way deeper into the castle.

He needed to be more careful. These people seemed more dangerous than he had given them credit for. If he wasn't at least a little more wary, it could easily get him killed. He hadn't even reached the demon he was searching for and had nearly gotten himself killed at least once. He needed to save his strength for his prey.

Michael had ended up in a rather nice-looking library. The whole place looked more impressive than everything else in the castle. The library appeared to have received the most attention. There was not even a single speck of dust on any of the books. Michael was on edge as he noticed it. Something wasn't right. He just wasn't sure what it was.

Each table he passed by had a candle placed in its center. The flickering light gave off an orange glow. Books were spread out over each table. It seemed quite dangerous being so close to the candles. He stepped across the rugs spread across the floor. He hadn't been cautious enough of his surroundings. He hadn't paid enough attention to what was below his feet. Several statues were displayed in the library, but Michael stopped in front of one that had caught his attention.

It was older than the others and had seen a great deal of damage. It was cracked and missing parts of its face. He hadn't even noticed that he had stepped off the edge of the rug onto something that shouldn't have been there. It was firm underneath his foot. He looked down, finding it uncomfortable to step on. He was looking down at a long, rustic chain. It brought him back to what the director from the secret organization had told him. Don't get caught in his chains. This was the moment he knew that he hadn't been careful enough. He saw the chain start to move.

"Shit!" he exclaimed.

The chains grabbed his legs and lifted him up into the air. He was pressed against a pillar nearby, and it wrapped itself around him. He was held against it rather securely, but that hadn't been enough, it seemed. For another chain rose up and bound his chest. He strained against the tight grip but knew it would do little good. The man from before was right. He had already fallen into their trap. As much as he struggled, he started to realize he wasn't going anywhere.

Michael noticed the cracks in the statue begin to glow in a radiant blue light. The light intensified before it rose up into a funnel of blue flames. As the flames dissipated, Michael saw that the statue was no more. In its place is a thin, pale blue demon with four arms. The demon sported a pair of curved horns with several spikes jutting through the top of its head. The demon looked down at Michael with his red, sunken eyes. This was the demon that Michael had been searching for. This is the Tomekeeper. The demon smiled maliciously as he saw Michael's discomfort.

"So, you must be the one I've been searching for," Michael said. "The only thing left alive of Chaos. The last remaining remnant of Chaos."

"That's right," the Tomekeeper cackled. "Although I must admit I'm a little disappointed you don't remember me from the war three years ago."

"There was a lot of shit happening then. I only remember the important demons."

The Tomekeeper's expression changed rather suddenly.

18

"I was the only one smart enough to hide amongst you," the demon snarled.

"And I still don't remember you," Michael replied.

"I know what you're trying to do, human," he claimed. "You're trying to rile me up. So, I loosen the chains, and you escape. I'm not going to fall for it."

"Damn," Michael said disappointed. "Was worth a shot."

Michael felt the chains tighten against his body, constricting him further. He could feel marks appearing on his skin from the ever-tightening grip of the chains.

"So how is it you survived?" he asked.

"I was smart," the demon replied.

"You must be the librarian that I heard about. The only demon so pathetic he couldn't fight to the bitter end."

"Librarian?!" the demon questioned angrily. "Is that what they have been saying about me?! I am one of the most powerful demons that was a part of Chaos' ranks!"

"Is that right?"

"Not only do I hold all the books. I create everything written within them."

"A librarian with original material, then."

"Shall I give you an example? Perhaps I could show you everything that your precious little brother has gone through while you were out here wasting your life away."

It was then that Michael began taking everything much more seriously. This demon was in fact far more dangerous than he had originally thought.

"What?" Michael asked.

"You don't know then?" The demon smiled. "Your little brother has been involved with the supernatural, despite your best efforts to keep him away from it. It has been a long couple of months for him, I'm sure. All the while, you struggled to shield him from it. How sad."

"How could it come to this?" Michael asked, hanging his head in distress.

"It's rather simple, Michael. You neglected him. You let your emotions blind you. You were so distracted that you didn't even notice when he was gone."

Michael lifted his head, his eyes blaring an intense stare. "What do you mean gone?"

"Would you like to find out?" he questioned. "I have the book right here."

Michael gritted his teeth as he glared at the Tomekeeper. "Do I have a fucking choice?"

"No, you don't," the Tomekeeper chuckled.

He opened one of his hands and a blue fireball formed on the palm of his hand. The flame changed shape into that of a book. Drenched in darkness, a red eye gazes back at him from its cover. The cursed grimoire fell into his hand on its back, and a gust of wind seemed to pull it open. The pages flipped through the book rapidly as the wind continued. Then the pages stopped as quickly as they had started. They stopped on the first page, and the Tomekeeper looked up at Michael expectantly.

"Shall we begin?"

"Enjoy this while you can, demon," Michael gritted through his teeth. "But when I am free of these damned chains, I will have your fucking head."

"You will never escape those chains. But I look forward to your attempts."

CHAPTER 2

THE CHAOSBRINGER

A year before Michael's capture, a series of events would change the life of his brother forever. Everything that was happening now marked the beginning of what was to come. It would lead to agonizing suffering for the Darsetts family. Their misfortune would be brought on by a single man.

The Chaosbringer is this man. He arrived on Khais with only one thing on his mind. He would reach the looming castle in the distance. He smirked to himself as he made his way across the barren wasteland. In no time he had reached his first obstacle.

The Chaosbringer trudged across a long, stone bridge suspended over a lake of lava. It was quite a different entrance from the one that Michael had used a couple months previously. Steam rose into the air, creating a rather noxious mist. It made it rather difficult to see anything, but it didn't bother him. He knew his path well enough that it would take a drastic change to throw him off. He reached the front doors, but there was something else as well.

Two decently sized demons stood guard at the gates. The demons had a bulky build and large horns sprouting from their heads. Their skin was filthy, ash gray. The demons saw him approaching and eyed him down with their yellow eyes. These demons are known as Archdemons. They usually would lead the vanguard within the demon army.

The Archdemon on the right grunted upon seeing him. He smacked the one on the left to get his attention. The left demon sighed. He knew something that the one on the right did not. The right one seemed almost excited. He probably never got to turn people away. It's not exactly a well-traveled path. The right Archdemon held out his hand, gesturing for the Chaosbringer to stop.

He did so, but at the same time shot the demon a nasty look. This didn't seem to faze the demon who didn't seem to know who he was. That being his first mistake.

"This is the Demon Castle," the Archdemon said. "Go back the way you came, or we will toss ya into the lava below."

The Chaosbringer whipped back his hood and revealed his face to the two of them.

"I knew it," the left demon sighed.

"Do you know who the hell I am?!" the Chaosbringer asked angrily.

"Chaosbringer," the right demon said shocked; his voice had dulled to a soft whisper.

He had not been expecting someone like the Chaosbringer to show up here. Quite frankly, it was unheard of.

"My apologies," he whimpered.

"Next time, my friend. I will rip out your fucking spine."

He pushed past the demons and opened the colossal doors. Then he marched into the castle, determined not to let anything else distract him.

"Dumbass," the left demon said, nudging the right demon in the rib.

"Shut the hell up!" The right demon shot back.

The Chaosbringer wandered through the halls, his footsteps echoing throughout the wide halls. The massive hallways were exquisite. If one took the time to appreciate them, they would be found to be truly breathtaking. Stained glass windows barred the view of raging lava outside. The Chaosbringer stepped onto a blue carpet that stretched to a flight of stone steps. Statues were lined up alongside the carpet all the way up to the stairs themselves. The torches placed on the walls were alight with blue fire, helping the statues stand out more clearly.

All of this did not interest the Chaosbringer, however. He was fixed on one thing and one thing only. He would meet with Barbatos, the Demon King. They had important business to discuss. He began climbing up the stone steps. He ended up in another broad hallway but knew the room at the other end was where he needed to be. That room was the throne room where the king surely awaited him impatiently.

He stopped in front of a pair of black double doors. Two skulls with crimson red gems shining vividly in their eye sockets served as the door's handles. It was time. It was time to meet with the king and warn him of the danger posed by a man with the last name of Darsetts. He pushed against the doors, and they swung open. Then he made his way into the throne room, where the king waited.

The Chaosbringer stepped into another vastly open room. Statues adorned the room, dwarfing the ones found in the hallways. A man sitting in a sinister-looking throne stared back at him. The throne was held by a platform three steps high. He seemed impressive even if he was doing nothing more than sitting upon a throne. A blood-red carpet leads up to the chair, adorned with statues running parallel to one another.

He has long, flowing gray hair with a goatee surrounding his mouth to match. He was staring at the Chaosbringer with bright red eyes. A shining gem sits in the center of a crown of bones, wrapping itself around his forehead. He also dressed himself with thick black armor, only to have it cut off at his shoulders. Allowing his muscular arms to be on display. Stitched to his armor was a ragged cloak. Beside him, the ground held a large, evil-looking sword.

"Chaosbringer," he said rather plainly. His voice was deep, and it seemed to echo in the large room. "To what do I owe the pleasure?"

"We have found him," the Chaosbringer said. "We have found the man who will get in the way of Chaos' resurrection."

He looked highly irritated after hearing this. He should have known. Why else would someone like the Chaosbringer come here to visit him?

"Why would I care about something like that?" he sighed.

The Chaosbringer balled his hands into fists. This clearly struck a nerve with him. He approached him and stopped at the top step so that the two of them could see eye to eye.

"Barbatos. Chaos is the one who put you in that seat. Being that he is a part of me, I could easily have you removed from it!"

"I keep order on this damn planet!" Barbatos bellowed. "If I am to be removed this entire dismal place will fall apart!"

"Remember your place, Demon King," the Chaosbringer said coldly.

Just then the doors burst open, and yet another man wandered into the room. He was sporting spiked black hair and wore bleakly shaded clothes. A scar in the shape of a wing stretched across the left side of his face. He wore a skull ring on his right hand. He is a minion of the demon king. Little did he know that this was probably the worst possible time to enter the room. He didn't even seem to notice the confrontation between the two men in armor.

The Chaosbringer slowly turned towards him in disbelief. He couldn't even fathom who this person could possibly be. The man obviously didn't recognize him as the Chaosbringer either. The title normally brought him immediate respect. But this man didn't pay him any attention whatsoever.

"Hey, Barbatos," he said eagerly, oblivious to the situation. "I need to talk to you about the state of my mansion."

The Chaosbringer glared at him. He couldn't believe the man would speak to a king in such a manner. It was repulsive. The man stopped at the base of the stone steps and finally noticed the Chaosbringer standing next to Barbatos at the throne.

"Who the hell is this guy?" he asked.

"I should be asking you that right now," the Chaosbringer said, sneering at him.

"I'm the Commander, One of the top Immortals in Barbatos' army."

"You?" the Chaosbringer asked. "You're the Commander that I've heard so many things about? You don't seem all that great from where I'm standing."

"That's only because you haven't seen me when I'm serious. Trust me, I'm as dangerous as they come."

"Is that right?" the Chaosbringer asked. He turned back towards Barbatos. "This is the guy you wanted to send after them? Seriously? **Him**?"

"He is a bit strange," Barbatos agreed. "But once he puts his mind to something he always gets it done in the end."

"If you say so."

He turned back to the Commander who had a look of annoyance directed at him.

"Well, I guess we have a job for you then. Just know that if you fail us, I will show you a fate far worse than death. Being an Immortal, we would have little choice."

"If I refuse?" the Commander asked.

Barbatos sighed and shook his head. The Chaosbringer walked down the steps and stopped in front of the Commander. He seemed to have an evil smirk on his face as he grabbed his face and lifted him into the air. Then he squeezed the Commander's face, making the crunching of his skull reverberate through the room.

"Enough of your games," the Chaosbringer scolded. "Or I swear I will crush your fucking skull."

"Fuck, fuck, fuck!" the Commander screamed.

The Chaosbringer dropped him onto the floor. The pain was excruciating. The power possessed by that man is simply ridiculous. He looked up at the intimidating man in front of him. He got to his feet, massaging his neck.

"I was joking, asshole," he gasped.

"Now was that so hard?" the Chaosbringer asked him.

"You're a real headache, you know that?"

"I've been called worse."

"What the hell do you want?" the Commander asked him.

"It's a simple job. You only need to kill the man who is standing in the way of our master's resurrection. And his friends."

"He must be a real piece of work to get in the way of Chaos' resurrection. But do you have anything that shows me what the fool looks like?"

"But of course," the Chaosbringer smiled.

He fished what looked like a simple pebble from within his cloak.

"You realize that's a freaking rock, right?" the Commander said.

"Oh, it's so much more than that," he said grinning.

He chucked the pebble onto the ground, and it exploded into a dark mist. The mist formed into a hazy gray screen, almost like looking at a phone or tablet.

"What the hell is this?" the Commander asked.

But then, as if to answer his question the screen changed shape again. The haze changed into the shape of a man. He looked sad and contemplated life itself. His long hair is unkempt, and his clothes are ragged. To be honest, he looked rather pathetic in his eyes.

"This is Roy Darsetts," the Chaosbringer explained. "He is a part of the prophecy. According to it, he will be the downfall of us all. He will be responsible for all our deaths."

"This guy?" the Commander asked. "He looks like a loser."

"That may be so. Just promise me you will not underestimate him."

"Whatever, man," the Commander said, rolling his eyes.

The Chaosbringer swiped his hand through the foggy screen, and it slowly began to change shape. Roy was no longer in front of them, but a powerful bald man sporting a tank top. He is wearing tight pants alongside the shirt, showing off his incredible muscles. He looked impressive, but that meant nothing to an Immortal. Their strength would easily dwarf his power.

"This is Vince Stranglehan," the Chaosbringer said. "He is a former wrestler and an ex-soldier to the secret society that fought us in the war a couple years ago."

The Commander couldn't help but feel like he seemed familiar. He may have seen the man during the war, but he wasn't sure. The Chaosbringer made another swipe of his hand, and the screen changed again. Another-average looking man had appeared. He has wild, spiked brown hair. A long and tattered trench coat billowed around him. There seemed to be several different assortments of guns peeking out from his jacket. Based on the grim look on his face, he had probably been through a lot in his lifetime.

The Commander felt that he had recognized every one of these people except for Roy. Each one of them had been an important part of the war for humanity. He would have to remember them in case he would have to deal with them himself.

"Phil Tyconian," the Chaosbringer stated. "Former mercenary but later joined the secret society."

"I'm beginning to remember these people," the Commander said, in understanding. "They seem more important than you were originally letting on."

"Right you are. Now would be a good chance to kill them for all the suffering they have caused, do you not agree?"

"You expect me to kill people who held back even the armies of Chaos?" the Commander asked, bewildered.

"Is that a problem?"

"No," the Commander sighed with a tinge of sarcasm. "Not at all."

He couldn't help but wonder what the hell he had gotten himself into. He knew there was no way out. He would have to kill these people no matter what. He just couldn't shake the feeling that doing so would probably get him killed in the process.

The Chaosbringer swiped the screen yet again, and the image formed into something else. His eyes widened at the woman he saw in front of him, and his hands clenched into tight fists. The Chaosbringer noticed and smirked at the Commander's response.

"I thought you might recognize her," he chuckled.

"Dedalia Sluvokia," the Commander growled. "Of course I remember her. She was one of my best and she turned on me in that war. I won't forgive her for siding with them."

He stared at the image and felt disappointment overcome him. The woman was beautiful with long dark hair. She wore the same pitch-dark clothes that he is wearing now. He was angry at her, but at the same time he feared her. He knew exactly what she was capable of, and that very thought terrified him.

The Chaosbringer made a quick swing of his hand, causing the image to change yet again. The woman was replaced with a man who also wore the outfit of an Immortal. He wore a Leather jacket and well-worn jeans. He had spiked his hair in the front, and he appeared to be neatly groomed. He wasn't sure if the man actually cared about his appearance or if it was for another reason altogether.

"Meet Derek Deathbed," the Chaosbringer said. "A well renowned assassin and another soldier from that secret society. He is very skilled at what he does."

"So, you are telling me he's probably one of the most dangerous?" the Commander asked. "How many more friends are you going to show me?"

"Just one. This one may be almost as important as Roy Darsetts himself."

He waved his hand through the clouded screen, and it changed again. Derek was replaced by an attractive woman, but this one the Commander didn't recognize. She had long, brown hair bound up into a ponytail. Her eyes seemed to pierce him as he stared at her figure. Her clothes were rather basic. She wore a simple blue tank top and ragged jeans. Her eyes were faded gray in color, but her smile was just infectious. He couldn't help but smirk as she looked down at him from the smoky image. He quickly shook his head to bring himself back to reality.

"Who the hell is she?" he asked.

"Lyn Darsetts," the Chaosbringer replied. "She is the one who will become the wife of Roy Darsetts."

"How do you even know that?" the Commander asked.

"That is of no importance to you. Now back to the point."

He waded through the screen, causing it to dissipate, and he grabbed the Commander by the front of his jacket. "Don't forget. You have a job to do. I would recommend you gather up your best. You fail this job, and I will make sure to kill you as many times as it takes for you to regret your fucking existence."

A dark burst of energy engulfed the Commander, propelling him out of the castle. He was thrown into a leather chair in his mansion. The Chaosbringer then effortlessly teleported himself out of the castle with a snap of his fingers. Barbatos had to witness all of this and couldn't help but wonder if there really was a point to any of it. Still, he was relieved that the Chaosbringer had finally left his castle.

"I really hate that guy," he sighed.

CHAPTER 3

THE JOB

The Commander landed rather uncomfortably on the leather chair in the office that he had made for himself in his mansion. The room itself looked like it had been created for someone quite important. The room was brimming with bookcases and neatly spaced statue heads on pedestals. The desk he was sitting behind had a certain new gleam to it. He was rather proud of the place he had made for himself.

He swiveled his chair around and looked out of the large window that looked down at the land beyond. The sight would be better if not for the muddy ground that paved the way for further destinations. He sighed. He had begged Barbatos for a place like this. He only wished the view could be a little more extravagant. Oh well. Not like there was much he could do about it.

Then his mind went back to the job that the Chaosbringer had given him. He would have to kill that nobody. Roy Darsetts. Not only that, but he would have to kill his friends too. It seemed beneath him, but that is what he has minions for. Might as well bring them in and brief them on the trip to Earth that they would be taking. Now he just needed them all to get along.

He slid open a drawer and fished out a phone. With a quick flick of his finger, his phone came to life. There was a particular icon he searched for among the cluster of apps and found it in no time. He pressed the icon to send out a message to four other people in the mansion. He knew that soon the four of them would grace him with their presence.

The first man to notice his phone vibrate is a man with buzzcut hair. He wore a green military jacket and torn jeans. His eyes were pale gray, and as he saw the message that had appeared on his phone, he couldn't help but smile. He is known as the General. It was finally time to show Earth hell. He had been looking forward to this for quite some time. He marched onwards to the Commander's office.

The second man to notice is a bald man with a simple physique. He wears a long, dark jacket that conceals a peculiar sort of weapon. This is the Lieutenant. He is wearing sunglasses despite being inside on a gloomy night. He began making his way towards the office where the Commander lay in wait.

"Oh great," he observed, rather disappointed. "Looks like it's time to go to work."

A third man clumsily fumbled his phone out of his jacket to see the message. He hung his head upon seeing the message. He had been enjoying the peace. Oh well. If the boss wants him to bust some heads, he knows he would be the best one for it. He had a very muscular build and stood no less than seven feet tall. His long black hair flowed behind him. He is known as the Sergeant. He hesitantly followed the others as they made their way to the office.

The last man stood out from the others. His hair is combed neatly, and he wore the suit one would expect from an office worker. His air was entirely different. The way he carried himself was more of someone who thought he was better than everyone else. To the others he would be known as the Worker, but soon he would be going by a different alias. Elliot Smith. He would need to be convincing in his role as Roy's coworker. He had worked very hard to bring himself to this point. For now, though he needed to go the Commander's office.

The four of them reached the door leading into the office at approximately the same time. The General opened the door, and the other three followed him inside. The four of them gathered in front of his desk. He looked up at them with the most serious expression etched on his face.

"I have been given a job," the Commander said. "That means that it will be **your** job."

"What's the job?" the General asked excitedly.

"Find Roy Darsetts and kill him," he replied.

"Sounds easy enough," the Lieutenant said.

"The Worker here will be doing the hard part," he said, pointing at him.

The Worker noticed the other three looking over at him expectantly.

"Why him?" the General asked, fuming.

"He will blend in with the other office workers at the building where Roy is currently employed," the Commander explained. "He will be under the guise of Elliot Smith. He will be a fellow coworker whom Roy can turn to in a time of need."

"So why the hell are we even here?" the Lieutenant scoffed.

"The three of you are backup," he responded. "The Chaosbringer believes that we will fail. I know the three of you are far stronger than the Worker. So, if he does fail, you will be cleaning up his mess."

"Back up?!" the General reiterated furiously. "Are you fucking serious?!"

The Commander was beginning to have some doubts about this, but he needed to keep his cool.

"You will be back up," the Commander repeated. "And I swear if you idiots fuck this up, I will come down there myself. If I come down there, I will find new ways of torturing you until you beg me for your untimely deaths. After all, it's not like I can kill any of you."

"So, when will we make our move?" the General asked.

"When it seems like the Worker has already failed."

The Commander looked over at the Worker from the vicinity of his desk with the utmost seriousness. "If you come crawling back to me before it is done, I will feed you to the fucking Void. Best you remember that in case you try to run."

"Don't worry boss," he said. "I don't plan to run. I would rather die than fail you."

"I like the enthusiasm. Just don't let it go to your head."

He opened another drawer at his desk and grabbed four Portoballs from its depths. He tossed each of them their own Portoball. The Sergeant turned towards the Worker and glared at him. The Worker felt his heart practically leap from his chest from the look. It wasn't just the look in his eye that terrified him. He was no less than twice his size. He was absolutely intimidating, and he knew how to use this to his advantage.

"Do not fail us," the Sergeant said.

"I'll do my best," he stammered in response.

"Now remember, only the Worker uses his right now," the Commander said. "I'll tell you when the rest of you are to dispatch, got it?"

He looked at the General, square in the eyes as he said this.

"Yeah, I got it," the General said disappointedly. "You're no fun. I have methods to make Roy wish he were already dead, expediting all of this significantly. But go ahead and do it your way."

"All of you get the hell out," the Commander commanded. "I will be watching your progress."

The Worker pressed the red button on the Portoball and vanished from the office. The other three put their shimmering orbs into their pockets and left the office. The Commander placed his head in his hands and sighed deeply. He glanced at the door of his office, now shut tight with only him in the room.

"For my sake, they better not fuck this up," he sighed. "I don't want to imagine what the Chaosbringer would do to me should we all fail."

They had to be successful though. After all, how hard could it be to kill a few humans?

CHAPTER 4

ROY DARSETTS

A man named Roy Darsetts is residing in a building deep in the heart of New York City. To say that his apartment is a mess is a severe understatement. The bedroom is filthy, with dirty clothes sprawled all over the place. He is the one that the Immortals were so scared of, just lying awkwardly across his bed.

He has long brown hair and is of average build at best. He isn't wearing a shirt, but he was sporting sweats that had seen better days. His alarm started going off next to him. Groggily he opened his eyes and glanced over at the clock. Seven AM. It was far too early to be awake but he needed to go to work. He sat up and hung his head in defeat. He would have to get out of bed. There was no way around it. He smacked his hand against the alarm clock to shut it up, nearly knocking it off its end table in the process.

"Time for another shit day," he groaned.

He climbed out of bed and grabbed a random shirt from the floor. He gave it a quick sniff. The shirt had an unpleasant smell, but he shrugged and grabbed it regardless.

"Good enough."

He put on the shirt and made his way over to his closet. He slid open the doors, and the clothes were barely hanging onto their hangers. He swapped his pants for ones that would have served as his dress pants. They weren't much of an improvement from the sweats he had been wearing, but they would have to do. He put on the rest of his suit over his shirt. He glanced at a mirror he had propped against a wall nearby. He looked better than he had before, but he still seemed like a bum.

"Just another day."

He walked out of the room and stepped onto papers. More clothes lay in a disheveled mess across the hallway. Everything crinkled under his footsteps, but it didn't seem to bother him. He had reached the kitchen, and the first thing he did was head to the coffee maker. A mug was rather conveniently placed next to it. The pot was already eagerly awaiting the steady drip of coffee that the machine would produce. He pressed a few buttons, and the coffee maker began to go to work. He looked around the room as the pot was filled with delicious coffee. Dishes were all over the place. Dishes were piled up in the sink, on the counters, and even the kitchen table. The whole kitchen looked like it really needed some work.

"I really should clean this shit," he said. Thinking about it more seriously. "**One** day I should clean this shit."

He noticed that the pot had finished filling up with coffee. He poured it into the mug and began savoring the fresh coffee he had just made. He brought his cup over to the clustered table and sat down. He enjoyed the bitterness of his coffee for about half an hour before he knew it was empty and knew he wouldn't have the time for more. The thought depressed him, but he got up and piled the mug atop the dishes in the sink.

He took another look around at the shabby apartment he called home. He sighed again. The place was a cluttered mess, but he would still rather be here than another day at work. He adjusted his tie to make it somewhat more presentable and grabbed his keys from the mess on the table. He made his way out of the apartment, locking the door behind him. He continued down the halls of the apartment building.

The rest of the building was in much better condition than his apartment. The carpet looked as if someone had replaced it recently, and the walls seemed to exude a shiny gleam.

"Time to make some money, I guess," Roy said.

He passed by a neighbor or two but didn't pay them any attention. Honestly, he felt there was no real reason to pay them any mind. He pressed the button for the elevator and waited. He just hoped that no one would approach him as he did. He wasn't so lucky. A man sporting spiked hair in his front passed by him but a woman with long black hair approached him.

"Damn it," he said. "Here we go."

"Roy!" she exclaimed.

"Dedalia," he said, unamused. "Just off for another fun filled day."

"Off to work?" she asked.

"Why else would I leave this wonderful hellhole?" he asked.

"Well, have fun."

"Yeah, fun," Roy said, flashing her a fake smile.

There was a ding, and the elevator doors slid open.

"Look at that," he said, eager to get away from her. "My ride's here. See ya later."

He made his way inside and pushed the button to close the doors. He made sure that Dedalia could see the overarching frown he had on his face as the doors slid shut. The smile she had been showing off quickly vanished. She knew Roy couldn't stand her, but she needed to keep an eye on him, and this was the best way to do it. She had to pretend to be someone that she really wasn't. She hated pretending to be so friendly, but she needed to make sure that he remained safe. It could be any day that the Immortals find them. Once they did, they would need to be ready.

"He thinks his job sucks," she muttered annoyed.

Roy had pressed the button for the lobby, and the elevator made its slow descent to the lobby. In no time, the doors slid open again. He wandered out into a rather spacious lobby. He walked past a small table with a basket full of apples. He was not interested in taking one, so he made his way over to the entryway doors. They slid open for him, and he stepped out into the brisk morning air. He shivered a little bit. These suits were not meant for this kind of weather.

"I hate the cold," he said to no one in particular.

He walked down the sidewalk, ignoring the usual distractions of the city. Even if he had the time for the festivities, he probably wouldn't be interested in them. He entered the subway nearby. He climbed down the stairs and made his way to his usual train. He got inside and cringed as he made his way through the crowded car. He grabbed a bar as all the seats were already taken. Just as they always were. This didn't make it any less annoying. It was going to be a long ride.

The ride was only thirty minutes, but it felt like it took much longer. He heard his stop over the intercom and was relieved. The brisk air greeted him as he gladly stepped off the train. At least the train was warmer. He sighed. He just couldn't win. He walked down the sidewalk for about another ten minutes before he saw the building that he was looking for. The thing that was slowly draining him of his soul. The office building where he worked. He passed a sign that confirmed it was in fact the place. Archon Corporation.

It was in this building that he would have to call all sorts of people and do his best to sell them crap that they really didn't need. Truly, it was a mind-numbing experience that he went through eight hours a day. He reached the front doors, and they slid open as if to greet him. He made his way inside cursing his own luck. He was sure that it was bound to be another long and dreadful day.

Roy saw the same old woman that he had been expecting. Confirming that nothing had changed. It kind of disappointed him, if he was to be honest. He could feel that this place was drawing out his limits. He wasn't sure how much more of this place he could take. It made him wish that something exciting would happen. Little did he know how much he would regret this in the near future.

The old woman squinted at the computer screen to read what was flickering in front of her. She slowly clacked the keys as her eyes glazed over everything displayed. Roy couldn't help but feel it was painful to watch. But she had been at that desk for so long that it felt wrong to interrupt her. He was sure she had been here since the beginning of this place. An impressive feat to say the least.

She wore her hair in a style typical to that of a grandmother. Her glasses sported thick lenses that almost seemed to zoom in on her eyes and enlarge them. Her bright pink office jumpsuit, which had matching pants, invaded his eyes.

She glanced up at Roy from her computer for a moment and noticed that he was approaching her. She locked onto him with her magnified eyes.

"Timmy!" she exclaimed, seeming quite excited to see him.

She never got his name right. Not even once. But she was just such a nice old lady that he just never had it in him to correct her. Not that it really mattered. He didn't converse with her much anyways.

"Janet," his tone couldn't match hers even if he tried. He knew that he would never be able to match her enthusiasm. More likely, though, it was because this place had begun to slowly drain him of what little sanity he had left. His attempt seemed rather pathetic when compared to hers.

"Good to see you, Joe," she said smiling at him, and went back to her work. She went back to her awkward clacking of her keys as she squinted at her desk. In hindsight, at least she was determined.

Roy shook his head and continued past her. It sure would be nice if just once she got his name right. Oh well, he had more important things to worry about. He plopped into the chair of his cramped cubicle and spun it around to face his own computer. He reached for the button to start it up, but a loud man's voice intruded upon his ears. He felt the shrill noise pierce through his skull. He hesitated to press the button as he knew that man's voice. It was the voice of his boss. Alan Samson.

"I want everyone in the conference room in five minutes!" Alan bellowed.

"This should go well," Roy sighed.

He gathered his phone and necessities. Then he followed his fellow confused coworkers in the direction of the conference room. He took a seat amidst a crowd of suits. He was fully aware that not one of the people in this room felt any genuine feeling toward one another. This is just how they dealt with their own work environment. It was a survival instinct when their boss was Alan Samson. He could be quite a monster of a man if he felt the need for it. This is the way of the Archon Corporation. Everyone knew how to focus more on their own work than to socialize. Alan had a strong vice on every one of them, and they were all aware of it.

He stood at the head of the table. He has balding gray hair with an ugly look on his face as usual. He is probably the least friendly sort of person anyone would ever meet. His suit shirt is untucked on one side, and his tie seems to be trying to escape by stretching out for his arm. His rounded gut tried to bust through his shirt, but somehow it contained it well enough.

He looked around at all of them with a look of disdain. One of the seats was empty, and Roy could tell Alan hated it. That spot belonged to Alan's assistant. Roy was sure that Alan was furious about his absence. He got confirmation by the expression on his face.

"Where the fuck is Wesley?!" he shouted.

CHAPTER 5

THE REPLACEMENT

No one had a clue what had happened to Wesley. They began chattering among themselves wondering where he had gotten off to. They could see Alan's expression slowly getting worse. It was only a matter of time before he would bring his frustration out on them.

"Meeting is cancelled!" Alan shouted. "Once I find that sorry son of a bitch, then all of you will be coming back here, and every one of you will be getting twice the work!"

Everyone grumbled among themselves. It wasn't their fault that his precious number two was a no-show. They got up and began making their way out of the room. Roy wasn't so lucky. Alan stopped him on his way out. He put a strong hand on his shoulder, and Roy turned to face him. He didn't have a good feeling about it.

"I know you're the most anti-social one here, but is there any chance you know what happened to Wesley?"

"Can't say that I have," Roy said, shaking his head.

"No matter. I took a shot. Now get your ass back to work."

"Of course, sir," he said and went on his way.

Roy couldn't help but feel his boss was the most emotionless being he had ever meant. He didn't care about the people he employed. The only thing that bothered him was how the work was going and how it would continue. Nothing else was worthy of his attention. Roy reached his cubicle and slumped back into his chair.

"Man, this place sucks," he sighed.

***

Wesley had been in the bathroom during the meeting. He had no desire to deal with Alan and his nonsense. He was just taking a break from dealing with his mentally abusive behavior. He stepped out of the stall after he had done his business and let the stall door close behind him. He trudged over to the sink and turned on the faucet. Then he hung his head as he gathered up his thoughts. No one had any idea how bad he had it being Alan's go-to guy. If anything, he had it worse than any of them. But still, he had to be in Alan's good graces, or else he would find a way to make him even more miserable. He lifted his head and saw his reflection staring back at him. His eyes looked dead inside. However, he needed the job. He just needed to remind himself of that.

When he left the bathroom, he would need to have a face that hid how he really felt as Alan's assistant. He couldn't risk his fellow coworkers getting suspicious of him. They didn't need to know how he really felt. In fact, he was probably more broken than any of them.

He brushed a hand through his slicked-back brown hair, trying to make it seem at least presentable. It didn't seem to make much of a difference. He sighed and noticed the neatness of his suit. At least he didn't have to worry about that for now. Alan would throw a fit about anyone sporting a messy suit, even though **he** was always in a tattered mess. One day, he would be liberated from this place, but for now, he would just grin and bear it.

Just then, the bathroom door swung open and a man that he didn't recognize entered. He turned towards him with a look of perplexity.

"Who the hell are you?" he asked.

"Name's Elliot," the man said, striding towards him. "I'm your replacement."

"My **replacement**," Wesley repeated in a daze.

Elliot grabbed Wesley's head and smashed it against the mirror. The glass rained down from the frame, and he was tossed through the stall door he had used just a moment ago. A bloodied gash had formed on the side of his face, and he could feel the warm blood running down his face. His face had slammed against the toilet bowl; if not for that, he may well have crashed against the wall beyond it. He weakly tried to lift his body and felt himself failing miserably.

"That's right," Elliot said, approaching him. "I'm to be your replacement."

"What do you want?" Wesley pleaded, nearing the brink of tears in his terror.

Elliot stepped into the stall and looked down at him with a smirk on his face. Wesley had managed to lift himself up against the toilet. The sight of Wesley groveling at his feet appeared to be rather pathetic. Elliot reached down and grabbed his tie. He hoisted him onto his feet.

"Weren't you paying attention?" Elliot asked.

He dragged Wesley out of the stall and flung him against the wall on the far side of the room. He crashed against the wall, leaving the structure quite weakened. He strolled towards the battered body of Wesley.

"You can never be me!" Wesley exclaimed. "I'm irreplaceable!"

Elliot stopped in front of him and grabbed the front of his suit. "I'm going to be so much better than you. They won't even remember your name, much less what you have done for this place. You will become an afterthought left behind in my success in the Archon Corporation."

"You bastard!"

Elliot slugged Wesley in the chest, and he smashed through the wall behind him. Rubble rained past Alan's office window. He was standing at his desk with his hands pressed against its surface.

"Where the hell is he?!" he wandered aloud.

Wesley's body tumbled past Alan's window while his back was turned.

"He seemed rather tense," Elliot said.

Then he leaped out the window after him. He fell past Alan's window, and the hunched-over man still wasn't any the wiser. Wesley had dented a car nearby with his fall. Elliot landed on his feet next to him. The impact caused his knees to buckle, but he quickly recovered. He pulled his keys out of his suit and pointed them at the car. He pushed a button, and the car chirped as it unlocked. This was his car after all. Exactly as he had planned it.

He walked around to the back of his car and flung open the trunk. Then he picked Wesley's body up off the roof of his car and tossed him in the trunk.

"Don't worry, Wesley," he chuckled evilly. "I will be sure to sabotage your legacy in this place."

Then he slammed the trunk shut. Then he made his way to the front doors of the Archon Corporation. He only hoped that his ruined suit wouldn't be an issue. He was still sure that he would be able to convince Alan that he would be more useful than Wesley had been.

He confidently waded past the workers, ignoring their surprised looks. He surely looked as if he had been in a terrible fight. He just let them think whatever they wanted. It meant nothing to him. He reached Alan's office and knocked on the door.

"Come in," a gruff voice said.

He entered a small office. Looking around everything in his possession seemed to be well out of date. His desk had a large crack stretching across its center. It didn't seem to be too promising. An ancient computer sat upon it, and he wasn't sure how the desk hadn't fallen over from its overwhelming weight. Books filled the poorly maintained shelves, barely held in place. He knew that the books hadn't been read in quite a while due to the dust layered on top of them. Alan was crammed in his chair with his gut pressing against the desk. It looked to be rather uncomfortable. He looked up at Elliot with a scowl plastered on his face.

"Who are you?" he asked, scowling.

"I'm here to replace Wesley," Elliot lied in a convincing manner. " It has come to our attention that Wesley is no longer fit to be your assistant."

"**Our** attention?" Alan asked. "What the hell are you even talking about?"

"Don't you worry about it. All you need to know is that I will fix this place better than **Wesley** ever could."

That seemed to be exactly what Alan had wanted to hear. A smile spread onto his face. It was not a pleasant sight. Almost terrifying.

"Just introduce me to your staff, and I will take care of all the rest."

"There's only one problem," Alan noted. "You never actually told me your name."

"Right. You may call me Elliot. I will be keeping a sharp eye on a certain Roy Darsetts."

"I wish you luck with that," Alan scoffed from behind the desk. "He used to be one of my best. He has fallen quite a bit since then."

"Not to worry. I will bring him back up. I guarantee it."

"Don't let me down, Elliot," Alan warned him. "I will remember this."

"I promise."

"Excellent. Let's turn all this around then."

Alan stood up and briskly walked out of his office. The sudden spring in his step was surprising for someone of his size.

"I want everyone back in the conference room in five minutes!" he shouted.

"What now?" a man grumbled.

Still, everyone made their way back into the conference room. They all settled into the seats that they had been in before. Alan stood at the head of the table once again with his hands on the table and seemed to be leaning towards them. But this time Elliot was standing next to him with a mischievous smirk on his face. Everyone

49

had their own distinct murmuring around the table about the newcomer standing next to their boss.

"That's not Wesley," a woman muttered to no one in particular.

"Who is that guy?" another man asked.

"Stop all your bickering," Alan barked. "I have a new addition to our corporate family to introduce. Just remember to treat him well, or all of you know full well what will happen."

He looked around at all of them as he said this. His gaze was intense, capable of piercing their very soul.

"Family?" a man asked skeptically. "Yeah, right."

"Just for that I am upping your workload," he declared. He looked directly at the doubting man.

The man who dared speak simply hung his head in silence. He knew he shouldn't have said anything. But he just couldn't resist the urge. He usually gets in trouble because of his mouth. Well, nothing he could do about it now.

"Anyone else got a smart comment?!" Alan asked, fuming.

No one dared to speak. They didn't wish to incur his wrath any further.

"I know we don't know what happened with Wesley, but Elliot here has graciously offered to take his place."

"Just like that?" a woman asked.

Alan shot her a look, and she covered her mouth with widened eyes. She couldn't believe that she had blurted that out. Luckily, it seemed that he had forgiven her, but she was sure to be on thin ice.

"If anyone has a problem with Elliot, you know where the fucking doors are," he said.

"Wesley was pathetic," Elliot said. "I'm here to ensure that all of you step up. I can promise that if you don't, your time here will be most unpleasant."

Alan smiled in agreement, and everyone bore witness to his sad attempt at a smile. He was sure that he had made the right choice.

***

Roy thought that his job was bad before, but with Elliot's arrival it was about to get so much worse. Elliot was practically on top of them for the next couple of weeks. On a positive note, they just about never saw Alan leave his office. He trusted Elliot completely to keep all the workers in line.

But one day things got even worse. The day was almost over, and Elliot was standing at Janet's desk.

"I know you have been here a while, Janet," Elliot ordered. "But I really need you to work faster. Either step it up or get the hell out."

Then Roy heard Janet's angry, shrill voice echo throughout the office. He almost felt bad for Elliot. He was just glad that he managed to stay on her good side.

"Listen here!" she shouted furiously. "I have put enough blood, sweat, and tears into this place to last three lifetimes. So, get the hell off your pedestal and go back to kissing Alan's ass in that sad excuse of an office!"

Roy had slid out of his cubicle on his chair to watch the confrontation. He was impressed. Janet can be scary. Not once had he ever witnessed her raising her voice quite like that. Elliot sure did look flustered. Upon seeing that, he decided to slide casually back into his cubicle before Elliot took out his frustration on him next.

"Just get back to work," he said in quiet anger.

Roy could tell from his tone that he was pissed, and he would rather not get in the way of that. Elliot stormed past him in a rageful walk. Roy finished his day and headed home. He had no idea how different things would be the next day.

***

Janet stayed behind while everyone else went home for the day. She had to finish up her work as is. She had a difficult time keeping up with the others. She didn't notice the woman sneak inside. The security guard didn't notice either and just continued along. The woman stopped at Janet's desk and cleared her throat. Janet jumped in her chair and clutched her chest. She felt wide-eyed as she looked up at the stranger standing in front of her.

"Who are you?" Janet asked. "Are you trying to give me a heart attack?"

"You may call me Lyn," she replied. "I have come here with a business proposition for you."

"Well, what is it?"

"I know you are tired of this place and are looking for an out," Lyn said in a sympathetic tone.

"Who wouldn't?"

"I'll offer you a million dollars to take your place," she offered. "I need to keep an eye on Roy Darsetts before he gets himself killed."

"A million dollars? Sure. Just to watch Ray, right?"

"Roy," she corrected. "But I assure you it's no joke, Janet."

Lyn hoisted up a briefcase and plopped it onto the desk. Then she unlatched it and swung it open. Dollar bills were crammed into the confines of the case. Janet couldn't believe what she was seeing. Her eyes lit up at the sight. She could finally be free of this place.

"Who exactly are you?" Janet asked curiously. "You're clearly a big deal."

"Details you don't need to know, Janet," Lyn replied. "Just take the money and enjoy your early retirement."

"Now how do I know this money is all real?"

"I know it seems strange, but it is all real. This is just the best chance I have of keeping Roy out of danger."

"If you say so," Janet said skeptically. "I'll gladly take it. I just hope that you know what you're doing."

"I appreciate you, Janet. Just know you may have very well saved many lives by doing this."

"Sure. Saving lives while sitting comfortably on my couch. Sounds about right."

"You just enjoy yourself, Janet."

Lyn closed the briefcase and slid it to Janet.

"You just make sure to keep your eye on Roy, alright?" Janet said with a smile on her face. "He's a good kid."

Janet picked up the case and made her way out of the building. Lyn couldn't help but smile. She was quite a silly old lady. She only hoped that Janet enjoyed her time away from this place. Based on what she learned in her research, Janet could probably use it. Lyn left the Archon Corporation shortly after.

CHAPTER 6

THE NEW RECEPTIONIST

The next day, Roy went through his usual routine. But things changed on this day as he wandered into the Archon Corporation. There was a woman sitting behind the desk, but it was not Janet. He had become accustomed to always seeing her there. So, seeing someone else seemed foreign. She was beautiful with a long ponytail. She appeared to be focused on her work and didn't even notice as he entered the building. He felt completely awestruck. He closed his eyes and took a deep breath. Then he opened his eyes, and she was still there. He wasn't hallucinating. Good, he's got enough to worry about.

"Damn," he said in disbelief.

Then she looked up at him and smiled. He froze. Her smile was just simply enchanting. Now what to do so he didn't look like a complete idiot. Roy felt himself gravitating towards the woman sitting at the desk, engrossed in her work. She seemed to stand out against the ugly gray of the rest of the office. He just realized how bland everything else seemed. He was unsure how he hadn't noticed before. He knew he would have to return to the dull confines of his own cubicle soon enough.

Roy wasn't worried about getting to his cubicle right away, though. He was more entranced by the woman sitting at her desk. The smile she gave him captivated him instantly.

"May I help you?" she asked pleasantly.

Even her voice was perfect. Roy realized he had become smitten almost immediately. It was possible that she was just trying to do her job, but he didn't really care. Her alluring aura was simply too strong.

"You're not Janet," he commented.

"No, I'm not," she agreed. "Janet has retired."

"Really? I must have missed that."

"It was rather sudden," she admitted.

He didn't need to know that she may have given her a large sum of money to do so. She adopted this disguise primarily to keep an eye on him. Minor details.

"So, who are you then?" he asked.

"You may call me Lyn," she replied.

"Where have you been all my life?"

"Trust me. You wouldn't be able to handle it if I told you."

"What?" Roy asked, taken aback.

"I'm fucking with you," she said, laughing.

Roy hadn't expected such a reaction and didn't really know how to respond to that. He felt a hand clap his shoulder, and he turned to see Elliot. He sighed. Once again, he was here to ruin all his fun. He just showed up one day after a mishap with a well-respected coworker had vanished. He was a real killjoy. Always work and no fun. He wasn't even in charge, but he was always at Alan's side.

"Don't you have anything better to do than harass the nice receptionist?" he asked.

"Not really," Roy said.

"Get out of here," Elliot said, ushering him on.

"I don't mind," Lyn insisted.

"I know you don't. But you are also trouble."

"Damn, you saw through my ruse," she said, un-amused.

"Just get back to work."

Elliot walked away, and she knew better than to antagonize him any further. She knew what he was. They had found them. He was one of them. An Immortal. They had already begun planning their next move. The only thing that she didn't know is how long that she had before he did so. Immortals were also incredibly powerful, so she would have to be quite careful in her planning.

Lyn returned to typing on her computer, while Roy entered his depressing cubicle. He slumped into his computer chair and stared at the blank screen in front of him. He sighed and booted up the computer. Elliot was already an assistant to the boss, and everyone had already hated him. He must be doing something right. His computer came to life.

"Man, I hate this place," he said miserably. "Nothing exciting ever happens."

Elliot stopped at his cubicle with a fake smile. "How's everything going, Roy?"

He glanced at Roy's computer screen and realized he had done nothing. "Do you even plan to work today?"

"Maybe later?" he responded lazily. "I'm not really feeling it right now,"

"Jesus. I can't believe we have kept someone like you around here for so long."

Elliot's phone vibrated, and he pulled it out to glance at it.

"Screw you, Elliot," Roy sneered disdainfully.

Elliot was barely even paying him any attention. He had just got a text from the boss.

"Great news, Roy," Elliot said smiling.

Roy knew that mischievous smile on Elliot's face wasn't a good sign. He didn't like where this was going.

"The boss wants to see you in his office," he said.

"Fuck me," Roy groaned.

Lyn observed them intently as Elliot escorted Roy to Alan's office. She watched as Roy wandered into the office and closed the door shut behind him. Elliot sat in a vacant chair nearby, and she saw him remove the shoelace from his left shoe. She didn't know what he was up to but knew it wasn't any good. She left the desk and marched toward the break room. She just needed to find a weapon that would help her deal with whatever that psycho was planning.

Roy walked into the office and sat down in a flimsy chair opposite Alan. Alan had his hands cradled together and looked at him with utmost seriousness. He could feel Alan studying him, sending a chill down the back of his neck. Whatever he was up to, he knew it wasn't going to go over well. He just had a feeling he couldn't explain.

Alan craned his neck at Roy and took a deep sigh. "Roy. I have begun to worry about you."

"Why is that?" Roy asked.

He was surprised by this. He didn't think Alan cared much about anything. Just the sentiment caught him off guard.

"You used to be such a good worker," Alan said. "Now your work is …well …shit."

"That's what this is about?" Roy asked, sounding amused.

"I need to know what has changed, Roy," he said bluntly.

"It's rather simple, sir. As the years have gone by, I have realized how shitty this job is. I have gotten to the point where I no longer care. I would rather this whole building burn to the fucking ground."

"Well, Roy, I appreciate your honesty. But none of that matters. I need your ass in gear, or you're fired. Simple as that."

"Well, that certainly sounds promising," Roy said rather coldly.

"Just get the hell out and get back to work!" Alan barked.

Roy couldn't believe how unempathetic Alan had become. He just sat there trying to process how one man could be so cold. His boss just glared at him intensely, but he hadn't seen what was coming next. Elliot had quietly snuck into the office with the shoelace in hand. He swiftly wrapped the lace around Roy's neck from behind him. He knotted the lace at the back of his neck and pulled it tightly. Roy grabbed the lace, but it did barely a thing against Elliot's powerful grip. He began gasping for air and flailing on the chair.

Lyn kicked the door open, holding a half empty pot of coffee. Elliot turned towards her in disbelief.

"What are you doing in here, girl?" he asked, noting the coffee pot in her hand.

He was so sure that no one was on to him. She must have been suspicious of him. This meant nothing. He would have to kill her after he was done with Roy. He had already begun his work on Roy as is. He refused to let down the Commander. Unfortunately for him, Lyn struck him savagely. She smashed the pot of coffee against the side of his head, and he screamed in anguish. Steam rose from his face where the coffee had splashed onto his face. The glass shards stuck to his face, exacerbating his agony.

"What in the hell is going on?!" Alan shouted.

Roy wanted to know that for himself. Now he was lying on the floor trying to catch his breath. He didn't have much time to think about it. Lyn grabbed a golf club free from the golf bag that Alan had leaning against a wall as Elliot continued screaming. She had managed to grab a nine iron and swung it into the side of his head. The club flew free of her hand as he stumbled back, and she grabbed his face. Then she quickly slammed his face against the shabby desk. The entire desk crumbled from the sheer impact. The desk was clearly in worse shape than she figured. She wasn't **that** strong.

Alan gazed up at her, a look of fury on his face. His expression looked rather comical with him sitting in his chair in front of the remains of his desk. Roy couldn't really believe everything that had just happened himself. Elliot was lying on the remains of the desk, unconscious.

"What the hell?!" Roy exclaimed.

"All of you get the fuck out!" Alan yelled. "You are all fired!"

Lyn helped Roy to his feet. He felt like he had finally caught his breath. With Lyn's help he made his way out of the office. He honestly hoped he never had to go into that abysmal little room ever again. He couldn't help but wonder who Elliot Smith truly is. He is clearly someone more important than he was letting on. He didn't trust the guy, but he knew that Elliot was clearly bad news.

After such a brutal beatdown there was no way that the guy could still be alive. Right?

CHAPTER 7

LYN

Roy felt himself being dragged through the office, not even noticing what was going on around him. He couldn't believe what had just transpired. It was a lot to take in. He didn't know what he could have to done to make anyone want to kill him. He didn't think he was so bad at his job that Elliot would reach that point. But then, Lyn completely beat the shit out of Elliot. He had no idea what was happening. It was already so difficult to process everything that took place. He wasn't sure how to accept everything that had come to pass.

The doors slid open as they made their way outside. As the cold air hit his face, he started to come to his senses. He was becoming aware of his surroundings. He heard the chirp of a nearby car and figured that was Lyn unlocking her car. Could he really trust her, though? Did she just kidnap him to have her way with him? Alright, the latter seemed a bit much. You can never be too careful, though, right?

Roy felt himself put into the passenger seat of a nice-looking car. He assumed it could be her car, but he couldn't help but wonder how she afforded it. He knew he couldn't swing it on his salary. The car started up as Lyn got into the driver's seat. He knew that they had left the Archon Corporation behind. He wasn't sure what he had gotten himself into, but he was sure it wouldn't end well.

***

Back in the office, Elliot weakly rose to his feet. A nasty burn had formed across the side of his face where Lyn had struck him. While black blood streamed down most of his face. She really had done a real number on him. Alan seemed surprised to see him on his feet again. But soon he went back to his normal façade. He stood up from the chair, being the only thing from the desk still in one piece.

"I thought I told you to get out!" he barked.

"I'm afraid I can't do that," Elliot replied. "Not that now you know my secret."

"Secret?" Alan asked. "What the hell are you talking about?"

Elliot pulled a pistol free from his suit and pointed it at Alan. He went directly back to his shocked demeanor.

"I don't know a damn thing!" he pleaded. Tears had misted his eyes.

"You should have called security," Elliot told him.

"Please!" he begged. "Don't do this!"

He had dramatically changed from his usual tough personality. It was rather amusing for Elliot as he pointed the pistol at Alan's face. His insignificant change in demeanor meant nothing to him. He still couldn't afford to let this man live.

He shot Alan in the head, and his blood splattered on the wall behind him. His lifeless body fell over backwards, and Elliot walked out of the office with the gun still in his hand. Everyone panicked at the sight of him wandering out of the office. Mostly it was the gun in his hand, but also the messed-up visage of his face. He was a mess, but he didn't care. He needed to get to Roy, and nothing was going to get in his way.

He passed through the sliding doors and made his way to his own car. He was not looking forward to the call he was going to have to make now. He climbed into his car, putting his head into his hands for a moment and took a deep breath. He was going to have to let the Commander know of his failure. He was not going to be pleased. He pulled his phone out from his suit and noticed the cracks on the screen. Probably due to his one-sided tussle with Lyn. Still, he dialed the number that would reach the Commander.

"What is it?" the Commander asked, sounding irritated already.

He was already in quite the mood. He was already off to a great start.

"You're not going to like this," he sighed.

"Don't tell me he got away," the Commander grimaced. "I put a lot on the line for you."

"That's exactly what happened," Elliot said wringing his hands in front of him. "But I will be on his tail soon."

"You fucking better be!" the Commander shouted.

Elliot had to pull the phone away from his ear due to the random outburst from the other line.

"I know. I will find the bastard and kill him."

"Just hurry the hell up. It's my ass being put on the platter. Don't forget that."

"I got it," Elliot shot back, annoyed.

Then he heard the phone click as the Commander hung up.

"Asshole."

Then he started up his car and turned onto the busy streets of New York. He didn't know where they went, but he did know that they couldn't have gone far.

***

Roy felt himself coming back to his own skin in a sense. Now that he was getting a good look at the woman who had just saved his life, he could tell that she was pretty. He needed to stop getting distracted.

"I never did catch your name," Roy said.

She glanced over at him. He seemed to be calming down now. It would probably be best to keep him in that state. So, it would be best to humor him at this point.

"I'm Lyn," she replied. "I'm your best chance at survival."

"So, what the hell was that back there?" Roy asked.

"That was just the beginning."

"Beginning of what?" he asked.

"I know you don't know what's going on. But you are in more danger than you realize. They have found you and will stop at nothing to kill you."

"Who is **they**?"

"I need you to trust me. No matter how insane it may sound."

"Should I be worried?"

"That man is more dangerous than you know. He is a being known as an Immortal. They are all powerful aliens who hide their true forms under a skin like our own."

This was starting to feel like nothing more than a bad joke. "Aliens? Really? Are they gonna bring out their ray guns and ask to see our leader too? I mean, c'mon."

"Look," she remarked, rather sharply. "I know how it sounds. But it's the truth and I need you to believe it. Only a select few people are left who even know of their existence."

"I want to trust you," he said, hesitantly. "But I really don't know if I can believe a story about an alien working a regular job."

"How else could you explain how you were unable to escape his grasp in that office, Roy?" she asked him. "If he had been a normal human, you should have had no problem getting out of his grip."

Roy couldn't help but think that she had thought too highly of him. Although he wasn't particularly strong, her belief that he could be at least slightly lifted his spirits. Maybe she wasn't so bad after all. Maybe he could bring himself to trust in her no matter how crazy it sounded.

"Alright, Lyn. You seem to believe in me more than I do myself. That's got to mean something at least. I'll believe you."

"That really makes this easier," she said, relieved. "Something you should know is that not only is he powerful, but he will also be very hard to kill."

"Wait," Roy said nervously. "We're going to have to kill the guy?"

"You must understand, Roy," she insisted. "He will only keep trying to kill you if we don't kill him first."

"It's just a lot to take it in," he replied, feeling his anxiousness coming forth. "I've never killed someone before, and I don't know how I'm gonna handle something like that."

"Just don't think too hard about it," she replied, unconcerned by the notion. "I'm going to do what I can to keep you alive."

"Do you often kill people?" Roy asked suspiciously.

"Not **people.** I only kill the Immortals that wish for the destruction of our world."

"You make it sound easy."

"Just stick with me," she assured him. "I can show you just how easy it can be."

"I don't think that's something to be proud of," he said quietly, expressing his disbelief. He was starting to wonder if he could really trust her. She seemed more dangerous than he had previously imagined.

"Believe me," she said, taking a heavy breath. "I'm not proud of what I have done, but I will do what is necessary. I know that they appear human, but we should **never** treat them as such."

"You seem like you have killed a lot of these Immortals."

"More than I'd like to admit," she agreed heavily. "But I assure you it gets easier after your first kill."

"You don't expect too much out of me, do you?" he asked, taking in everything that she had told him.

"For now, I'm going to take you to meet a friend of mine. He may be able to help us."

"Is he an alien slayer or something?" Roy asked.

"Something like that."

She turned into a parking lot to the right and Roy saw a bar in front of them. She pulled the car into the backlot, hoping to avoid any pursuers. She parked the car and turned towards him.

"I know all of this seems rushed," she apologized. "But we need to keep moving."

"Yeah, I got it," he said.

The two of them got out of the car and made their way into the bar. The building seemed to greet them with the clink of glasses and casual conversation. It looked like a nice place. Everything was organized neatly. Roy was rather surprised. He honestly enjoyed the atmosphere of the place.

Roy hadn't realized it, but they were heading towards the man that Lyn was searching for. He would be the one giving them the advice for moving forward. Hopefully this person will be a great help moving forward. Lyn saw him with his back toward them enjoying his beer. He is a buff, bald man wearing a tank top. His muscles seemed to ripple through his shirt as much as they could. Roy sat down opposite him with Lyn sitting next to him. The man smiled at him. He seemed genuinely happy to see him. Not an expression he was expecting from a stranger.

"Roy Darsetts," the man said, smiling. "At last, we meet."

CHAPTER 8

VINCE STRANGLEHAN

Roy didn't know what to think of the man smiling at him from across the table. He was pretty sure that the two of them had never actually met.

"Do I know you?" Roy asked.

"I'm sorry," he apologized. "I'm Vince Stranglehan. I worked with Michael for some time. He told me so much about you that I feel like I already know you so well."

"So, you knew my brother," Roy said surprised. "I didn't think he even had any friends."

"Michael had lots of friends," Vince replied. He paused and looked around the bar suspiciously. "But he also had lots of enemies."

"I can only imagine," Roy said. He was beginning to feel that Michael had kept a lot from him. He was sure this was only a small fraction of everything that had been kept from him.

"He had always told me he was a simple business-man. Which is why I had decided to go into a similar profession," Roy replied, feeling deceived.

"No offense. But that sounds incredibly boring."

"It is," Roy agreed. "What do you do?"

"Me?" Vince asked. "I was a wrestler at one point. But now I'm a simple soldier trying to keep humanity safe. To do that, though, we need to make sure that you're safe."

"What makes me so special?" Roy asked.

Vince shot Lyn a quizzical look. "So, you didn't tell him?"

"Didn't really have a chance. We had a superpowered killer chasing us."

"Fair enough," he sighed.

"Tell me what?" Roy asked curiously.

"Would you believe me if I told you were a part of a prophecy that could change the course of the very world that we live in?" Vince asked.

"Prophecy?" he asked. "That sounds like bullshit to me."

"I figured you would think that. However, there is a prophecy that was made by a demon among the Immortals. They believe in it wholeheartedly. You are kind of a big deal in the said prophecy."

"How did I get so lucky?" Roy asked.

"According to the prophecy the one who will strike down the king of demons will have the last name of Darsetts," Lyn interjected. "The Immortals are servants to the demons so they will do whatever it takes to stop you on the course that you have taken."

"Demons too?" Roy asked. "This just keeps getting weirder. It's getting harder than ever to believe all of this."

Vince glanced over at Dedalia. "You really didn't tell him a damn thing."

"Like I said, we were a little busy," she replied.

"Well, that's just great," Roy said. "Do I get a say in any of this?"

"Sadly, Roy, you don't," Vince said, grimly. "They will hunt you down for as long as it takes to put you in the dirt."

"I'm no one special."

"I know you don't like any of this, Roy. But this is your fate. You will be the one to put an end to the Immortals once and for all."

"Fate?!" Roy shouted. "Fuck fate! I'll live my own damn life!"

He slammed his hands on the table without even realizing it. Vince's cup had nearly toppled over. His smile from before had turned into a frown. People were beginning to stare at them nervously. He had just wanted a more fulfilling life. A better life than the one he was currently in. This was no way to live life. He felt as if his life was in the hands of someone else. The thought infuriated him.

"I understand your frustration, Roy," Vince said. "But when the time comes, you **will** answer the call."

"You don't know shit."

"Now I have some business I need to attend to," Vince said, looking almost betrayed. "Go with Lyn and maybe she will give you the answers you are searching for."

"Whatever, man," Roy said getting to his feet.

He followed Lyn out of the bar and back into the car. After sitting in his seat for a few moments, he suddenly just lost it.

"Fuck!" he screamed.

Lyn tenderly grabbed Roy's hand. Then she looked into his eyes. His eyes welled up from his level of anger.

Something about her eyes looking back at him made him begin to calm down. He started to take deep breaths and felt himself become his normal self.

"Look, Roy," she said. "I know this whole thing is a lot, but Michael only did all of this because he cares for you deeply. He would do anything to know that you are safe. Even if it means you may have to go through some shit that you probably don't want to. This is the only way that he was able to do so."

"You're right," he said anxiously. "I just really don't know what I'm supposed to do."

"Don't worry about it," she said. "I don't either."

"How is that supposed to help?" Roy asked.

"You need to embrace your fear, Roy. Once you do, it will be easier to find your path forward, and the Immortals won't be able to do a damn thing to stop you."

Roy didn't know what to say. He opened his mouth to speak but no words would come. But something about the look that she continued to give him calmed his nerves.

"Lyn, I have to be honest with you," he said.

"What is it?" she asked.

Suddenly, Roy felt compelled to ask her something. He didn't care if she ended up shooting him down. "I know you're supposed to be like my protector or something. But would you consider going out with someone like me?"

"Well, you certainly are forward," she said, surprised. "And what makes you think that you can handle a woman like me?"

"I don't know," he replied honestly. "But I appreciate you for who you are. I would offer my undying loyalty to you."

71

"You realize that in my profession, you will constantly be at risk? I will need you to keep up with me, never falling behind. If you do, you may very well die."

"I don't care about any of that. I will better myself and help you in your battles, so you never have to be alone."

She considered this. His eyes seemed to be pleading with her. "You will have to promise that you won't fall behind. I can't be carrying you around like a dead weight."

"Not only will I fight beside you, but I will also offer you a shoulder to cry on after a rough day. I will take care of you. I will free you of your shackled darkness."

Lyn just stared at him, seeing him in a new way. Roy was offering her a life free of the strife that she had come to terms with. He was proposing a life of peace and tranquility. Something that she hadn't realized that she had wanted.

"You really are something else," she said, having a hard time believing it herself.

"Take my hand," Roy said, offering it to her. "I will fight beside you to the point that you no longer will have to. Then I will lead you to a relaxing life that you deserve. A life where the two of us can enjoy our days as they go by."

Lyn could feel herself tearing up, a world without struggle. It felt like a fleeting dream. She only hoped that Roy would be able to keep his promise. She had made up her mind. She would give this ambitious man a chance.

"Why the hell not?" she said, smiling at him. "But don't make me regret it."

"I wouldn't dream of it," Roy said, grinning at her.

Lyn sure hoped that she knew what she was doing. Roy was already so clueless about the life he would become a part of. But maybe he was **exactly** what she needed. Perhaps he could bring some light to the bleak life that she had lived.

"Don't get too excited just yet," she said with a mischievous smile. "We're gonna start by building up your muscle. That's the only way you will be able to survive being with me."

"I'm looking forward to it," Roy replied, unfazed.

Maybe she could finally be some light in the darkness that was his life. It made him feel hopeful for the future. Maybe after all this was over, he could finally have a life like he had always wanted.

***

Vince sat at his table in silence. There was a slight chance he may have sprung too much on Roy at once. He sighed. Maybe it was too much to expect of him. After all, taking out the Immortals would be quite an undertaking. As he finished his beer, he caught the glimpse of a man approaching him. He presumed that the man inching towards him was the one that had been following the two of them.

Vince waited patiently for him to stop behind the chair. He could hear his heavy breathing. The encroaching man seemed excited about something. Surely, he thought he had the advantage over Vince. He saw Vince as just another easy kill. Perhaps now would be a good time to turn the tables on him. Vince saw his face in the reflection of his glass. His face appeared to be in rough shape to say the least.

"What the hell happened to your face?" he asked, without turning around.

"You knew I was here all this time?" Elliot asked. "Why didn't you go after me before?"

"I was awaiting the proper moment."

Elliot drew a pistol from the confines of his suit. People started screaming and fleeing from the bar. A typical response from a man holding a gun.

"Is this moment you were hoping for?" Elliot asked, sneering at him.

"Of course it is," he said, gripping the edges of the table.

He pushed off from the table, and his chair slammed into the man behind him. Elliot had collided with the table behind him. Vince got up and lifted his chair up into the air. He whacked him across the face and wood splinters flew as the wooden chair shattered. Elliot slid across the table next to him.

"What the hell are you doing?!" the bartender shouted.

Vince walked over to where Elliot was lying on the floor. He knew all this only worked because he caught the man off guard. If Elliot had gotten a hit on him, it would have ended rather badly for him instead. Vince knew he needed to keep up this momentum if he wanted to stand a chance. For now, he was ignoring the bartender.

Vince grabbed Elliot off the floor and lifted him up. He carried him over to the bar's counter and smacked him hard against it.

"You want me to call the cops, asshole?" the bartender asked fuming.

"That's exactly what I want you to do," Vince strained.

"Are you serious?" he asked, taken aback.

He wasn't expecting that. He must not have realized that he would be reporting him to the cops. None of what he was saying made any sense. Vince grabbed the gun from Elliot's hand and slapped it on the counter. The bartender's eyes widened in disbelief.

"This man was going to shoot me," Vince said. "There's no telling what he would have done after that."

"Shit," the bartender said.

He wandered over to the phone and began dialing the number for the cops. Vince saw Elliot trying to reach for the gun on the counter.

"No, you don't!" he shouted.

He twisted Elliot around and smashed his face against the counter. Then, for good measure, he put his arm into a rather elaborate arm lock. This was a handy move he had learned from his wrestling days. Then he looked over at the bartender.

"Hurry the hell up, would you!" he demanded.

The bartender waved him off with his hand and continued conversing with the officer on the phone. Vince knew that Elliot wasn't fighting back solely from the wounds he had suffered. The pain he was in was probably unbearable. They would heal quickly, but there were still a lot of wounds to heal.

Vince kept Elliot in the grappled lock until the cops arrived, and they hauled him away. Elliot had still been glaring at him as they pushed him into the back of the police car. Vince knew he had made a new enemy that day. But hopefully they would be able to stop him from whatever it was he was planning. He only needed to figure out how to do it.

CHAPTER 9

A BUDDING RELATIONSHIP

Lyn pulled into the driveway of a rather lavish-looking house. Roy's mouth dropped in amazement. He assumed that this was probably her house, but he couldn't help but wonder how it was that she could afford it. They continued down the paved driveway, and he saw hedges lined alongside the drive. This looked like the design of a rich person's house. She brought the car into a circular parking area and parked near the front door.

"Holy shit!" Roy exclaimed. "Are you rich or something?"

"No," she replied, smiling at his excitement. "The company I work for gave me the house. They are the ones who are rich."

"It's amazing," he said, awestruck.

"Do you want to see the inside?" she chuckled.

"Oh, right."

He realized they were both still in the car. He was too busy staring at the shimmering house. The two of them got out of her car and made their way towards the house.

"By the way, what is this company?" Roy asked. "I can't imagine they would just give you a house like this for no reason."

"Well, we fight against the unknown," she said. "Such as the Immortals. Being so extravagant is part of the cover. They wouldn't expect us to be in such a flashy place."

"I can't believe how lucky I am that someone like you would even be interested in me," he said excitedly.

"As long as you can keep your promise to me, you will be surprised by just how much fun that we can have," she said, beaming at him. "But you also offered me something that no one else has. I have never actually had the chance to just enjoy my life. I'm willing to give you a chance, but you better not give up on me. If you do, I may have to kill you."

She opened the front door and led him inside, with Roy feeling rather nervous. He had hoped the last thing that she had said was another one of her jokes. Unfortunately for him, he wasn't so sure. However, he was curious about the house that he was entering.

If he thought it looked amazing on the outside, the inside was even more impressive. Just the entryway alone was massive. The ceiling was way over his head, and he honestly didn't know where to look first. He kicked off his shoes and after she gave him a look, he placed them neatly on a mat nearby. His shoes fit quite nicely alongside hers.

Then she guided him into the living room. He plopped down onto a luxurious white couch. She sat down next to him and clasped his hand in hers.

"This is a nice place," Roy observed.

"Just shut up," she demanded playfully.

Next thing he knew, he felt her lips brushing against his own.

"You're cute," she said, breaking apart their kiss.

"I don't know what I did," he said, surprised.

"You don't have to do anything. Just be yourself, and I'll help you feel like the happiest man alive."

"You really are just incredible."

"Just stop talking," she said. "You're ruining the moment."

She kissed him again but this time more passionately. She pushed him onto his back with fervor as she continued to kiss him. Roy couldn't believe all this was happening. He had girlfriends before, but Lyn seemed so different from anyone else. It just felt right. Suddenly she stopped and he felt a twinge of disappointment.

She had climbed off the couch, and he gazed back at her, feeling betrayed. She turned back towards him with a playful look on her face.

"Be right back, boy," she said seductively. "I'm gonna get more comfortable."

Roy had been left alone, lost in the clutter of his thoughts. She was so different from most other women he met in his life. Even when she first appeared at that desk at work, he could feel he had no choice but to gravitate toward her. He couldn't stop himself from being infatuated with her. He didn't know if she had felt the same about him. But maybe if he just kept being himself, then maybe she would reciprocate his feelings.

Lyn reentered the room, leaving Roy captivated by her alluring body. Her lingerie leaves little room to the imagination. Lyn's toned stomach gripped his attention, and he could see the cleavage from her breasts desperately trying to be liberated from the confines of her outfit. He didn't know what he had gotten himself into, but so far, he knew he was enjoying where it was heading. She wandered towards him seductively, and she bent down towards him. Her cleavage stood out in front of him as she pressed her lips to his ear.

"You ready for me to rock your world, boy?" she whispered seductively. "I promise I won't bite, unless you want me to."

"Absolutely!" he said excitedly.

"Then you better follow me to the bedroom, boy."

She turned back towards the bedroom from where she had come. This was when Roy got a good look at her rounded butt peeking out from the back of her lingerie. As she walked, she purposefully swayed her butt, keeping him completely enraptured. He really did feel like the luckiest man alive. She could feel his eyes mesmerized by her, and she couldn't help but giggle. He playfully chased after her into the bedroom.

Roy joined her in the bedroom. She was already lying atop the blissful mattress eagerly. He crawled on top of her and kissed her. She kissed him back passionately, their tongues dancing across each other. Then he lowered the fabric barring his access to her breasts. He licked along her nipples, getting a pleasurable response from her.

Then the two of them helped each other out of their confining clothes and made love. That moment was the beginning of their relationship; it could be argued that it was far from the normal sort of relationship. But everything changed on that day for the better.

***

After about six months of the dating scene, Roy had gathered enough courage to go and buy her a ring. He was planning on making his intentions clear that night. Little did he know, fate hadn't forgotten about him.

That night, as they nestled together in bed, Lyn's phone rang. Groggily she grabbed her phone and saw that it was two in the morning. She took the call well into the kitchen, where Roy would not be able to hear her. She noticed Vince was the one calling, and he usually only called about something important. She only hoped that it had nothing to do with the Immortals. Somehow, she doubted that she would be so lucky.

"What is it?" she asked sleepily.

"I have bad news, Lyn," Vince said on the other line. "The Immortals are up to something."

"What do you mean?" she asked.

"Well, it's been six months. And they still haven't made a move. I don't like it."

"That's a good point. So, you think they're scheming something?"

"I'm sure of it. I know it's not just Elliot that they sent. There are three others as well."

"How do you even know that, Vince?" she asked.

"Because the other three arrived last week. I'm sure that they plan to break Elliot out of prison, but I don't know how they are going to do it."

"Shit," she sighed heavily into her phone. "We had a hard enough time with just Elliot. Do you know how much harder this is gonna be if all of them get together?"

"I know," Vince remarked. "I got eyes on the bastards, but there's only so much that I can do."

"Right. This doesn't look good. Just let me know the second that Elliot finds his way out of prison."

"Will do. In the meantime, keep Roy out of any unnecessary trouble."

"I should be able to keep him occupied," she replied.

"Whatever you have to do," he said.

There was a click as he hung up his phone. She placed her phone on the kitchen counter and sighed frustratedly. This didn't look so good. So much for a happy and peaceful life. She gripped the counter and hung her head.

"Fuck," she whispered.

A groggy Roy wandered into the kitchen. "What's going on, babe?"

"Nothing at all, dear," she smiled.

Being as tired as he was, Roy couldn't see through the fakeness of her smile. She had counted on it.

"Cool," he said and turned back around.

She watched as he waddled back to the bed. It looked like their time of fun was quickly coming to an end. Four Immortals would be at their doorstep soon enough. She just had to figure out a way to deal with them before they could hatch whatever scheme it was that they were up to. Hopefully they will be able to see through whatever it is in time.

CHAPTER 10

THE PROPOSAL

The next day, Roy woke up with the intention of proposing to the woman of his dreams. He was excited for the date that they had planned for the evening. He had eagerly been waiting for this day. The day that he finally made Lyn his other half. He already felt like she could be, so it just felt right.

He plucked the box containing the ring from a drawer in his nightstand and went on his way. He had many things he wanted to get done before their dinner that night. He shut the door behind him as he left and seemed to skip down the busy streets of New York.

Lyn, however, did not share his enthusiasm. After all she wasn't a morning person. Before she had replaced Janet, she never had to worry about getting up early. Now, though, she had to do it constantly, and it was not an easy adjustment by any means. Roy was more used to it, even though she knew he hated it. She rolled over to her own nightstand and tapped her phone to see the time. It was eight in the morning; way too early was all that she knew. She had a whole day to figure out what to do before their dinner. She closed her eyes in anticipation of falling back asleep.

***

An hour passed and she heard a loud banging at her door. She opened her eyes and blinked them into focus. She hadn't even sat up as the doorbell had begun to ring. "You have got to be kidding me."

She roughly shoved her blankets aside and hurled herself out of her bed. She stormed towards the door in what she deemed sleepwear. She was dressed in a comfortable tank top and underwear. A normal ensemble, she figured. She whipped the door open and saw two people standing there. It was a man and a woman. She recognized both of them. The woman was Dedalia, while the man was Derek.

"We talked about this," she said to them. "You shouldn't be here."

"We know that Vince told you what is happening," Dedalia said. "We came here to speak to you of something else."

"Yeah, what is it?" she asked.

"We're coming inside," Derek said bluntly.

He rudely forced his way inside and Dedalia reluctantly followed behind him. Lyn followed them, rather irritated, into her living room.

"What the hell is this about?" she asked hotly.

She plopped on a chair opposite the couch they had occupied.

"You need to tell Roy what's going on," Dedalia said. "He needs to know the danger that he is in. Keeping him in the dark like this only makes it worse."

"I'm only doing what Michael had wanted," Lyn debated. "He made it quite clear he didn't want Roy to experience any of the supernatural."

"You're only delaying the inevitable at this point," Derek replied. "He has already witnessed the supernatural. He needs to be ready for the shit that is coming."

"Why are you guys so worried about it?" Lyn asked.

"Because we have a bad feeling," Dedalia insisted. "Elliot will find a way out of prison soon, and he will either kill you or kill him."

"What are you talking about?" Lyn asked, surprised.

"We have found out the two targets at the top of the list are you and him," Derek informed her. "So, when he gets out of the place the both of you will be in for the worst of it."

"How did you even find that out?" she asked.

"We have our ways. But trust me, if you don't tell him what's happening, it won't end well for either one of you."

"Fuck," she breathed. "I really don't know what I should do."

"We can have Vince train him. Then he can fight the Immortal bastards. But it won't mean a damn thing if you don't send him to Vince."

"I just wanted a normal life," she sighed.

She felt tears begin to well up in her eyes. The whole situation was unbearably frustrating. Already their time together was coming to an end. Fate is a cruel creature.

"Too bad," Derek said. "This is what happens when you want to join the fight against freaks like these guys."

"Do you have to be such an asshole?" Dedalia asked.

"Get the hell out!" Lyn screamed.

Derek looked over at Dedalia, surprised.

"What?" he asked. "Was that too much?"

Dedalia began dragging him out of the house by his jacket. Derek strained against her strong grip.

"Just remember, Lyn!" Derek managed. "Get him trained! Then we can all fight together!"

"Fuck off!" Lyn shouted after him.

She slumped against a wall and clenched her hands into tight fists.

"Fuck!" she screamed.

Derek was right, and she knew it. It didn't make this any easier. The Immortals would be coming for them both in no time. Especially if they were at the top of Elliot's list. At the same time, she couldn't help but wonder who else was on his list. It couldn't be the other people who were chosen to protect Roy. Dedalia and Derek were only two among those picked to protect him. Michael had been rather meticulous about those that were assigned to keep Roy safe.

But for now, she needed to get ready for the evening that the two of them had planned. Maybe then she would bring up the fact that they needed to get ready for the fight that was coming for their bleak futures. She spent the rest of the day getting ready for the night.

***

Roy and Lyn met each other at the restaurant at about six o' clock that night. They were surprised at how quickly they were given a table. It seemed like the restaurant wasn't having a very busy night. This worked out well for them. They were enjoying the night the same as they normally would on any other date. But Roy noticed that she seemed rather distant.

"Babe?" he asked.

He felt her staring past him. Something was clearly off.

"Lyn?" he asked, worriedly.

She seemed to come back into reality. She tried to play it off as if she had been paying attention.

"What is it?" she asked, unable to hide her distracted demeanor.

"Everything alright?" he asked. "You seem like you have been in another place the whole night."

"It's nothing. I'm here. That's all that matters."

"Well, I wanted tonight to be special."

He pulled out a small box from his jacket and placed it on the table. He flipped it open to reveal a rather luxurious ring.

"I wanted to talk about maybe making our relationship even more meaningful," he said with a shimmer in his eyes.

Her eyes widened at the sight of the ring that he had placed before her. She couldn't believe that this was happening.

"I'm listening," she said, drawn in by the beautiful ring on the table.

"There's no point if you're going to be someplace else," he said. "I need you to really be here."

"You have piqued my interest."

"I did have a whole speech planned."

"A whole speech?" she asked. She seemed to be completely focused on him now. "Please do go on."

"Lyn," he said nervously. "You are my everything. You are my beacon in the darkness. I know you will be the one to help me fight the dark. You are my queen forever and always. Will you take my hand in marriage and brighten up the rest of my days?"

"Absolutely," she said happily. "Just as I said the first day I met you, I will make you the happiest man alive."

"I love you," Roy said, smiling.

"And I love you too," she said, beaming back at him.

After that moment, the two of them really enjoyed the evening even more. Roy had put the ring on her finger which gave her the biggest grin he had ever seen. At least he knew that he had picked up a good ring. He couldn't wait to start their lives together.

She knew her friends had told her that she needed to tell Roy about all the dangerous things that were coming their way. She just couldn't do it. Seeing how happy Roy was, she couldn't bear to take that away. She would just try to live their happy lives for as long as they could. If the Immortals dared to get in the way of that, then she would simply have to kill them.

CHAPTER 11

THREE VISITORS

Back on the foreign planet known as Khais, the Commander grew increasingly anxious. He spent most of his days hiding away in his office, still awaiting news of Elliot. It had been six months since he had dispatched Elliot to Earth. He hadn't heard anything in the entirety of his time down there. Either Elliot had met his demise, or he had been captured by the humans. If he was in their captivity, then he didn't understand why he hadn't just broken out. He knew even Elliot would be able to escape any confinement the humans would throw him into.

The Commander knew that he would have to take drastic measures. This was to send the other three of his men to finish the job. He hadn't wanted to do this, but it seems that now he has little choice. They would have to make their way to Earth and find him. Either they would find him as a heap of ash on some deserted street, or he would be stuck somewhere against his will.

He brought his phone out as he had before to summon his three minions. Throughout different rooms of the mansion, each minion had received the message from the Commander. In mere minutes they each had reached the Commander's office. The General was first to enter the room, followed by the other two. If all of this was for naught, then he would make sure that Elliot suffered severely.

"So, what do you need?" the General asked impatiently.

"We haven't heard from Elliot in six months," the Commander explained. "I need you three to go to Earth and find out what has happened. Then you will tell me if he is alive or dead. If he is still alive you are to bring him to me, and I will deal with him personally."

The General smiled wickedly. He had been hoping to go to Earth for some time. He was eager to show Earth the terror that the Immortals could bring them. If he managed to find Roy and his friends, then it would be even better. Barbatos himself would reward him greatly for bringing their corpses to him. He knew their deaths would disprove the prophecy and they would no longer have to worry about the mortals. He would prove just how feeble they were.

"Once you do that," the Commander continued. "You will finish what Elliot started. Kill Roy and his pitiful friends."

"I would be glad to," the General said excitedly.

The Sergeant and Lieutenant exchanged glances. They both understood that the General was out of his mind. But they would still have to follow him anyway. The Commander was quite clear that the three of them were to go to Earth to find their missing ally.

The General had already left the two of them behind. In the hallway, he fished out the Portoball he had been given some time ago. He pressed the red button in its center and vanished from the mansion.

The Commander saw the other two just standing opposite his desk and felt his anger start to boil up.

"What the hell are you two idiots still doing here?" he asked annoyed.

The two realized that they looked ridiculous right now. The Lieutenant looked up at the Sergeant.

"Yeah, man," he said. "Why the hell are you still here?"

The Sergeant snarled down at him as the Lieutenant shook his head disappointedly. He walked past the Sergeant out into the hallway.

"Jackass," the Sergeant growled, following after him.

"Dumbasses," the Commander sighed.

The Lieutenant was still in the hall with the Portoball in his hand. He saw the Sergeant walking towards him with a nasty look on his face.

"Shit," the Lieutenant said.

The Sergeant grabbed him by the throat and lifted him up into the air. He felt the Sergeant's overwhelming strength crushing his windpipe, causing him to gasp for air.

"My bad," he wheezed and pressed the button on his Portoball.

He disappeared from the Sergeant's grip, and the large man tightened his empty hand into a fist. He couldn't stand the Lieutenant, but he was an important part of their operation. He would just have to tolerate him for now. He grabbed the Portoball from his jacket and pressed the button. He vanished into the air and left Khais behind.

The Sergeant had appeared on a sidewalk on the busy streets of New York. He had a difficult time coming to grips with everything around him. All sorts of distractions and sounds engulfed him. It was very different from Khais. Khais was the only place he had ever known. His home was more of a place stuck in the past. This felt like a future many decades ahead of what he was used to.

He saw the Lieutenant standing nearby, caught up in the same trance as him. Seeing him brought back the feelings he had just a moment ago. He approached him, and the Lieutenant slowly turned towards him. His eyes widened as he saw him standing in front of him.

"Jesus, man," he said, startled. "Can you not sneak up on me like that?"

"Pull a stunt like that again and I will rip off your damn head," the Sergeant snarled.

"Fair enough," he said. "Right now, though, we need to work together. We'll have to find the General first. Seems that he left us behind in whatever fucked-up plan he has in the works."

"You may live," the Sergeant growled. "For now."

The General had already been on Earth for at least a week by the time the two of them had arrived. Time passed very differently on Earth than it did on Khais. As they had suspected, he had indeed left them behind. He didn't need them at the time, and if he did, he would easily be able to find them. He had made quite an impressive life for himself already.

He had procured a semi, which he was currently using as a base of sorts. The trailer contained all the equipment that he had gathered. Most of his supplies consisted of firearms. He also managed to obtain an SUV for easy transportation through the city. He even managed to find the prison withholding Elliot from them. He simply needed to come up with a plan that would benefit Elliot's escape. He needed to make it count.

He was wandering in his trailer, taking stock of all the different weapons he had in store for the battle to come, when his phone chirped. He looked down and saw what he had been expecting. The two buffoons he was to work with had arrived on Earth at last. Time did pass very differently here than on Khais; still, he hadn't realized that they were that far behind. Just a few moments up there would translate to a week down here. He realized it was a good idea after all to place trackers in the pockets of their jackets. If not for that, he never would have realized their arrival when he did.

Still, he didn't need their help just yet. He would first need to infiltrate the prison in the disguise he had picked out. He glanced over at the uniform of a security guard hanging next to him. He would assume the role of a security guard, passing notes to Elliot while he made his rounds. Once he has enough information, then he will formulate his plan. He knew he would have to do something extravagant to get as many officers' attention as possible. All in due time.

"Soon enough you both will become pawns in my game," he said.

He changed into the guard's uniform and walked out of the trailer. He got into his SUV and started it up.

"Time to go to work," he said.

Then he rolled down the streets in the direction of the prison where Elliot was being held. The poor fools had no idea what was coming their way. He relished the thought.

CHAPTER 12

LETTERS TO A PRISONER

After Roy's gutsy proposal to Lyn, in a prison a good twenty minutes away, Elliot lay upon his bare bed. The officers had been kind enough to give him solitary confinement. He was sure it was because Vince had convinced the officers that it would be for the best. He had a lot to thank Vince for, it would seem. When he got out of this dreary place, he would make sure to pay him back in kind. He was lucky he had a bed and a toilet; apart from that, his room was empty.

Elliot could have easily broken out of this place. He decided against it. He figured that the others would come for him after enough time. For now, he was playing the waiting game. He was sure that once they came for him, they would have an elaborate plan to make the mortals suffer. Still, he was growing impatient. He had been in this tiny room for six months already. If they had a plan, he wished that they would implement it soon. His boredom was driving him insane.

Just then a wrinkled piece of paper slid underneath

his thick metal door. He descended from the bed and glanced at the paper curiously. He bent down and picked it up off the floor. He smiled as he realized it for what it was. He was right after all. They had arrived, and they already had a plan. Based on what he was reading, the mortals would have a tough time getting out of this one. Then his smile faded as he finished reading it.

"I have to be in this shithole for another six months?!" he shouted furiously.

***

A day ago, the General had grabbed the uniform of a security guard from the back of his truck. He grabbed a briefcase that he had stowed nearby and carried it out with him. He needed to look the part for what he had planned. He walked out of the trailer and made his way over to the SUV he had parked nearby. He climbed inside and brought it to life. He drove the vehicle out onto the road and blended into the traffic as he made his way towards the prison where they were keeping Elliot. It wasn't too difficult to find.

He had a letter handcrafted for Elliot nestled safely in his back pocket. He just needed to find a good moment to sneak it into his cell as he did his rounds at the prison. He pulled into the parking lot and gathered his things before exiting the SUV. He looked around and squinted at the building, as the sun was shining in his eyes. It was already a bit later than he had anticipated. But there wasn't much he could do about that, unfortunately. It didn't seem very busy, at least. Which seemed to be a good sign for his intentions.

He made his way inside and approached the front desk. He noticed that the place looked disgusting. He saw cracks in the tiles and tears in some of the walls. The desk he was approaching looked like it was nicer than everything else in the room. Officers were bustling around the room. He could tell this would be incredibly annoying.

Then he reached the officer at the front desk. She was probably the worst thing in the whole place. Just judging by her face, he could tell that she would have an attitude.

"Great," he muttered under his breath.

The officer peered up at him, her eyes seemingly glazed over. She seemed like she would rather be anywhere else but here. She sighed dramatically.

"What do you want?" she asked in a monotone voice.

"I'm here to see the Warden," he said.

He needed to keep his negative emotions trapped behind his face. He could feel his irritation trying to break out onto his face. He needed to fight it. He needed to seem remotely sane. At least he felt he was more collected than the woman staring up at him now. She was starting to weird him out. It was like she was analyzing him. He was starting to feel like a science project.

Finally, the unnerving tension broke with another loud sigh from her.

"Fine!" she blurted out. "Tyconian, take this guy to meet with the warden, would ya?"

She had glanced over at another officer with spiked hair. A man got up from a desk and wandered over to them. Tyconian. The General felt as if he should know that name from somewhere. It looked like one of the people he was searching for. His appearance reminded him of Phil, one of the men that the Chaosbringer had shown to the Commander. It couldn't be, though. The man from that picture didn't look like a police officer. If this really was Phil Tyconian, then this could prove to be more difficult than he had originally thought.

"Gladly," the man responded as he approached them. "I was getting tired of all this deskwork anyway."

"I can only imagine," the General said.

"What was your name again?" he asked him. "I'm Phil by the way."

The General had thought of many different outcomes, but this hadn't been one of them. He just needed to keep calm and quickly come up with an identity. He found it to be quite difficult to come up with an identity on the spot.

"Uh…Bill," the General lied.

"You got a last name, Bill?" Phil asked him.

"Jackson?" the General said rather unconvincingly. "Jackson."

"Well, let's go then, Bill."

Phil guided him towards the warden's office. He had looked at the nametag on the General's jacket before he stepped in front of him and knew that the General had lied to him. The name on the nametag wasn't even close to the name that the General had given him. He knew that something was up. However, now wasn't the time to bring it up. He would have to deal with it later.

Phil stopped at a rather ragged-looking door. He ushered the General towards the door. The General wasn't sure, but it looked as if he was suspicious of him. Did he already blow his cover? He would have to be even more convincing from here on. He hesitantly reached for the door and swung it open.

The office looked worse than the lobby he had stepped into earlier. The tiny office was a mess. Paper and trash were lying across the floor. Phil closed the door behind him, and the General heard his footsteps as he returned to his desk. For now, he felt that he may have been in the clear, but in the future, he would have to be more careful. The warden was cramped behind a small, beaten desk.

He had thinning hair, combed back with a beard that hadn't been properly groomed in who knows how long. His rounded gut seemed to be pushing against the desk. He was surprised the flimsy desk hadn't already flopped over from the constant straining of the man behind it. The General couldn't believe that this man served as the warden.

The warden was hunched over a computer, seemingly straining his eyes to see the screen in front of him. He suddenly stopped typing at the computer and looked up at him. He seemed surprised to see him. He had been so focused he hadn't even noticed him enter his dingy little office.

"Who the hell are you?" the Warden asked gruffly.

"The name's Bill Jackson," the General said.

He might as well stick with the lie at this point. Else everyone would get suspicious of him. Just as Phil had been. Not really something he could afford at this point.

"I'm a new transfer," he replied.

"A rookie, eh?" the Warden said, stroking his unruly gray beard. "I don't really know if I need another guard around here. I did just hire that fella a few weeks ago."

"I'll make it worth your time, sir. You can never be too careful."

"A fair point."

He seemed to ponder for a moment, stroking at his beard. "Hmm, I guess it couldn't hurt. Why the hell not? I'll have Phil show ya around."

"Thank you, sir," the General said gratefully.

"Just none of that sir shit. Just call me Doug."

"You got it, Doug."

The name just sounded ridiculous coming out of his mouth. Mortals really had rather strange names for themselves.

"Now get the hell out," he ordered. "I got important shit to do."

The General exited the office and nearly jumped as he saw Phil standing right outside the door.

"Let me show you around, Bill," Phil said in a convincing manner.

After they were about halfway down the hallway, he pushed the General against the wall. Phil was lucky he had a cover he had to worry about, else he would have killed him right there.

"Listen," Phil sneered at him, poking him in the chest. "I don't know who the hell you are or why you're even here, but I know you're not who you say you are. I don't know what kind of shit you're trying to pull here, but I will find out and get your ass kicked out of here faster than you can blink. Got it?"

This guy is smarter than he had anticipated. This didn't look good for the facade he was trying to put on. If he wanted to be convincing for now, he would just have to play along.

"I got it," he strained.

He tried his best to make it look as if Phil had been causing him pain even though he barely felt it. This would make him feel like a big man, and this is what the General needed him to believe. He needed to act like a victim.

"You aren't fooling me," Phil growled. "Walk with me, asshole."

He began wandering down the hall, and the General followed him, looking rather distraught. He glanced at the prisoners behind the caged doors. They looked stranger than the weirdest Immortal he would have seen on Khais. Then he noticed that they had stopped in front of a thick metal door with a slot etched into it. He figured that would be how they gave the prisoner food. Other than that, he couldn't imagine it would serve much purpose.

"This is the cell of a very dangerous man," Phil explained. "I don't **ever** want to see you coming over this way. I don't trust you, so I will take care of anything needed for this prisoner, alright?"

"Sure thing," the General replied.

Phil turned his back on him for a moment, and he took his chance. He bent down and freed the letter from his back pocket. He briskly slid the letter underneath the door. Phil turned around with a skeptical look on his face. The General made it look like he was tying his shoes.

"What the hell are you doing?" Phil asked, irritated.

"What's it look like?" the General asked, trying to sound innocent in the matter.

"Whatever, man," he sighed. "Let's get going."

Phil led him back to the lobby. He knew that this guy was up to no good. He would have to find a way to figure out what he was up to before he would be able to do it.

"Be back here at nine AM tomorrow," Phil said.

"Don't worry," the General said. "I will be."

Phil watched the General walk out the door, feeling uneasy about all of this. That man was trouble. But he would need proof that he was scheming something. He returned to his desk and slid open a drawer. He removed his phone from the drawer and dialed a familiar number.

"What's going on?" Vince asked from the other end of the line.

"We got a problem," Phil said. "I'm pretty sure that the General is here."

"Shit."

"He hasn't done anything yet. I'll try to keep an eye on him."

"Tell me the moment he does something. We need to be ready the second he makes his move."

"If he's here, doesn't that mean the others will be here too?" Phil asked.

"I would count on it," Vince said. "We need to be ready for the worst possible outcome. I will need to get Roy ready. He won't have a choice in the matter."

"I don't think he'll appreciate that."

"I won't let humanity lose to the Immortals because one lazy son of a bitch refused to step up."

Phil heard his phone click. He wasn't sure if Vince was upset with him or if he was done with the conversation.

"Well, he is determined," Phil said, putting his phone back in its drawer.

The General had returned to his SUV and dialed a number of his own. The Lieutenant was the one to answer.

"Yeah?" he asked.

"It's time to meet," the General said.

The General hung up. The Lieutenant noticed that the General had sent the location of where to meet to his phone. He helped the Sergeant to the spot where the three of them would meet, and they waited for the General to arrive. They leaned against the truck that the General had made his base of operations. It only took a few more minutes, and the General's SUV parked nearby. He climbed out of the SUV and walked towards the two of them with a big smile on his face.

"Friends!" the General exclaimed. "I know how to stop Roy and his irritating friends!"

"Are you going to enlighten us then?" the Lieutenant asked, unimpressed.

"You're going to love it. But we will need Elliot's help. But it will be worth it. Trust me."

"So, you found him?" the Sergeant asked.

"Of course I did," the General said. "Did you think I was fucking around while the two of you were screwing around on Khais? I never did understand what you idiots were waiting for."

That's what they expected from the General. It still seemed strange being said with a large smile on his face. Yet they were relieved that he was still his normal self.

"I even have a plan for if he fails," he said. "Or if somehow he gets himself killed."

"You seem rather proud of yourself," the Lieutenant said with a raised eyebrow. He didn't trust it.

"You have no idea how well this is going to work," the General said. "Now come with me my friends. This is just the beginning of the end for the mortals. Now we will make this old truck into the most dangerous weapon they have ever seen."

This excited the Lieutenant. He may not like the General very much, but one thing he enjoyed more than anything else was mindless destruction.

"C'mon, Sergeant," he exclaimed. "Let's build this son of a bitch!"

The Sergeant rolled his eyes and wandered over to help them. He wanted nothing to do with whatever they were planning, but he still knew that it would surely benefit them in the long run.

***

Elliot had unfurled the piece of paper that had slid into his room and began reading the letter that the General had so painstakingly crafted for him. He read it again, as he didn't want to accept his fate to this place for another six months.

Elliot, we have found you. We have a plan that will break Roy and his pathetic friends. However, we will need you to stay here for a bit longer for the plan to come to fruition. We are in the process of developing an incredible weapon that will strike fear into the very hearts of the mortals. Once it is finished, we will come for you, and together we will show everyone exactly what it is that we are capable of. After we bust you out of your cell, you will find Roy and destroy him while we keep everyone in the city busy. Until then, you will need to remain in your cell. It should be a quick six months. We will send another letter to update you on any changes to the plan. Just know that if you fuck this up in anyway, we will kill you ourselves.

Sincerely, your friendly Immortals

Elliot finished reading through the letter; he crumpled it up and tossed it over his shoulder. They had to be kidding. The outcome had remained the same. He found himself ensared, a mere pawn in the General's sinister scheme. These six months had been torture enough for him, and now they expected him to wait another six months. He didn't know how it was that he got so lucky.

This had better be worth it. Roy Darsetts had no idea how much that Elliot wanted to kill him. He would make him suffer in the most unimaginable way possible. Not to mention that, if somehow, he failed to kill Roy, he was sure that the General would kill him himself. No pressure, right?

CHAPTER 13

TRAINING

A week has passed since Roy's proposal to Lyn. He had been the happiest he had ever felt in some time. He was enjoying life to the fullest. However, Vince had a lot to consider after the conversation he had with Phil not too long ago. Elliot had friends that followed him down to Earth. This could be catastrophic for them if they aren't careful. He knows that Roy won't like it, but he will have to get him ready in case the worst happens.

He got into his gray pickup truck and headed over to Roy's apartment. It didn't take too long for him to reach his apartment door, and he rang the doorbell. He was sure he heard loud sensual moaning from the apartment and hoped it wasn't what he thought. It took a few minutes, but then Roy answered the door shirtless, wearing sweats. He saw that Roy was putting on some muscle. He guessed he could thank Lyn for that. But still, he would need combat experience as well. Constant sex would not help with that.

"For fuck's sake, Roy," he said in disbelief.

"What's up, man?" Roy asked.

"I see your day is going well. You realize there is more to a day than just fucking all the time, right?"

"What's your point, Vince?" he asked.

"Get dressed. I need you to come with me. We have a lot to talk about."

Roy could read the seriousness on his face. "Alright, fine. Be back in a minute."

Roy closed the door, leaving Vince alone in his thoughts. He couldn't believe that Lyn had corrupted him so much. This was just a bit much. They wouldn't be able to do much in terms of defense if the Immortals caught them while they're getting busy.

"How did it come to this?" Vince sighed, pondering to himself.

The door swung back open, and Roy stood there in a leather jacket and jeans.

"That's what you're wearing?" Vince asked.

"Yeah, man," Roy replied. "It's much better than that shit I wore before."

"How original. Well, let's get going."

The two of them made their way down to Vince's pickup and climbed inside. Vince started it up and drove it into the busy streets.

"So, what did you want to talk about?" Roy asked.

"We need to talk about the man who nearly killed you six months ago," he said reminiscing the moment.

"Why?" Roy asked. "Isn't he in prison?"

"Yes, he is," he responded. "Unfortunately, there has been a development that doesn't bode well. Three of his friends arrived a couple of weeks ago. And I'm sure it's only a matter of time before said friends bust him out of that prison."

"Wait," Roy said processing this. "Are there others like him? I had hoped once he was put away than we would have nothing more to worry about."

"There are many Immortals, Roy," Vince explained. "That man is the weakest among them. His friends are much stronger than he is."

"When were you going to tell me all this?" Roy asked.

"I had hoped that Lyn would bring you up to speed. It seems she was so blind by the prospect of a happy life she refused to tell you about any of this."

"Well, that's just great!" Roy shouted, frustrated.

"Don't worry, Roy," he assured him. "That's why I brought you with me today. I plan to train you. I will help you in the fight against these sons of bitches."

"How in the hell are you supposed to train me to fight people with inhuman strength?" Roy asked.

"I'll put you through your paces," he said with a rather mischievous smile.

Roy didn't like the smile that had adorned Vince's face. He was beginning to get worried about what he had gotten himself into. Then Vince turned the truck into an abandoned parking lot. He parked the truck, and Roy took in the scenery.

The place looked awful. Rubble was all over the ground, and a fallen telephone pole was sprawled out right in front of them. There was a building in the distance, but it was so beat up he wasn't sure what it was exactly.

"What is this place?" Roy asked.

"This is where I trained," Vince said. "And now it will be the place where you will do the same."

"Is this supposed to be a gym?" he asked, taking in the battered building.

"You catch on quick."

"What the hell happened here?"

"I can imagine you don't remember the great battle that happened not too far away from here, do you?" Vince asked.

"What are you talking about?" Roy asked.

"I figured as much," he said. "It was a brutal battle to decide the fate of humanity. A secret society of humans that fought the supernatural in our stead. We fought against the armies of a demon deity known as Chaos. This is just a small portion of the city that was affected. There just hasn't been enough time to repair the destruction the demons wrought."

"Demons," Roy said, skepticism ringing in his voice. "You said something about the demons before, but I still don't know if I can wrap my head around it. I mean what's next? Vampires? Werewolves? Maybe some mystical fairies?"

"I wouldn't dismiss the possibility if I were you."

"Still not sure if I can trust you; it just sounds way over the top."

"I know it sounds unbelievable," Vince remarked. "One day, though, you will see it as the truth. I feel that fate will show you what I mean soon enough."

"I don't even know what you're talking about, man."

He was looking at Vince like he was a complete weirdo. Maybe he was. But Vince knew that, based on the way events were unfolding, he would begin to meet the demons sooner rather than later.

"Don't think about it too much," Vince said. "Lemme show you around."

The two of them got out of the truck and headed to the ruins of the gym in the distance. As they made their way towards the building, Roy couldn't help but notice that the condition worsened as they approached it. Eventually they reached the front doors, which miraculously slid open as they neared them. Then they stepped inside the building and Roy realized it was just as terrible on the inside as it was outside.

The only thing that looked to still be intact was the large wrestling ring in the center of everything. Shards of concrete of varying sizes littered the building. Roy wasn't sure what exactly Vince had been hoping to accomplish here. He stepped on a large crack on the floor, causing him to look down and notice several others just like it.

"How are we supposed to train in a place like this?" Roy asked.

"The only thing that we need is still in one piece," Vince replied with determination.

"Wait. I thought we were training. How are we going to do that with all this broken shit."

"You won't need any machines. We are going to improve how you fight. I heard about your tussle at your office. That was rather pathetic."

"Well, I haven't really needed to fight people before."

"These aren't **people**, Roy. These aliens will kill you without a second thought. This is why you need to be better in a fight."

"So, what?" Roy asked. "Are you gonna fight me?"

"That's exactly what we're doing here," Vince said, flashing him a smile.

"Seriously? You think I'll stand a chance?"

"Probably not. I used to be a wrestler back in the day. But I won't be holding back either. You're going to have to hit me with everything you got."

"Sounds fun."

Vince climbed into the ring and stood up, ready for what was to come. "C'mon, Roy. We don't have much time."

Roy took a deep breath and followed Vince up into the ring.

"Now, Roy I need to see what you are capable of," Vince urged him.

"Alright," Roy said, rather unconfidently.

He removed his jacket and tossed it on a chunk of debris. His gray T-shirt showed off the improvement he had made in the last six months. Although it wasn't a significant improvement, he was still more defined than he had been six months ago. He ran at Vince and was stopped in an instant. All Vince did was stretch out his hand, and Roy's head collided with it. He held him in place with such a simple move. Roy tried to push against it, but it did little good.

"I really got my work cut out for me here," Vince sighed.

He brought his knee up into Roy's stomach, forcing him to reel forward.

"You have to expect resistance in a fight, Roy," he said.

"I know," Roy groaned. "You moved a lot faster than I thought you would. Real fights are hard."

Vince couldn't help but bring a palm to meet his face. It was worse than he thought. He lowered his hand.

"Try again," he said.

Roy ran to him once again. Vince allowed him to try to launch a fist at his face. It seemed he had learned nothing from before. This time Vince grabbed Roy's wrist and twisted it, causing him to cry out from the pain. Then he kicked him onto the mat. Vince then offered him a hand, and Roy reluctantly accepted it. Vince helped him get back on his feet.

"You need to do better," Vince said.

Roy felt woozy. The pain shot through his body all at once. It was a strange feeling.

"I know!" he shot back. "It's not as easy as you make it look, man!"

"Roy, look at me."

Reluctantly he looked up at Vince.

"I'm not putting you through this to show off," he said seriously. "But I need to know if anything happens to me or even Lyn, you will be able to step up. Maybe even save the day."

Roy accepted his words and knew that Vince was right. He needed to believe in himself more and not let everyone else do all the hard work.

"I'll do better," he promised.

"Good," Vince said genuinely. "If you want a fighting chance against these bastards, you will have to be better than me."

"No pressure, huh?" Roy asked nervously.

"Again," Vince demanded.

Roy sighed. He needed to anticipate Vince's counterattack, but he had no idea what he was going to do. He just had to read his movements, and maybe he would be able to break through his defense. He ran to Vince and saw the large man's arm move towards him. He ducked under his attack, and he thought he saw Vince show a slight smirk at this. It made it seem like Vince was pleased with his efforts, giving Roy a glimmer of hope.

Roy walloped Vince in the stomach, making the larger man stagger back. However, he hadn't expected his next move. He was excited that he got a hit in. Vince let loose a mighty kick that connected with his gut. He felt his body involuntarily lurch forward. Then Vince charged at him and knocked him onto the floor with a powerful blow from his arm. This was a perfect clothes-line move. After all that, he was still knocked on his back. It was incredibly frustrating. Vince stretched out his hand. He ignored it and got up on his own. He needed to beat this guy, but he didn't need his sympathy.

"That was better," Vince said. "But still not enough."

Yeah, I know," Roy scowled.

He took a few steps back and psyched himself for the next attack.

"I will beat you," he promised. "I have to."

"Your confidence is refreshing," Vince replied.

Roy ran towards him in a blind rage. He needed to beat him. If he couldn't, he might as well just hand his life over to the Immortals. Vince was disappointed by his movement. He grabbed him by the throat and lifted him up into the air. Then he choke slammed him onto the firm mat below. Roy groaned in pain. It looked like he was a little too eager. He could see the wrestler in the man before him. Vince said he wouldn't take it easy on him, but he clearly was. Still, Roy couldn't win against him.

Vince spent the next six months training Roy. They would meet up once a week. His combat prowess gradu-ally improved, but he was never able to best Vince. It usually ended up in a one-sided match. At the same time, he learned many things about being in a real fight. Next thing he knew, he had a wedding to get ready for. Hoping that somehow Vince was wrong and that nothing would ever happen to either of them. If Vince and Lyn were out of the picture, he wasn't sure if he would survive the destructive power of the Immortals.

CHAPTER 14

PRISON BREAK

Elliot managed to get through another six months in prison. Though he hated every minute of it. On this day he received a letter that changed everything. He saw it slide under the door and dared to feel a slight twinge of hope. He climbed off his bed and wandered over to the letter. He bent down and picked it up off the floor and couldn't help but smile as he read it.

Elliot, it is time. Today is the day you will break free of your cell. Roy is to be wed on this day. Destroy your confines and reach him and the others at his wedding. Crash the wedding and remind them of how dangerous we are.

Your friendly Immortals.

He could almost feel himself beaming with excitement. It was finally time. Now he just needed to figure out how exactly he wanted to break out of his pathetic cage. He crumpled the letter and tossed it aside. He walked towards the heavy door that barred his way. Then he knocked on it hard, hoping to get the guard's attention.

He heard nothing from the other side. So, he knocked even louder. He felt the door tremble under his fist. Still nothing.

"Hey, guard!" he shouted.

"Shut the hell up in there!" The guard barked.

Well, he finally got a response at least. "You seem like a lot of fun."

"I told you to shut the hell up!" the guard shouted.

The guard turned towards the door exactly as he had hoped.

"Are you gonna make me?" Elliot asked.

"Listen here, you motherf—" he managed.

A powerful force knocked the door off its hinges, cutting off his words. The guard was thrown on his back, the door pressing against his body. He couldn't move. The weight of the door had him pinned down.

Elliot stepped out of the cell and breathed in the musty air happily. Then he ripped the chains apart that had bound his wrists for so long with ease. He stepped onto the door that was lying on the guard. He looked down at his terrified face.

"What the hell are you?" the guard whimpered.

"I'm just the start," Elliot said, smiling down at him. "My friends are much worse than I am. We're going to take this world by force. And there isn't a damn thing you can do about it."

Elliot heard the shuffling of more guards running down the hall. He could see at least three more guards.

"Are you mortals truly so eager to throw your lives away?" he asked.

They extended their nightsticks and continued running at him.

"Guess so," he chuckled. "Fuck it then."

He stepped off the door and grabbed the handle. He lifted it up like it was nothing more than a briefcase on a daily commute. Then he hurled it at the guards like a giant Frisbee. The heavy door slammed against the guards and smashed them against a wall on the other side of the hallway. They had been knocked unconscious, and he walked towards them leaving the scared guard behind him. He didn't feel the need to bother the cowering guard. The guard didn't know how lucky he was.

He stepped back onto the door and made his way around the corner into the next hallway. More guards were lying in wait for him. Another group of three. It seemed rather peculiar. He had thought his friends were supposed to keep these guys busy. Oh well. More fun for him.

The one closest to him was holding his nightstick rather nervously. He ran at Elliot and swung his weapon in his face. The nightstick stopped in front of Elliot's face as he had grabbed it in a fierce grip. He tore the nightstick from the guard's grasp, flinging him against a cell door. Then Elliot quickly chucked the object at another guard's face. It reflected off his face, and he was thrown onto the floor.

The third guard just looked at his fellow guards in paralyzed shock. Elliot had taken them both out so easily. He doubted that the guards were dead, but they were definitely unconscious. The guard raised his taser up nervously and pressed the button, causing sparks to emanate at the end. He hoped this would help scare him off. Elliot just kept walking towards him. For him, this was just a casual stroll. There was something seriously wrong with this guy.

He fired the taser into Elliot's chest. He shook wildly as the volts struck his body, but he didn't even fall back. He removed the bit the taser shot into him and threw it onto the floor. Then Elliot grabbed the guard's wrist before he could reach for his own nightstick. He twisted the guard's wrist, and the man cringed in pain. Then Elliot flipped him against a cell door, just like he had with the first guard.

Elliot had almost wished the other guards hadn't been preoccupied. It would have been more fun to fight more of them at once. He continued down the halls but met with little more resistance. In a few minutes, he had reached the lobby. He saw that only one guard remained. He was sitting comfortably at a table with a newspaper in front of him. Even he knew that newspapers were well out of date in this age. Something about him seemed strange.

Then the man lowered the paper, and he saw Phil staring back at him.

"Well, shit," Elliot said.

Phil got up from his chair and looked at Elliot rather sternly. "You've been causing a lot of trouble for us. You should go back to your cell before you get hurt."

"You're nothing more than another human getting in my way," Elliot said confidently. "Why should I be scared of you?"

Phil showed a slight smirk on his face. He pulled out his pistol and aimed it at Elliot.

"Give me a reason," he warned. "I've been hoping for this ever since your ass was dragged in here."

"If you already know what I am, then you know using that won't do a **damn** thing to me," Elliot replied, unconcerned.

"Try me. See what happens."

"You don't scare me," Elliot declared.

He walked towards Phil. "You are nothing human. Your weapons are pathetic."

Phil took a deep breath and shot Elliot in his right knee. This was to prove a point. He was sure that based on his reaction that it had worked. Elliot had screamed in pain and fell to his knees. He cringed as the wound grazed on the floor. This was not a sensation that he was accustomed to. He felt pain before, but this was something else. Somehow, he knew that this wound would not heal like his previous injuries would.

He didn't know what was with that gun, but it was more threatening than he had originally realized. He needed to get out of here. Now.

"What were you saying before, Elliot?" Phil asked. "Something about our weapons being pathetic?"

Elliot looked up, and tears had welled up in his eyes from the pain. He opened his mouth to counter with a smart remark, but then the wall furthest from them blasted apart. A large, armored semi had burst through the wall. This wasn't a part of Phil's plan. He leapt out of the way. He saw that the others he had been warned about were inside.

"Son of a bitch," he said disdainfully.

The General got out of the truck on the other side and walked over to Elliot. He helped him onto his feet and helped him up into the truck. Phil couldn't believe that all of this was happening. He honestly didn't know what to do in this situation. He could probably handle one of them, but dealing with all of them at once was out of the question.

He lifted his gun up towards the large man sitting in the driver's seat. The Sergeant glanced down at him. He growled and jumped out of the truck. He landed heavily in front of Phil. Phil looked up at him, still hearing the ringing in his ears from the collision the truck had made just a moment ago.

"I can't let you or your buddies leave," Phil said grunting as he stood up.

"You are lucky," the Sergeant replied.

"Why's that?" Phil asked.

"You are not a priority. Thus, you will live. Even though you hurt my friend."

"Not a priority?" he asked. "Is that supposed to be a joke?"

Phil had enough of this. He had to do something. He lifted the gun up to point at the Sergeant's face.

"You will live," the Sergeant repeated.

He grabbed Phil's wrist, and Phil felt pain shoot through his arm as the large man crushed his bones. He shouted out and dropped his gun. Then, before he could react, the giant of a man grabbed him by the throat and lifted him into the air. He gasped for air and felt himself flung through the wall behind him.

"Follow us and you will die," the Sergeant snarled at him.

However, his warning would fall on deaf ears, for Phil had lost consciousness. The Sergeant got back into his truck and started it back up. He carefully navigated the large, armored truck back on the road.

The General had guided Elliot into the trailer of the semi. There was a secret door behind the seats in the front. Elliot stood there limply looking at a police car in front of him.

"You want me to get into that thing?" Elliot asked.

"Yes," the General said. "This will help you reach Roy's wedding much faster."

"Where did you even get that thing?" he asked.

"You don't need to know," the General replied.

"Crash a wedding?" he asked. "Let's do it."

He got into the car and started it up. He turned the sirens on as the Sergeant pressed a button on his console. The door at the end of the trailer slid open, and Elliot pushed down onto the accelerator. The police car sped out of the trailer and flew towards the traffic coming towards him. He narrowly missed several cars and veered off into his own lane. Now he just needed to find the pain in the ass who calls himself Roy Darsetts. This should be fun.

CHAPTER 15

WRATH OF THE IMMORTALS

The three Immortals spent six months working on the truck that the General had obtained during his time on Earth. They would use this truck to hatch their plan to break Elliot free of his prison. The truck had been improved significantly from the husk that it had been before. The armored aspect made it seem more like a long tank. This would be the weapon that would gather the attention of the law enforcement.

Before all that, though, they would have to inform Elliot that today was the day. It just happened to be the day of Roy's wedding. They would free him and have him crash the sacred ceremony.

"Are you guys ready to break some shit?" the General asked.

"Hell yeah!" the Lieutenant exclaimed.

"I'm driving," the Sergeant stated.

"This was **my** plan," the General said.

The Sergeant glared at him. He didn't seem to like the General's logic.

"I don't care," he scowled.

"Fine. It won't mean anything anyway."

The Sergeant climbed into the driver's seat. He didn't know what the General meant about him driving not making a difference. But he knew that his main purpose was absolute destruction, and what better way to achieve that than this truck. It felt good just sitting in the seat.

The Lieutenant sat in the middle with the General on the other side of him. The General didn't look pleased. He probably thought of this truck as his greatest creation, and someone else plucked the reins away from him. While the Lieutenant felt incredibly awkward between the two of them.

"Well, let's get going, tough guy," the General said bluntly.

"Gladly," the Sergeant smiled.

He started up the truck and pressed down on the gas pedal. He brought the truck onto the streets, immediately barging into the busy traffic. The truck sped down the road, shoving the cars aside. It plowed through the cars with ease, making the Sergeant giddy with excitement.

The civilians never even saw it coming. One minute it was just a normal day, and the next thing they knew, a maniac in a crazy-looking semi was plowing through the local commute. Some would try to get out of his way, but he would either veer towards them or knock another car into them. The Sergeant was having more fun than he had ever dared to dream of. Then he had another idea to **really** get the cops' attention. He sharply turned through the building next to him. The truck smashed through the building as if it were nothing but a feeble design. If this didn't get their notice, he wasn't sure what would.

**

Back at the prison, it was chaos. Police officers were on the constant move. Officers were rushing out of the building or on the phone about a horrid crash somewhere in the city. Phil was sure that the General was somehow behind this. He didn't know how exactly, but he was sure that he was. He sat at his desk calmly while everyone else ran around in a panic.

He noticed that nearly everyone had left the building and decided to take matters into his own hands. He got up and headed to the warden's office. He knocked on the door.

"Come in," a gruff voice said.

Phil swung the door open and stepped inside the clustered office.

"You wanna tell me what the hell is going on?" the warden asked.

"What do you mean, sir?" Phil asked.

"You were the only one who was suspicious of that guy who I hired six months ago. It seems he was the only one who wasn't here when this shit hit the fan. So, I think you know something about him that you weren't letting me in on. I want to know what it is."

"Honestly, sir, you couldn't handle it," he replied, trying to dodge his accusations.

"What?" the Warden asked sounding annoyed. "Do you think I'm stupid?"

"No, sir," Phil said reluctantly. "He's just a very unbelievable kind of person that would take a lot to explain."

"Why don't you try?" the Warden snarled.

The look was rather frightening. He figured he probably shouldn't piss him off any further.

"He's an alien from another planet called Khais. He disguised himself as one of us but is super strong with rapid healing powers, and he wants to destroy everything that we love and hold dear."

The warden just stared at him for a moment like he was nuts. Then he shook his head in what Phil assumed was disbelief. Then he stood up.

"If you don't know anything, just say so. Now I gotta go out there and deal with this shit myself."

"I don't think that's a good idea."

"Now you think you're better than me?" the warden asked.

"I wouldn't say that sir," Phil replied rather hesitantly.

"You are a real asshole," the Warden said storming past him.

"This isn't going to end well," Phil sighed.

***

The Sergeant crashed through another building and noticed all the flashing lights behind him. He smiled widely. Everything was going exactly as they had planned. Just then he felt the entire truck tremble as something crashed into them like a battering ram. Even the General seemed surprised. There shouldn't be anything that could create trouble for this truck. He had made sure of it.

"What the hell was that?" the General asked.

There was slight concern in his voice. The Sergeant glanced in his sideview mirror. It appeared to be a much smaller armored truck. However, this armored truck had the word "SWAT" stretching across its side and had its own flashing lights of red and blue. The Sergeant wasn't sure what it meant, but it seemed to be a viable threat. He had an idea but wasn't so sure if it would work.

"Here goes nothing," he said.

He slammed on the brakes; the many pursuing cars with flashing red and blue slammed into the back of the truck.

"What the hell are you doing?" the Lieutenant asked.

"Just wait," the Sergeant said calmly.

He shifted the truck into reverse and pushed down on the gas. The truck's wheels rolled over the tops of all the cars behind it and just kept moving backwards. The SWAT truck had gone into reverse as well and kept alongside them well enough. A door on the side slid open, and a man in an armored uniform stood there holding a bazooka. He fired a rocket into the side of the truck.

An explosion ripped through the driver's side of the truck, and the Sergeant did his best to protect himself from the blast. Despite the armored plating covering the truck's side, the explosion tore through it all with ease. Most things could not mortally injure an Immortal, but flames were one of the few things that could. The Sergeant didn't even have the time to register for the pain as the right side of his face became severely burned.

He turned the truck sharply. He needed to balance it out. The blast had nearly toppled them over. He needed to get it back on all its wheels. At the same time, being on top of all the cars that they had wrecked was only making it more difficult. He managed to get out of the pile of cars, and the truck swung into a massive circle, smashing through another building as it went. The truck finally came to a stop, and he regained his bearings. He took a deep breath and saw the SWAT truck come racing towards them.

The Sergeant could now feel the intense pain from the burn on the side of his face. He knew that the burn would take decades, maybe even centuries, to heal. If he hadn't lifted his arm when he did, he would surely be dead. He gripped the steering wheel tightly in his rage. He now would have a permanent scar for the rest of his days, and it's all thanks to the ones in this SWAT van.

"Motherfuckers!" he screamed and kicked down on the gas pedal.

In his anger he saw only red. He didn't care about the two sitting next to him. He would put an end to these encroachers, whether it killed him or not. The men in the van brought down the windows and fired upon them with machine guns. The one with the bazooka needed time to reload such a powerful weapon, it seemed. They would just take advantage of this.

The Sergeant squinted as the windshield became more and more cracked from the bullets. He grew tired of not being able to see them coming and pushed the window out of place. He continued over the remnants of the windshield lying helplessly on the road. He saw the man with the bazooka had climbed onto the roof of the van and directed the large gun towards them once again.

"I really hope you know what you're doing," the General said nervously.

"I got this," the Sergeant said with overbearing confidence.

He abruptly turned towards the SWAT van, and the

truck spun towards the van. The man with the bazooka seemed to be taken off-guard. The truck's trailer collided with the van, and it flipped through the building next to it. Unfortunately, for the people in the van, they were next to a pier. The van rolled right into the ocean, with the people inside scrambling to reach the water's surface.

The Sergeant breathed a sigh of relief. His crazy plan had worked. He was unaware that the man with the bazooka had been thrown against the side of the truck. The man had managed to grip the side of the truck and was now climbing up the side of the trailer.

"You can't tell me that you meant to do that," the General remarked skeptically.

"Of course I did," the Sergeant replied.

"You're a crazy motherfucker!" the Lieutenant exclaimed, nudging his arm. "That was badass!"

"Don't encourage him," the General replied. "Don't forget we got a passenger to pick up."

"Oh shit," the Sergeant remembered.

He had plumb forgotten all about Elliot. He got the truck going again and, in a few minutes, they were closing in on the prison. Then the man with the bazooka from before dropped onto the hood of their truck. He had his bazooka locked onto the three of them. If he fired that rocket from there, it would be the end for all three of them. It wouldn't matter what crazy maneuvers they did. The Sergeant grew tired of this thorn in their sides.

"I don't know who you people think you are," the man said. "But I'm putting an end to all of you right now. You are too dangerous to stay alive."

The Sergeant moved quickly. He used his long arms

to grab the bazooka and wretch it out of his hands. He tossed the gun aside and grabbed the man's arm. He yanked him across the hood, forcing him to slide directly in front of the Sergeant.

"You are right about one thing," the Sergeant declared. "We are too dangerous to stay alive."

The Sergeant smacked his face against the truck's hood and flung him through the air. He crashed atop a dumpster in an alleyway. He dented the lid with his fall, and he groaned in pain. As he recovered from the fall, the truck kept on going.

The Sergeant turned the truck through the fencing surrounding the prison where Elliot lay in wait. Then he drove the truck straight into the prison. They saw Phil. But the three of them took care of him. Then the General helped Elliot into the truck and escorted him into the trailer. It was here that he showed him to the car that he had stolen for their purpose. He helped him into the car as he had suffered a nasty wound from Phil's gun.

The Sergeant had guided the truck back onto the road as the General had told him what was going to happen next. He heard Elliot start up the police car as well as the sirens. Then he pressed a button on his console, and the trailer's door slid open, and Elliot drove out of the truck. The General rejoined them and looked over at them, looking rather grim.

"It seems he was having just as hard a time as we were," the General sighed.

CHAPTER 16

FATED WEDDING

During all the craziness that was happening in the city, Roy stood in front of a mirror trying to psyche himself up for what was coming. He took a deep breath and sighed. He could only focus on the nerves that he was feeling. After all, he had a heavenly woman awaiting him.

"I really don't know what she sees in me," he sighed.

Just then the bathroom door swung open, and Vince walked inside. "What are you doing, man?"

"Just contemplating life decisions," Roy replied.

"It's a little late for that, isn't it?" Vince asked.

"I suppose you're right about that," he agreed.

"Of course, I am."

"So how do I look?" Roy asked.

He felt inferior in the luxurious setting that everyone else seemed to be enjoying so much. He had hoped that Vince would at least give him a blunt response.

"You look like a trainwreck, but the suit looks great," he joked.

It seemed that Vince wouldn't be disappointing him at least. "Thanks, asshole."

"My duty as best man is to be completely honest with you."

Roy couldn't believe that he had got to this point. It seemed like a dream that he never woke up from. Still, it made him feel so much happiness. He had someone who would be glad to see him. Someone who lit up the room just by being there. He shook his head to boot the doubting thoughts from his mind.

"You of all people need to be in high spirits on this day, Roy," Vince said, trying his best to calm him down. "You just let me handle everything else. I won't let anything get in the way of this day. We may never have another moment like this for a long time. So just enjoy yourself while you can."

"You may be onto something," Roy assented. "Can't believe that I even thought of doubting you."

Roy wandered out of the bathroom. Vince clasped the sink in front of him and hung his head in distress. He didn't have the heart to tell him that this whole ceremony was a terrible idea. His phone began ringing. He stopped staring at his reflection for a moment and pulled out his phone. Phil was calling him. Normally he would text, so he had a feeling that it was something serious.

"What's going on, Phil?" he asked.

"This is bad," Phil said, sounding panicked. "This is so fucking bad."

"Breathe, Phil. What happened?"

Vince cringed as Phil took deep breaths over the phone. It initiated an obnoxious static noise in his ear.

"He's coming straight for you guys," Phil sighed.

"Who is?" Vince asked.

"Elliot," he replied anxiously. "I tried to stop him. He's wounded, but he could already be there for all I know."

"You wounded him then? In what way?"

"He'll have a limp. I shot the bastard in the knee. I should have shot him in the head. Stupid!"

"Calm down," Vince said. "Everything will be fine."

"No, it won't. I ran into the other Immortals too. I don't even know how I'm still alive. They wanted me to stay alive for some reason."

Vince rubbed his temple with his free hand. He thought he knew exactly what they were up to.

"I know what they're doing," Vince grasped. "They want Elliot to make an example of Roy. They want him to kill Roy in front of us. They have blind faith in Elliot's success."

"Doesn't that mean that they will be right behind Elliot?" Phil asked.

"I don't think so. For some reason I think they are leaving this up to Elliot."

"But why?" Phil asked.

"That I don't know. But imagine what will happen if Elliot fails. The three of them will surely be after us next."

"Shit!" Phil shouted in his ear.

He had to pull the phone away for a moment. "Phil, I need you to listen to me. You need to call Dedalia and let her know what's going on. Then get her to bring **him** in on this. The assassin."

"Are you serious?" Phil asked. "The guy's an asshole."

"We don't have a choice," Vince grimaced. "He has his own debt to repay. He will comply or I will kill him myself."

Vince heard Phil sigh in disgust through the phone.

"Get your shit together, Phil!" he ordered. "Lives depend on this!"

"Alright, alright!" Phil exclaimed. "I got it."

"Good, now get it done," he commanded.

He heard the phone click as Phil hung up. Vince put his phone back into the confines of his suit. It seemed likely that Elliot was already here, hidden among the crowd. All he had to do was find him before he made his move. The only problem was that he didn't know when he was planning to strike. He needed to get out there now. He practically burst out of the bathroom and immediately looked around the room.

"Shit!" he exclaimed.

The room was packed with men in suits and women in fancy dresses. Elliot would effortlessly blend in with the crowd. He just had to wait for him to do something an ordinary human wouldn't do. Maybe he would be lucky enough to find him limping down the aisle at some point.

***

Elliot swerved in and out of the heavy traffic as he approached the church where Roy's wedding was in full swing. He only knew about it due to the information that the General had uncovered during his time in the prison. Finally, he found it. He sharply turned the car into the parking lot and lazily parked the police car he had used. Then he began his slow limp towards the church.

Elliot noticed several people giving him nervous glances as he hobbled up towards the building. Not that it mattered to him. There was only one thing that he needed to worry about. He just had to blend in with these people and find the right time to take his moment. He reached the door and grabbed the handle, but then his hand slipped from it of its own accord. A woman opened the door for him.

"Are you okay?" she asked.

"It's been a day," he groaned.

"I get it. I've had days like that."

"You have no idea."

"Well, shall we?" she asked. "I can help you if you want me to"

So, humans are capable of good things after all. He knew that over the years, humans had a habit of triggering bloody acts of violence, often among anyone who disagreed with them. His fellow Immortals weren't much better. This woman seemed to be a truly good person. It had caught Elliot off guard. She was now standing there offering her arm to him. Maybe humans weren't so bad after all.

"Gladly," he said, smiling.

He cradled his own arm into hers, and she helped him inside. It seemed that she was one of the guests that hadn't come with anyone else. The two of them took a seat in the back, and the woman held his hand in a rather comforting way. He didn't know what to think. This all felt so new to him. He glanced over at her, and she flashed him a bright smile. He couldn't help but wonder what he had done to deserve such friendliness. It appeared that humans were capable of kindness after all. Not something they felt was important to mention while he was on Khais.

Then he saw Vince scoping out the room. He knew that Vince was looking for him. He wouldn't expect him to be with this woman though. Perhaps he could use this situation to his advantage. Now he just needed to find the right time to make his move.

Just then a familiar tune began to emanate through the church from a piano. Having never heard it before, Elliot felt entranced by it.

"Damn it!" Vince shouted.

He would have to be a part of the ceremony involving the bridesmaids and groomsmen. He was sure that Elliot was in there somewhere; he just couldn't quite pinpoint him. After the pairs of men and women traveled down the aisle, they stood at the front of the church. They looked over at the crowd as the priest began the service, which he had probably rehearsed many times before.

The ceremony also gave Vince the opportunity to look at everyone at once. He was sure that he found Elliot sitting next to a woman. She seemed happy to be next to him. She didn't know or understand how dangerous the man sitting next to her truly was.

"Isn't this nice?" the woman next to Elliot asked, smiling.

Her nice demeanor was intoxicating. He couldn't help but smile back.

"If you're into this sort of thing," he whispered back, feeling that it was the best way to respond in this ceremony.

"Oh, stop," she chuckled.

***

Vince bent down and whispered into Roy's ear. "I'll be back. Going to the restroom."

Roy nodded as Vince snuck off the altar. Elliot needed to get his head back into the game. Eventually he would have to break free of the woman's charms. He would figure out the opportune moment to strike. He just needed to ignore the woman's wiles. Then the pastor said a line that he knew was the perfect moment.

"If anyone has a reason for these two not to be wed, then let them speak now or forever hold their peace," the pastor announced.

Elliot knew that this was his moment. He stood up, breaking free of the woman's grip to her dismay, and limped to the aisle.

"What are you doing?" she asked.

"You should get out of here," he said. "Shit's about to go down."

This didn't seem to happen often. Everyone was staring at him in disbelief. Normally there was just a silent moment, and nothing happened. However today was different. Then he did something even more blasphemous. He pulled a pistol out of his suit.

"I do, motherfuckers!" he shouted.

The pastor looked upon the scene in utter shock. All the guests began screaming and running around in a panic. Not that he could blame them. This whole moment seemed unreal. Elliot was walking towards Roy with the pistol aimed at him. The pastor had produced a handkerchief and began blotting at his sweaty bald head.

"I knew I should have just retired," he sighed.

"I finally found you, Roy Darsetts!" Elliot shouted. "And right now, in this moment, you got nowhere to go. I get to kill you in front of all your friends. All your family. The Commander will shower me with praise when I return to Khais with your mangled body! And there isn't shit you can do about it!"

"I don't even have any family **left**, asshole," Roy said through gritted anger.

"Are you fucking kidding me?!" Lyn shouted. "Listen here, you son of a bitch! You are **not** ruining my wedding day for this!"

Elliot felt fear travel through his body for a moment. No. This was his moment.

"Shut up, bitch," he demanded. "You can die first if you want. It doesn't fucking matter to me."

"Can I kill him?" she asked Roy.

"Not yet," Roy said, looking past Elliot.

"Why not?!" she asked furiously, clenching her jaw.

Roy nodded his head towards the man who had appeared behind Elliot. Vince had snuck behind Elliot and now cradled his arms under Elliot's armpits. He lifted him up into the air, and the two crashed onto the floor. Elliot winced as a fresh pain shot through his leg. He had fallen onto Vince's body, and the strong man had already put him into a tight grapple. It was hard to bring his pistol up toward his target. He knew full well that this had been his intent. He flailed against Vince's strong grip, but it only seemed to make his hold get even tighter.

"Fuck this!" Elliot shouted.

He found the floor with one of his feet and pushed himself up onto his feet. It looked rather comical as Vince was lifted into the air still atop the smaller man's back. It was quite the scene to look upon. Elliot's strength truly was something else. The next thing Vince knew, he was flipped over Elliot's head. He crashed through the wooden pew next to them.

"You will not stop me from my mission!" Elliot barked. "My reputation rides on my success!"

Vince picked up a pair of long and jagged pieces of wood. They seemed to be about the right size for what he was planning to do next.

"You hear me, asshole?!" Elliot asked.

Vince got up with his back still facing him. "Yeah, I heard ya,"

Then he swung around fast like a hurricane and smashed Elliot's face with one of the pieces of wood. He knew that he caught him by surprise. The wood shattered against his face. Elliot winced as he felt the pain from the splinters of wood now lodged in the side of his face. Vince didn't even give him the chance to process what just happened. He had already begun swinging the other piece towards his face. He had to be relentless. If he gave him the chance, Elliot could easily turn this fight around.

Elliot lifted his arm to brace himself for the wood coming down at him. The wood shattered against his arm. He didn't have the reaction that Vince was hoping for. He tackled Elliot across the aisle, hoping for it to faze him long enough to figure out what to do next. Elliot's back slammed against the pew on the other side, and Vince riddled his face with a barrage of punches.

Then Elliot grabbed Vince's wrist after a third punch and clobbered him in the face with a punch of his own. He hadn't been expecting that and was thrown onto his side. He was lucky that Elliot was one of the weaker ones. Any other Immortal would have knocked him clear down to the doors easily enough. He got up and saw Elliot limping towards him. It reminded him of Elliot's injury that Phil had given him. He was grateful that Phil had run into him before.

Elliot hurled a punch at Vince, and he sidestepped him. Then he quickly brought his knee up into Elliot's gut. Elliot hunched forward, and Vince brought him into a different wrestling hold. He spun Elliot through the air and smacked him against the pew nearby. The result merely cracked the wooden bench.

"Well, that was anticlimactic," Vince said, disappointed.

Elliot was still in his grasp, and Elliot delivered a kick to Vince's face as he was held sideways. This caused Vince to stumble back, and he felt warm blood streaming from his nose. He was certain that his nose was broken from the blow. He spit out the blood running into his mouth and wiped off the rest on the back of his sleeve. The suit was instantly stained, but he didn't care about that right now. He had to deal with the man in front of him.

Elliot ran at him as fast as his limp would allow him to. This looked like Vince's last chance. He punched Elliot in the face with swift precision. Elliot staggered backwards, and Vince hastily hurled a kick into his chest. Vince had knocked him onto his back. He walked up to Elliot and stomped on his bum leg.

"Motherfucker!" Elliot screamed.

Vince kicked him in the face for good measure. Elliot seemed to be growing weaker, just as he had at the bar. His eyes were barely open anymore, but Vince could still see that he wanted to go on. It was time to end this before he could cause any more problems. He reached down and grabbed Elliot's tie. Then he began dragging him to the altar. He only hoped that this would work. It wasn't the most ethical way to eliminate an Immortal, but surely it would be worth a try.

The Pastor came out from behind his podium and pointed a finger at him angrily. "This behavior is unacceptable in the house of God! Stop this madness at once!"

Vince just stared at him coldly. "Move, old man. I will hurt you."

The Pastor stepped aside and blotted at his sweaty face. "People nowadays are so rude."

He reached the tub that was filled with holy water. He looked down at Elliot and saw him flailing his arms in a desperate attempt to break free of his grip. Perhaps this would work after all. He knew what fate was in store for him after all.

"Do it, dumbass," he snarled. "You're only fucking yourselves over by doing so."

"Shut your damn mouth!" Vince ordered.

He used all his power to toss Elliot into the holy water. A loud shriek echoed in the church as steam rose up from his suit. It seemed that he was right after all. His body was rapidly cracking and turning into ash.

"You're all fucked!" Elliot shouted, making sure his voice was loud enough for everyone to hear it. "Once **they** find out. You're all dead!"

Then his face cracked and fell into the tub mixing with the rest of the ash that was floating in it. Roy couldn't believe what he had witnessed. Is this what the Immortals were capable of? He couldn't help but wonder just how many more there were. Or maybe he would be lucky, and this was all there was. Could it be possible that it was all over? Elliot's death bringing about the end of the Immortals? Somehow, he didn't think he would be quite so lucky.

"What in the hell was that?!" the Pastor asked exasperated.

"You wouldn't believe me if I told you," Vince said, fatigued. "But you wanna maybe finish what you started?"

He glanced over at Lyn and Roy. "You never finished this very important ceremony."

The Pastor wandered over to them, grumbling as he went. He fished a pair of rings out of his robes. He must have grabbed them at some point. But Roy wasn't sure when he even had the chance.

"Here," he said, roughly shoving the rings into their hands. "Kiss the bride already."

Roy couldn't help but feel that this Pastor was terrible. But there wasn't much that they could do about it now. They put on each other's rings, and they shared a quick but passionate kiss. Roy felt giddy now. For that single moment everything seemed to stop, and he could enjoy himself. But then the moment stopped, and he felt a twinge of disappointment. Lyn turned towards Vince and the anger in her eyes was quite terrifying.

"You single-handedly **ruined** my wedding day!" she shouted. "I will not forget this!"

"I didn't—" he started.

Then Roy couldn't believe what she did next. She grabbed his nose, and there was a loud crunch as she twisted it back into place. He hollered from the pain that he felt, but then the feeling faded, and it did indeed feel better.

"There, asshole," she growled.

Then she turned towards Roy with a smile on her face. "Are you coming, husband?"

"Of course, dear," he replied, not sure what to think.

He was in a state of shock from what he had just witnessed. She could have done much worse, judging by the fiery look she had burning on her face.

"You put a ring on it," Vince commented.

Roy just glared at him but then followed Lyn out of the church. After all, he didn't want to be on her bad side. Not after what he had just seen. Vince let out a small chuckle and followed them. At least he wouldn't be bored protecting these two. Perhaps he should thank Roy's brother for that at least.

"You're all insane!" the Pastor shouted. "I fucking quit!"

CHAPTER 17

THE HONEYMOONERS

It has been a couple of weeks since Roy's wedding, and it felt like a lifetime already. He may not have known Lyn all that long, but it seemed like she was the one that he had always wanted. They would do just about everything together. The only real downer that they had come across was the disaster that had happened during their ceremony. But they still were officially married now and were able to spend all their time enjoying each other's company.

It was even more difficult to believe that one of their greatest adversaries wouldn't be bothering them anymore. That holy water in the church had successfully brought him down into nothing more than a pile of dust after all. But they would have to worry about their future now. In Roy's eyes, they were now free to live their lives as they wished. No more unnatural threats to disturb their life of peace.

Yet now he had a beautiful woman at his side. She had spruced up his apartment and made it her own. He still wasn't sure why she would have left that mansion behind. Supposedly, she was only meant to use it when it was completely necessary. But that didn't really explain why she had been using it before. Maybe she had her reasons. Oh well, he wasn't going to complain. He noticed her shift next to him and slowly opened her eyes groggily.

"Hey," she said sheepishly. "Morning."

"Morning," he replied drowsily.

Even though he woke up before her, he still found it difficult accepting this as his reality. He had become accustomed to nothingness being his company upon waking. It was a refreshing sight. Something to look forward to, something exciting.

"Time to wake up," she giggled.

It seemed so strange to see her act so different from the persona that she presented to other people. He had to admit to himself that he kinda liked it.

"It's so early though," he grumbled.

"Oh, I think I know a way to fix that," she purred.

"Is that right?" he asked, smiling.

They practically ripped their clothes off each other and made passionate love in the dusk of the morning. After they had both reached satisfaction, they just lay there looking into each other's eyes. They breathed heavily as the sex took a lot out of them. But now they were just enjoying the quiet moment. They had so few of these moments; most of their time had been about merely surviving. Being wanted by the Immortals put a bit of a damper on their relationship at the beginning of it. Yet now they could actually enjoy their time together.

"I love you," Roy said happily.

"I love you too," she replied with a big grin on her face.

Lyn had thought she was using Roy to escape her old life. But now she felt that she really did love him. He was her everything. She would do everything in her power to make sure that he lived a long and happy life. It didn't matter what she went through as long as they could be as happy as they are right now.

The two of them spent most of the day together. Just frolicking around Roy's apartment. They enjoyed everything from savoring their piping hot coffee and watching TV together to eating lunch together. However, this blissful fantasy would have to come to an end. There was a loud knock at the door. Before she even glanced through the peephole, Lyn knew that their day was about to be ruined. She saw Vince standing outside and knew it couldn't be good. She swung the door open, and he looked rather impatient.

Vince made his way past her and entered the living room. Roy was sitting on the couch quite comfortably. When he saw him enter the room, he knew it was time. This time of day had become the daily watch. Vince would come over and spend the day scanning for adversaries down on the streets just to make sure that the Immortals weren't planning anything sinister. Roy sighed and leaned back into the couch. Vince stood at the window peering down on the streets below.

"So, to what do we owe the pleasure?" Lyn asked sarcastically.

"You know the drill, Lyn," he said without turning to face her. "I have to make sure that the two of you are safe."

"That's just super," she sighed.

She leaned against the doorway to the living room. She hated this. They should just take the fight to them. That way they wouldn't have to keep an eye over their shoulders.

"You know what?" she said. "I think we are out of beer. I'll be back."

She grabbed her keys and was out the door before Vince had even noticed.

***

A few minutes passed as Vince watched the traffic go by. "Lyn."

He turned and saw that she was nowhere to be seen. His eyes hadn't betrayed him after all. He had seen her down there and the worst possible scenario had formed in front of him.

"Roy, we have a problem," he noted.

"What is it?" Roy asked genuinely.

Roy knew that Vince was trying to get in the way of Lyn's enjoyment. Vince being here all the time made it quite difficult to enjoy their time as husband and wife. He knew that she was just trying to get out of the house. Vince being there made it rather insufferable. Nothing like being a newlywed with a third wheel always there.

"Lyn may be in danger," Vince said seriously. "I'm pretty sure that I just saw **the** truck go by. I saw her down there as well."

"The truck?" Roy asked. "There's a lot of trucks out there, man."

"Not just a truck. The same truck that destroyed most of the city during your wedding."

"Shit."

"We need to get going, Roy," he demanded. "Now!"

"I don't even know which place she went to for the beer," Roy said in a panic.

"Damn it!" Vince shouted. "It may already be too late."

***

Lyn had taken her car to the nearest gas station. She just couldn't handle another minute of Vince. She needed to get out for a minute. This was just an excuse to get away from him. She walked into the gas station not noticing the large, armored truck parked alongside the street. Even if she had seen the truck, she wouldn't know of the danger that it posed.

***

A couple of weeks ago in the aftermath of Roy's wedding, the Sergeant pulled his truck into the parking lot of the church. They were expecting Elliot's overwhelming success. The three of them climbed out of the truck and approached the church, feeling confident in their plan. They were completely oblivious to Elliot's demise. As they wandered down the aisle, they couldn't help but appreciate the destruction that had occurred here. They were quite proud of what Elliot had managed to accomplish.

However, there was something that wasn't adding up. There was no sign of any of the mortals who should have been killed. Vince didn't matter to them, but the other two were a big deal. The Commander was very clear that those two needed to be killed more than anyone else. Together, those two would be the most hazardous to their cause. They didn't really get it, but he seemed to be afraid of what they could do if they managed to live.

They saw a priest at the front of the church wiping at his sweaty face with a soiled handkerchief. He turned towards the three men walking towards him.

"Oh great," he muttered under his breath.

"What happened here?" the General asked.

He was genuinely curious. It was beginning to seem more like Elliot had failed, but he wouldn't be able to punish him if he couldn't even find his body. Knowing how Immortals die, he was starting to get nervous. Maybe they had killed him. Surely that couldn't be the case.

"What happened here was a disaster!" the priest shouted. "It was supposed to be a simple wedding, and some nutjob came out of nowhere. He had a gun, and I was sure he was going to start shooting people! Then he just casually walked up to the bride and groom and threatened them."

"Calm down, old man," the General ordered. "What happened to the man with the gun?"

"Some big guy beat the shit out of him," the priest replied, trying to catch his breath. "Somehow, he did the same to the guy who was stupid enough to attack him. Then he tossed the guy who had the gun into the holy water I have prepared for baptisms."

"Do you understand what any of that means?"

He was afraid that perhaps the old man had figured out what they were.

"No," the priest said, wiping more sweat from his brow. "Should I?"

"There's only one thing I need to understand. What became of the man with the gun?"

"Why are you so curious about that psychopath?"

The General was rapidly losing his patience. He wasn't sure, but he was assuming that the holy water that the priest was referring to may have been the thing that killed Elliot. If so, things wouldn't be going well for any of them. This meant the mortals had discovered a major weakness of theirs. This is not something that they could afford to come to light.

"I don't know if I should tell you," the Priest said. "You got a scary look in your eyes."

The General had enough of the games. He grabbed the priest by the throat and lifted him into the air.

"Fucking tell me what happened!" he shouted furiously.

The Priest grabbed the General's hand, desperately trying to pry the man's hand off his throat. He could feel his windpipe becoming gradually crushed. He started wheezing as he became more eager for air.

"Tell me, or I swear I will snap your fucking neck!" the General bellowed.

"Alright!" the Priest exclaimed.

The General dropped the Priest onto the floor with a heavy thud. He began breathing in the air deeply. He didn't think he would ever be so grateful just to breathe.

"He dissipated into a pile of ash in the pool," the Priest said weakly. "It was the strangest thing."

"Fuck!" the General shouted furiously.

He turned towards the other two. "This isn't good. We need to get the fuck out of here now."

"What's going on?" the Lieutenant asked.

"They have figured out one of our blaring weaknesses," the General said, dismayed. "They know now how to kill us all, just as they have already done to Elliot."

The General stormed out of the church, with the other two struggling to keep up with his pace.

***

Back in the present, the General was taking the truck for a drive through the town and couldn't believe his luck. He saw Lyn pull her car out from the parking lot of Roy's apartment complex. She was all alone, too. He smiled to himself. It looks like their luck was about to change. It was about time to execute plan B.

The General followed after her without getting too close. Lyn reached a gas station and wandered inside. She heard a jingle as someone else entered after, oblivious to who it could be. Nothing for her to worry about.

She spent her time looking at the different assortment of beers and finally found the kind that she had been searching for. It was the last case they had left. A man next to her picked it up. Her eyes widened as she recognized his face. She really **hated** it when Vince was right. The General was standing there smiling at her. It was rather unsettling.

"This what you were looking for?" he asked.

"What are you doing here?" she asked nervously.

"I think you know why I'm here."

He flashed the pistol he had stowed away in his jacket. "You're coming with me. Don't make a scene or I will kill you."

She sighed. She knew she didn't have a chance. She was sure that the other two goons would be right outside waiting for her to try something. She wouldn't be able to take on all three of them at once.

"Fine," she sighed.

He led her back to her car. They left the beer behind in the gas station. It wasn't exactly a priority right now. She got in the driver's seat, and he sat in the passenger seat next to her. It turned out that the General was alone after all. She had assumed that the three of them would be here. But there wasn't much she could do now to get out of the situation. He had a pistol pointed at her, giving her an unbearable feeling of helplessness.

"Drive," he ordered. "My friends will keep yours occupied."

CHAPTER 18

DEADLY BUSINESS

After Phil hung up the phone following his discussion with Vince at Roy's wedding, he panicked. So much was happening all at once and he wasn't sure quite how to handle it. He knew that Vince was right. He would have to call Dedalia. She would have to bring the assassin into the fold. He just really wished that they didn't need his help. He is a true asshole. Well, nothing much he can do about it now.

Phil was sitting at his desk watching the insanity unfold outside. He probably should try to stop the psychos driving the armored truck, but this could be just as important. He had to let Dedalia know what was happening. He grabbed the phone at his desk and dialed her number.

"Yes, Phil?" a pleasant woman's voice asked.

"How did you know it was me?" he asked, surprised.

"I have my ways."

"Enough about all of that. I think it's time for us to repay our debts to Michael's brother."

"And why is that?" she asked.

"**They** are here. They're running through the city as we speak."

"If that really is the case. Why the hell are you sitting on your ass right now."

"What?" he asked confused.

"We all need to get together and find Roy," she replied. "His very life depends on it. Yet there you are, sitting comfortably on your ass."

"Are you spying on me?"

"Something like that. Now, get over here now. I will deal with the other one."

"Alright," he said confoundedly. "I'll be there soon."

She hung up before he could blurt anything else out. Well, it looks like everything is coming together. They would finally be able to join Roy in his battle against the Immortals. The only thing is that Roy didn't know who most of them were. But of course, she was right. He needed to stop sitting down and start to do something. The Immortals are incredibly dangerous, and if they got to Roy, there is no telling what they would do to him. He would just have to deal with the jerk that would soon be a part of their group.

He slid himself out of his chair and made his way to his car with a feeling of purpose. They would beat the Immortals. He didn't know how yet, but still he knew that they would. He pushed the door open and walked briskly towards his car. He crawled inside and started it up. Then he drove towards the apartment building where Dedalia would be lying in wait.

As it happened, her apartment was in the same building as Roy's. It was two apartments down the hall.

This made it quite easy to keep an eye on him and make sure that he was safe. He was sure that he heard sensual noises coming from Roy's apartment as he passed. But he dismissed the thought from his mind. Then he stopped in front of the door that barred the way into Dedalia's apartment.

He hesitated at first but then pressed down on the doorbell. The chime rang throughout her apartment and soon she was at the door.

"Took you long enough," she said.

"You going to let me in?" Phil asked, ignoring her remark.

"I don't really have a choice," she said, stepping aside. "We all have our obligations."

He stepped into her apartment and made himself cozy on her couch. He looked around and saw that it wasn't the nicest apartment, but she could have done a lot worse. The TV opposite him looked rather small compared to what he had been expecting. An armchair was nestled nearby with the footrest stuck out. He was sure that the chair was broken. Living here alone, he doubted that she had planned to even use it. He could tell that the apartment had been around for some time, but the location was ideal for what they were trying to accomplish. He knew that the others would come in and go from this place. He knew that the assassin they were bringing to fold soon had also been through here quite often.

"Sure, make yourself at home," she judged. "Just don't forget we're working, alright?"

"Yeah, yeah, I know," Phil said, brushing her off.

She left him sitting in the living room, leaning against the kitchen counter. The color of the kitchen seemed to have faded a while ago. Pots and pans were cluttered behind her. Despite the mess around her, she paid it no mind. Dishes filled the sink, and a couple more cluttered on the table. She was more occupied with the phone now in her hand. She dialed a number and waited for the man to answer. An assassin who goes by Derek Deathbed.

Further into the city, a warehouse was situated that had somehow avoided the destruction brought on by the General and his cohorts. A man stood in the elevator, flanked by a pair of suspicious-looking men on either side. The man in between them sported hair spiked in the front. He adorned himself with a dark leather outfit. Currently, he had a headphone in his right ear to drown out the obnoxious noises that emanated through the factory.

The two men in the elevator with him had the look of a basic thug. One is bald, and the other has long, greasy hair. Each of them had a scruffy beard and bloodshot eyes. They both seemed exhausted and the look of one who has seen a lot. They wore ragged vests over ugly gray T-shirts and torn jeans. They seemed to be eyeing the man in between them cautiously. They didn't seem to trust him. The man in between them barely paid them any attention.

The man cramped between the two thugs in the tiny elevator is Derek Deathbed. He is a well-respected assassin in many shady circles. For him this was just another job. He had managed to get as little trust from these two buffoons as he could. He even convinced the two of them to take him to his client. They didn't seem none the wiser. This whole thing seemed to be almost perfect. He really enjoyed it when his plans went well. He only kept these two alive, because he didn't believe it necessary to kill them. He didn't enjoy killing for no good reason.

Hopefully the two skeptical men didn't give him a reason for that to change. But then his perfect plan fell apart in an instant. His phone began to ring. Sadly, he hadn't put it into silent mode.

"For fuck's sake," he said, rolling his eyes.

"Who the hell is that?" the man on his right asked.

Derek pulled out his phone and squinted at the name emblazoned on the screen. Dedalia. "You gotta be kidding me."

"Who the hell is it?" the other man asked.

"No one, either of you, would know," Derek replied quietly.

"Are you bringing trouble here?" the man on the right asked, his eyes showing rising anger.

Derek laughed at his question. He was quite clueless. "Buddy, I **am** trouble."

"You gonna answer it?" the man on the left asked.

"I really should," Derek said, considering it. "But know that if I do, I'll have to kill you both. I really don't wanna do that after we built such a great friendship."

"Fuck you," the man shot back.

"Now that's not very nice," Derek replied coldly.

He pressed a button on his headphones to transfer the call to his ear. "What's up?"

"We need to talk," Dedalia said.

The man on his left released a fist at his face. Derek tightly grabbed his wrist and twisted it, causing him to cry out. Then he pushed him into the other man, and the two of them collided against the elevator wall.

"Is now a bad time?" she asked.

The bald man scrambled to his feet and produced a knife in his hand. He swung the knife down towards

Derek's face in a wide arc. He grabbed the man's wrists and strained to keep the blade of the knife away from his face.

"No," he said, straining against the knife. "I'm just working."

"Are you sure?" she asked. "You sound a little out of breath."

"Just tell me whatever the hell you are so worried about!" he exclaimed.

He thrust his knee up into the man's stomach, causing him to reel forward. Then he quickly kicked him against the elevator wall.

"Well, it's the General," she replied worriedly.

The other man had grabbed the knife off the elevator floor and ran at him.

"Fucking hell!" Derek blurted out, annoyed.

"What was that?" she inquired suspiciously. She wasn't sure if he had been talking to her or not.

Derek sidestepped his lunge with the knife. Then he kicked the thug against the opposite elevator wall.

"Don't worry about it," he panted. "Please continue."

"Well, we think that the General is behind the attacks that happened a couple weeks ago," she said.

"Finally," Derek said, sounding relieved. "Sounds like the bastard is making his move. Now I'll have to make mine."

The elevator doors slid open at the sound of a pleasant ding. Derek stepped out of the elevator, and the doors closed behind him before the two thugs could get back out.

"He has found us, Derek," she said. "It's only a matter of time before he comes for us."

"It's about fucking time," he responded. "I look forward to putting the bastard down"

Derek stepped onto crumpled papers on the floor. In fact, this whole office was a disgusting mess. A man with slicked-back hair sat behind an outdated desk. Papers were all over the place. This must have been the least organized person he had ever seen. Any wonder he was able to keep his shady crime ring intact. He looked up at him with disgust.

He wore a jacket meant for a suit, but he had a filthy, well-worn shirt underneath. His jeans were in shambles, somehow still stitched together. This was clearly a man who didn't care about anything at all.

"I don't know how you run a business in this shithole," Derek declared.

"Who the hell are you?!" the man demanded sneering at him.

"Just the man delivering you back to hell where you belong. I'll be doing the world a favor."

"Listen here, you shit!" he shouted.

"Can you hold, Dedalia?" Derek asked.

"Uh…what?" she asked perplexed.

"This asshole won't shut the hell up," he said disdainfully. "Be right back."

She really didn't know how to respond. The whole situation just sounded so intense. Surely, he knew what he was doing.

"Vladimir," Derek said. "I don't normally do this, but I think you should know that I'm the man that was sent here to kill you. But on a positive note, you're gonna be making me a shit ton of money. So, I truly thank you for that. You ugly sack of shit."

156

"Motherf—" he managed. The rest of his words were cut off as Derek drew a pistol faster than the blowing of the wind and shot him in the head. His blood splattered the wall, and his head smacked against the desk. Then he slipped onto the floor.

"Thanks for holding," Derek said gratefully. "Now what the hell were we talking about?"

"What the hell was all that noise?" she asked.

The elevator doors slid open, and the two thugs from before came running out with determination in their eyes.

"Hold that thought," he replied.

He shot the two of them in the head with alarming precision. The two of them were thrown onto their backs, and their blood was soaked into the loose papers on the floor.

"What's going on over there?" she asked.

"Nothing to worry your pretty little head over," he reported. "Just killed three shitstains that won't be bothering anyone anymore."

"You did all that over the phone?" she asked. "That's rather impressive."

"Just imagine if I hadn't been on the phone," he said darkly.

"You're insane. You know that, right?"

"Maybe just a little bit," he chuckled.

"Just get over here," she urged him.

"Yeah, yeah, I know," he said cockily. "We can't let Roy die on us. I can assure you if I'm there to protect him, you have got nothing to worry about. Be there soon, babe."

He pressed the button to hang up the phone call. Then he made his way out of the factory he had just made such a mess of.

B. Storm

***

Dedalia just stared at the phone in front of her blankly. She couldn't believe what that man had just called her.

"What the hell did that son of a bitch call me?!" she shouted furiously.

Phil had wandered into the doorframe. "Talking to your boyfriend?"

"Shut the fuck up!" she demanded.

"Oookay," he said, exiting the room.

He seemed to have struck a nerve. He knew how to take a hint. Good to know though that he wasn't the only one who got riled up by Derek's obnoxious behavior. Still, they were going to need his help.

Derek had reached the apartment complex in approximately ten minutes. He knocked on the door and was greeted by Phil. He was no longer in his guard uniform but in a long trench coat and comfortable clothes. He looked exactly as the Chaosbringer's Void Stone had shown him not too long ago before the Commander's eyes.

"Heard you got your ass kicked," Derek said.

"Missed you too, asshole," Phil replied.

"No, you didn't," he said, walking past him.

"You're right," Phil muttered under his breath. "I really didn't."

CHAPTER 19

BREAK IN

Vince was pacing back and forth in the room. Lyn had left, and they only had a basic idea as to where she had gone. They needed to find her, and fast. Otherwise, there was no telling what would become of her.

"We have to find her, Roy," he urged.

"I don't know what you're so worried about," Roy replied. "I'm sure she can handle herself. She was one of the soldiers from your secret society, right?"

"That doesn't mean anything, Roy," Vince replied urgently. "She might be able to beat one of them in a fair fight if she had any of her equipment, but she is unarmed. Not only that, there are sure to be three of them. Not exactly fair odds. They will kill her without a second thought."

"Wouldn't it be difficult to tail someone in an armored semi?" Roy asked, skeptical of the Immortals being able to tail her so easily.

"I'm sure it would be," Vince agreed. "But the General is a very crafty bastard. He would find a way."

"I don't know, man," he replied. "The whole thing sounds rather ridiculous to me."

"You need to take this more seriously, Roy. Your **wife** is in grave danger."

"What do you want me to do, Vince?" Roy asked irately. "Should I start kicking in the doors of every place near here that sells alcohol? Is that what you want?"

"I don't know," he replied. "I just wanted you to take this more seriously."

"If these guys are as dangerous as you say, how the hell am I supposed to survive anyway, man? They are clearly much stronger than either of us. So how would we even stand a chance?"

"Just stick with me, and I will get us through this."

"Why are you so confident that you'll be able to do so?" Roy asked. "Last I checked you're just another human like me. Are you better than me? A superhuman? A **god**?!"

"No," Vince sighed. "But I've spent a long time dealing with these sons of bitches."

"So, you're better than me?" he asked.

"I didn't say that, Roy," Vince said apologetically. "That's not what I meant."

"No?" Roy asked, his irritation bubbling in his tone.

If things kept going like this, he wouldn't be surprised if Roy tried to take off and deal with things in his own way. That would not be good for anyone. He needed to keep his promise to his brother. He would keep Roy safe from harm no matter what.

Then there was a loud knock at the door. Roy pried himself up off the couch, ready to answer. He began walking towards the door.

"Roy, wait," Vince pleaded.

"You worry too much," he said. "It's probably just Lyn back with the beer. You can stop freaking out now."

He stopped in front of the door eager to open the door and greet his adoring wife. He really wanted to believe that. However, a destructive kick knocked the doors off its hinges, slamming into him. It was definitely **not** Lyn at the door. He slid across the floor and crashed into the wall behind him. The door fell forward, and he collapsed on top of it in an unconscious state.

"Well, that was easy," the Sergeant chuckled.

"Son of a bitch!" Vince shouted.

He charged at the large man standing in the doorway of the apartment. He tackled him out into the hallway, and the Sergeant slammed against the wall opposite the busted doorway. He needed to regain Roy's trust. Maybe protecting him now would be a step in the right direction. The Sergeant glanced down at him and smirked. He was unfazed by his act of desperation.

"Is that the best that you can do, mortal?" the Sergeant asked him. "No wonder your kind are destined to perish."

He grabbed the back of Vince's shirt in a powerful grip and hurled him up against the ceiling. Rubble rained down on the Sergeant as Vince fell back down to his feet. The dust from the debris dirtied his jacket, but he didn't seem to even notice. Vince slammed onto the floor in front of him, and he savagely stomped on Vince's back. Vince cried out in pain, and he was sure he felt the floor beneath him tremble.

"Simply pathetic," the Sergeant belittled.

The Sergeant stomped on him again, and Vince burst through the floor. Sometimes he hated being right.

He landed perfectly on a poor cleaning lady's cart. Her cleaners scattered across the hallway as he smacked onto it with a heavy thud.

"Where did you come from?!" she exclaimed.

He looked up into the lady's baggy eyes. She looked to be a middle-aged Mexican woman who would rather be doing something else with her life. He could tell by looking into the tiredness in her eyes. She looked exhausted. Weakly, he climbed off her cart.

"Sorry," he apologized.

She just stared at him as he limped towards the nearest elevator. She began gathering her cleaning supplies but still watched him go. She couldn't help but think that he was a strange man. But still she had important things to do. She didn't have time to let him distract her.

Vince knew he had to get back up there and fast. Roy, being unconscious, would make it all too easy for the Sergeant to either capture him or finish him off. That was something that he couldn't risk. He knew that the others were here, but he couldn't just rely on them to be here. It was just too much of a risk.

The Sergeant had looked down at the hole in the floor he had made with such precision. He was rather pleased with his destructive prowess. He knew that Vince was alive, but it would still be some time before he would be able to reach him and try to stop him. However, he hadn't noticed a man wandering out of Dedalia's apartment. The man had brought out a pistol and aimed it at the Sergeant's face.

"Hey, dickhead!" he shouted.

The Sergeant turned towards him slowly with a gnarly sneer on his face. He looked down to see Phil standing in front of him, pointing a pistol up towards his face. He remembered the last time that he had dealt with him. Back then it was easy. He would just have to make sure the same would be true this time.

"What—" the Sergeant started.

Phil shot him in the head, cutting off any of his words. Black blood spilled into the air as the large man fell over backwards. He narrowly missed the hole in the floor that he had made earlier. Then Phil heard the elevator ding behind him. He turned towards it with his gun at the ready.

"Now what?" he asked rhetorically.

The doors slid open, and the Lieutenant stepped out into the hallway. He recognized him as one of the three he had dealt with on the day of Roy's wedding. He was holding some sort of staff in his hand. The Lieutenant shook the staff, and it extended at the top and bottom. He twirled the staff in front of him with a smile on his face. He felt quite confident that he would be able to take on Phil without getting a single scratch.

"You shouldn't have done that," the Lieutenant said, grinning.

"And why not?" Phil asked. "Be doing everyone a favor."

"You really think he's dead?" the Lieutenant asked.

"Doesn't matter," he said, unworried. "Right now, he isn't moving."

"I'll enjoy killing you. You cocky shit."

Phil brought out another pistol for his other hand and aimed it alongside his other one.

"Go ahead and try, motherfucker," he beckoned.

He shot at the Lieutenant with both his pistols, but the man spun the staff rapidly. The staff was spinning so quickly it seemed to create a vortex. The bullets ricocheted off the staff, keeping him perfectly safe. Phil advanced towards the man, spinning the staff. If he could just get close enough, he could try to pry the staff from his hands.

He reached the Lieutenant and lunged at him. The Lieutenant was ready for him, and he smacked Phil across the face with the staff. He was thrown against a wall, his pistols sliding across the floor. He rolled onto his back and sat against the wall. He cursed the fact that he hadn't been fast enough. He tried to get himself up, and the Lieutenant struck him again with a violent swing from his staff. The blow struck his face, and he fell back onto the floor.

Now, the Lieutenant stood over his body, smiling as he had before. He lifted the staff well over his head and looked ready to bring it down onto his helpless body.

"Damn it!" Phil exclaimed. "I can't go out like this. Not by a piece of shit like you!"

"This is the end of your story, mortal," he gloated.

Phil couldn't help but feel as if maybe this was really his end. Is this freak right? Is this really his end? But then someone else appeared and snatched the staff out of the Lieutenant's hands. He turned towards the man who had just stole his staff from him and saw Derek standing in front of him.

"I remember you," the Lieutenant reminisced.

"I get that a lot," Derek replied nonchalantly. "But I really don't give a shit."

Derek whipped the staff across the Lieutenant's face, and his sunglasses were thrown off his face. They shattered as they collided with the wall. The Lieutenant glared back at him after slowly turning his face back towards him.

"Those were my favorite pair, asshole!" he snarled. "I won't forget this!"

It seemed that the Lieutenant was a little too attached to something as trivial as sunglasses. It didn't matter to Derek in the slightest. He swung the staff up into the Lieutenant's face, and black blood sprayed up into the air. Then, before he could recover from the attack, Derek struck him across the face. The Lieutenant was thrown against the wall and slid to the floor.

The staff was not a normal weapon. It gave the user unnatural power. Something that someone like the Lieutenant could use to his advantage. Even Elliot could have benefitted from its properties. He lay there unconscious after Derek's vicious onslaught. Now they just needed to find a way to get Roy out of here as well. It could prove to be rather difficult considering he was unconscious as well.

Derek turned around and looked up to the Sergeant standing in front of him. He really had to appreciate how tall the bastard was. He felt small in a way that he didn't think possible. Still, this was a bad situation.

"Fuck me," Derek sighed.

The Sergeant clasped his large hand on Derek's throat and hoisted him into the air so that the two of them could be eye level. The staff had fallen from his hands, making him feel rather helpless. He didn't stand a chance against a man like this. He gripped the large hand and tried his best to pry it from his throat. He felt the struggle to breathe intensify. He needed to get this psycho to release him somehow.

"You and your friends are nothing more than a pack of fucking parasites," the Sergeant growled. "We will put all of you out of your misery. Just like the feeble rats that you are."

The Sergeant flung Derek through the wall next to him and slid across a floor he felt that he recognized. He looked around and realized it was, in fact, Dedalia's apartment. He chuckled to himself. The Sergeant surely hadn't realized it, but he had tagged in a **real** monster. Dedalia ran past him, and he knew that he was right.

She vaulted herself into the air and readied a fist for the Sergeant's face. He grabbed her in the air and hurled her down the hallway. She slid down the hallway on the balls of her feet. She flashed an intense stare up at the large man in front of her.

"You dare show your face, bitch," he snarled.

"It's time to put you down," she said bitterly.

She ran at him and tackled him. He had tried to grab her once again, but his hands slid off her jacket. The two of them tumbled through the open space in the floor, smashing through the outer edges of what was left of it. The Sergeant slammed onto his back, and he winced from the pain that shot through his back. Still, he grabbed her and tossed her against the wall next to them. The wall cracked where she smacked against it, and she fell to the floor. He groaned as he stumbled onto his feet.

***

The cleaning lady that Vince had encountered before just watched this scene play out in absolute shock. Her mouth hung open as she stared over at the two of them. She had no idea what she was looking at. It seemed like something that would only happen in movies. She blinked, and the craziness was still happening right in front of her eyes. Then everything went even more insane.

Dedalia tackled the Sergeant through the window nearby. It was unreal to witness. It didn't seem like she should have been able to pull off such a feat. Still, she forced him off his feet and smashed him through the window. The two of them went tumbling down to the street below. There was an explosion of glass as they crashed onto the roof of a car. The two of them nearly flattened the car when they fell. The Sergeant hadn't felt such pain in quite some time. Dedalia was certainly a worthy adversary. She was far more dangerous than he had remembered.

"Well played," he groaned weakly.

He lifted her into the air and launched her into the air. She rolled across the parked cars alongside the road. She was sent spinning into the air, and her foot smashed through a windshield, stopping her momentum. She saw the Sergeant grunt as he got to his feet. She knew what she needed to do, but she would have to hurry. He was already running atop the cars in her direction.

She fumbled with the depths of her jacket but found what she needed. It was a strange device that somewhat resembled a gun. She began assembling it as the Sergeant ran towards her. As she finished, it was clear that it was in fact a rifle. She lifted it up to meet the madman rushing towards her. He jumped into the air, and she shot him in the head. He was thrown against the car behind him.

She forced her foot out of the windshield it had been stuck in and climbed off the car. The Sergeant wasn't dead, but that would at least keep him occupied for the meantime. She needed to get back into the building. They had only encountered two of the men that were coming for Roy. The General hadn't yet appeared. She knew he is the most meticulous. She needed to get to him as soon as she could.

Roy woke up to the sound of his phone ringing. He had thought he had it on silent. It appeared that was not the case. He glanced down at the screen and saw a number he didn't recognize. He had a feeling that he should answer it. Normally, he wouldn't, but he had a grim feeling that he really should.

"Roy Darsetts," a man's voice said.

Something about his voice gave him chills. He could sense a form of danger behind the calmness of his voice. He knew he would have to respond. He just had to be careful how he did so. There was something off about the voice on the other end of the line.

CHAPTER 20

FATED MOMENT

"Who the hell is this?" Roy asked hesitantly.

"All you need to know is that I'm the man pressing a gun to your pretty little wife's head," the voice said.

Roy practically leapt onto his feet. Somehow this man had got the jump on Lyn. It was up to him to save her. He felt his muscles ache, but still he ran to his bedroom.

"Now how fast can you get here?" the man asked. "Depending on your urgency, maybe I will let her live."

"Don't you fucking touch that trigger!" Roy demanded.

He was scrambling through the drawer on his end table. Then he found it. The pistol that Lyn had convinced him to get in case things went wrong. This felt like the moment. If he had the chance, he would fill this man full of holes. He didn't know who he was. All he knew was that he was holding the only good thing in his life hostage. He couldn't allow his brightness to be taken from him. He grabbed the gun and ran out of his apartment.

"Now I would be careful of how you speak to me, Roy. I may just shoot her now before you even have a chance to reach her."

The elevator dinged, and Vince walked out of it. Roy ran past him and pushed the button to close the doors behind him. Vince looked around at the scene, rather confused. Then he realized that Roy had taken the elevator down without him.

"Shit!" he exclaimed.

He didn't know what was happening, but he had a bad feeling regardless. He looked around and saw it looked like a storm had gone through the hallway. The only thing left of the madness was an unconscious Lieutenant lying against a wall. He had decided that he had wanted some answers and approached him. Then he saw Derek wander out of a hole in the wall at Dedalia's apartment. Not too far off, Phil weakly got to his feet.

"What the hell is going on?" Vince asked.

"We kicked their asses," Derek said confidently. "But they kicked ours first."

"Where's Dedalia?"

Phil pointed at the broken window. "She's a fucking nutjob. But at least she got the Sergeant off our backs."

"It was badass," Derek said respectfully.

Vince stopped at the Lieutenant's limp body. He grabbed him and lifted him into the air. Then he forcefully slammed him against the wall. His eyes flicked open.

"What the hell happened here?" Vince asked.

"Isn't it obvious?" the Lieutenant asked him, smiling. "We won."

"What was that?!" Derek asked.

He drew a pistol and pressed it against his head. The Lieutenant chuckled.

"That gun won't do shit against me," he chuckled. "But I think you already know that."

"Don't tempt me, you son of a bitch," he growled.

"What do you mean, you won?" Vince asked.

"We were nothing more than a distraction. The General was the one who got what he wanted."

"Shit!" Derek shouted and lowered the gun.

"Where the hell is Roy?" Phil asked.

"He went down to the lobby already," Vince replied.

"That's exactly what the General wanted," the Lieutenant laughed. "That's where he is waiting."

"Then why the hell are we still here?!" Phil demanded.

Phil and Derek ran towards the elevator. At least they had good intentions.

"Next time I see your ugly face, you're dead," Vince threatened.

"Funny," the Lieutenant mocked hatefully. "I wanted to say the same thing to you."

Vince tossed the Lieutenant onto the floor roughly and then he ran off to join the others. The Lieutenant could feel the black blood trickling down the side of his face.

"Well, that was annoying," he weakly grimaced. "But for now, I'm out."

He fished a Portoball from his jacket and pressed the red button. He vanished from the hallway into another place entirely.

***

"Just, please, don't hurt her," Roy pleaded.

The wait as the elevator made its descent was unbearable. He heard the voice laughing from his phone.

"Look at how quickly you changed your tune," he chuckled. "Hopefully you get here before I change my mind."

"I'm coming as fast as I can."

"Would you like to talk to him, dear?"

His heart sank as he heard her voice. It sounded pained yet strong. "Roy. I know things look bad right now. But you need to be strong. Don't let him get into your head. Keep calm and think clearly. It's the only way to beat this bastard. And remember above all, I love you with all my heart."

"Stupid bitch," the General growled.

There was a loud smack. It sounded as if the General had smacked her on the head with the butt of his gun. He heard sobbing afterwards. He felt his anger boiling to a dangerous point.

"Don't tell me you hit her," Roy gritted his teeth.

"What if I did?" the General asked. "Not as bad as if I **shot** her, is it?"

"Just you wait, asshole," Roy gritted, feeling his rage peak.

"I'm sensing hostility, Roy. Shall I just shoot her now?"

Roy punched the elevator wall in frustration. His knuckles dripped with fresh blood. He would kill him, no matter what it took. He had heard enough. The doors slid open, and he bolted into the lobby. What he saw was the thing of his nightmares. The man who had been talking to him was indeed pressing a pistol against the side of his wife's head. He was smiling sinisterly at him and hung up his phone.

"About time you showed up," he said impatiently. "I was this close to blowing her brains out before you got here."

Roy dropped his phone onto the solid floor and felt his anger flow through him. But seeing the tears streaming down Lyn's face pulled hard at his heartstrings. There was also a bloodied gash on the side of her face from where the General had struck her. So, he was right. His rage overwhelmed him, making it difficult for him to keep his composure. There was no telling what the psychopath might do to her.

"Roy," she sobbed. "I'm sorry we couldn't have a normal, peaceful life like we both wanted. I know I'm not making it out of this. Just promise me you will make the Immortals pay for what transpires here. Never give up. Keep fighting til each of these bastards are eradicated from existence. This asshole is just the beginning."

"Lyn," he whispered, hanging his head.

Even in her hopeless state, she was staying strong. Roy fought back his own tears. He knew that there was nothing he could do. He had to stay strong for her sake as well. He had an inkling of what the General planned. He just didn't want to accept it. She knew that she wasn't going to make it. The man pressing the gun against her head had no intention of letting her live. The two of them knew it, but neither wanted to accept it.

"I love you," she said.

The tears poured down her face, and Roy could feel his own eyes fill up like an eager basin.

"This is sickening," the General said.

Lyn smiled nervously at Roy through her raining tears and the General fired the gun. Her blood splashed onto the floor, and she fell limp to the floor.

"I couldn't take another second of that shit," he said, disgusted.

Roy looked down at her lifeless body and didn't want to believe it. The love of his life was taken from him in an instant.

"Son of a bitch!" Roy shouted. "I can't believe you acfually did it!"

"I think you already knew what the outcome was gonna be," he said, smiling. "You just didn't want to accept it as truth."

"Motherfucker!" Roy screamed.

He brought out the pistol he had been carrying and fired at the man in front of him. Of all the things the General had been expecting, this wasn't one of them. A bullet dug into his right shoulder. He ran towards the nearest window as Roy shot at him erratically. Another bullet bit into his leg just before he jumped through the window.

The General limped towards his car. It was a long and painful walk, as his car was a few blocks away. Once he reached his car, he all but collapsed into the driver's seat. The bullet wounds would heal, but the pain was still dreadfully unbearable. He was desperate and just needed to get anywhere but here. He gripped the steering wheel tightly.

"Fuck!" he screamed.

He should have been better than this. He wasn't sure where it was that he had gone wrong. Roy **shouldn't** have had that gun. It didn't fit with his plan. Still, he was lucky. It wasn't the kind of a gun that could kill him, no matter how many shots would have been fired into him. Now he lacked the time to let his body heal its fresh wounds. He would have to return to his hideout. His SUV would work just fine to get him there, but not much else. He started up the car and went on his way. He would leave everything up to his two cohorts. He only hoped they were successful. He knew all too well what the Commander was capable of when he was angry.

Dedalia wandered into the lobby and saw Roy on his knees. He was sobbing uncontrollably. Lyn's body was lying in front of him. She couldn't believe it. Lyn wasn't the kind of person to go down easily. There must have been a good reason for her not to fight back.

"What the hell happened?" she asked.

He looked up at her and wiped the tears on the back of his sleeve.

"The General," he said quietly.

The elevator dinged, and the others came flooding out of it. Vince and the others looked around at the scene in shock. None of them had been expecting it to play out like this.

"Are you alright, Roy," Vince asked.

"I'm going to kill them," Roy said, failing to suppress his rage. "I'm going to kill every last one of these bastards."

"Easy, Roy," he urged. "Your emotions are out of control."

"I don't care!" Roy shouted. "I will kill every last one of them!"

"That's very noble," Derek said bluntly. "But frankly, you have no fucking idea what you're up against."

"Nice touch, Derek," Dedalia scolded.

"Well, he's right," Phil said, agreeing with Derek's sentiment.

"Can both of you idiots just shut up and read the room?" she asked.

"All of you are here to protect me, right?" Roy asked.

"True, we are," Vince confirmed.

"Then I guess you better come with me, or I will do this on my own," he promised.

"Fuck it," Derek said excitedly with a smile. "I'll help ya out."

"Of course, we all will," Dedalia assured him. "We all owe so much to Michael. We wouldn't be able to leave you behind."

Vince grabbed Roy's hand and helped him to his feet. Roy's tears had dried. Now he looked more determined. Which is good. If he truly wanted to battle with the Immortals, he needed to give everything that he had.

"Just remember what I told you, Roy," he reminded him.

"I'll have to be better than you," Roy remembered.

"I'm looking forward to that day."

"As am I. Then I can finally kick your ass."

"We'll see, kid," he chuckled.

"This is all good and all," Phil said. "But do any of you realize we aren't properly equipped to battle these sons of bitches?"

"Don't you worry about that," Derek insisted. "I know a guy."

"That sounds suspicious as hell."

"Just walk with me," Derek replied

"Should I be concerned?" Roy asked.

"Someone that Derek knows?" Phil asked. "Most definitely."

"Heard that asshole," Derek proclaimed.

"What am I getting myself into?" Roy asked.

"Just remember you wanted this," Vince said with a slight smirk.

Chapter 21

Callahan Delkeg

"So, who is this person that Derek knows?" Roy asked.

"Callahan Delkeg," Derek said. "He's the best chance that we got."

"Are you serious?" Dedalia asked. "He's not really all that sane."

"Could say the same about you," Derek remarked.

"Anything I need to know about this guy?" Roy asked.

"He's right," she replied. "He really is our best chance. Especially going against the Immortals. But he can be a bit intense."

"You have to be," Derek said. "Going through the shit that he does."

They all followed Derek out into the parking lot. He took them to Roy's car. They all climbed into the car with Roy in the driver's seat. Derek sat in the front passenger seat so that he would be able to guide him efficiently. Roy started up the car and pulled out into the busy streets.

"So how do you know this guy, Derek?" Roy asked.

"Actually, we all worked together," Dedalia stated. "We were all part of a secret society."

"So, what happened to this secret society?"

"There was a great battle. Most members of the society died. Chaos was the one who wiped out nearly everyone. All of it happened in but a single moment."

"It was a damned tragedy," Derek said sadly. "A lot of good people died."

"Who even is this, Chaos?" Roy asked in disbelief. "What happened to him?"

"He was killed, by your brother. I still don't understand it myself."

"As for who he was," Dedalia explained. "He was a great demonic deity who ruled over absolute darkness. His realm is truly the place of nightmares."

"Wait," Roy processed. He was trying to understand what they were telling him. "Is my brother some sort of celebrity?"

"Not in the way you think," Derek clarified. "No one knows all that he has done for humanity. He is popular among us and the other members of the secret society, but no one else even knows that he exists."

"That is rather distressing."

"Turn right," Derek interrupted.

That took Roy off guard. For a second, he forgot that they were even going somewhere. He turned right, a stunning sight greeting him. He appeared to be driving up to a rich man's abode. Neatly trimmed hedges lined alongside the driveway. It was rather distracting.

"Keep in mind, Roy," Dedalia reminded him. "We want to stay on his good side."

"Should I be concerned?" he asked.

"As long as you don't piss him off," Derek assured him.

"That's comforting," Roy sighed.

He stopped at a gate with a speaker placed next to it. It felt almost like he was in some sort of movie. Suddenly a voice filled the vacancy of the car as a man made himself known through the speaker. Roy hadn't expected it and shuddered in his seat. He had expected a voice, but not so sudden.

"You got an appointment?" the voice asked. Roy wasn't sure how to respond. He knew full well that they didn't but at the same time they needed his help.

"Should we?" Roy asked, unsure.

A loud scream shot forth from the speaker, and the voice returned shortly after, sounding out of breath.

"I'm very busy," he said tiredly. "I may not have time for you."

"It's us, Callahan!" Vince shouted from the back.

"Why didn't you just say so?" he asked. "Just a moment."

There was a clicking sound, and the gate in front of them began to slowly slide open.

"That's all we had to say?" Roy asked, surprised.

"Well, it probably would have had to have been one of us," Vince retorted. "He doesn't know who you are."

"Would have been good to open with that."

Roy drove the car through into the parking lot of an impressive-looking mansion. The driveway engulfed a massive fountain. In the center of the fountain, a statue spewed up water into the bowl below. He drove around the fountain and parked near the vicinity of the front door.

Roy got out of the car and looked around at the place, awestruck. He felt like he had been to more mansions in the past few days than he had all his life. It was rather mind-boggling. He had certainly come a long way from an ordinary businessman. All of this seemed like a dream. One he had never expected to be brought into existence.

"I'm beginning to feel underdressed," Roy said.

"Don't worry about it," Vince said, clapping his back.

Everyone else joined them at the front door, and Roy reached for the doorbell. He figured that would be the proper way to get someone's attention that they had arrived. To his surprise, the door swung open and a man in a business suit stood in front of him.

"You're early," he noted. He seemed to analyze Roy's appearance. He seemed to be trying to get a feel for who he really was. The way that the man's eyes seem to scan him up and down was rather uncomfortable. "So, you're Roy Darsetts."

The man in front of him had his gray hair slicked back, which matched the shade of his goatee. The goatee, however, was nothing more than a simple line beneath his lips. He was looking down on Roy with faded gray eyes.

"Do I know you?" Roy asked uncomfortably.

"No, I suppose not. I've heard a lot about you already. You remind me of your brother in a way."

"Really?"

"Back when he was still a novice at the very least."

Roy scowled. It seemed to him that the man wasn't here to make friends. Wasn't sure yet how he felt about him.

"Name's Callahan Delkeg," he said. "I've been expecting you, Roy. Just call me Delkeg. I'm the only chance you have against the Immortals after all."

"What was that?" Roy asked. "You've been expecting me?"

"That's right, Roy. Now follow me."

He turned his back on him and wandered into the house in front of them. Roy looked at the others in disbelief and they gestured for him to follow. He shook his head but decided to follow him regardless. Delkeg guided him through the incredible mansion.

Roy couldn't help but stare at the various shining objects that Delkeg had placed in the wide hallway as they walked.

"I knew it would be a matter of time for you to come to me," Delkeg said. "Now the Immortals have made their move, you will require weapons. Weapons that I possess, but no one else does."

"Only **you**?" Roy asked. "What makes you so special?"

"Do you know anything about the secret society?"

"I have only heard it mentioned."

"Then it's not yet your time to know about it. Just know that I was a big deal within the society. I was the one who created these weapons in the first place and changed everything in the battle against the supernatural monstrosities."

"You did all that?" Roy asked, taken aback. That was a lot to take in. This one man did so much. He was having a hard time believing it.

Delkeg couldn't help but let out a small chuckle. "You've got a lot to learn, kid."

They had reached the living room, and Roy noticed an obscene number of expensive vases surrounding the furniture. It made him nervous to just walk into the room. The fear of breaking a multimillion-dollar vase was overwhelming. He managed to reach a couch and took a seat. The others joined him in the room, with Delkeg sitting across from him.

"One thing you need to know if you truly want to take on the Immortals," Delkeg said. "You need to understand them if you want to be able to best them."

"What do you mean?" Roy asked.

"Well, do you know how to kill an Immortal?"

Roy thought about that question for a minute. He didn't have a clue how to kill one. It wasn't something that he had ever even needed to consider. "No, I don't."

"That's my point exactly. Would you like to know?"

"I will do whatever it takes. I promised Lyn as much."

"Typical. A wonderful story of vengeance brought on by the death of a loved one. How fitting."

"What the hell does that even mean?" Roy asked, feeling his annoyance in his tone.

"Don't worry about it. You wish to learn about the Immortals? I can help you with that."

"Just tell me," Roy urged him.

He was losing patience. Based on the smirk on Delkeg's face, he knew it too. His response seemed rather drawn out.

"Obviously you noticed that they give the image of a perfect human," Delkeg stated. "However, there is much more to them than that. They have superhuman strength and rapid healing. Making the illusion of them being practically invincible. Hence, where they get their name."

"That's all good and all, but how the hell do you kill something like that?"

"Remember your wedding, Roy?" Vince asked him. Roy glared over at him.

"You would bring that up **now**?" He shot back.

"Think about it, Roy. Think about what happened to Elliot in the holy water."

Roy closed his eyes and took a deep breath. He brought his mind back to Elliot's death. He dissolved in the tub of holy water in a steaming mess. He didn't seem to understand why that meant anything. But then it clicked in his brain.

"Holy water," Roy said in awe.

"Exactly," Delkeg said. "Holy water or something with holy properties is how you kill an Immortal. You can use it to kill other things as well, but I sincerely hope that you never encounter a monster quite like that."

"So, you have holy water?"

"Oh, I have much better than that. I have dipped all my weapons in holy substance myself, making them perfect for fighting the Immortals. If they fail, then just burn the bastards."

"Where can I get your weapons?"

Delkeg smiled and stood up. "That's what I was waiting for. Allow me to show you."

Everyone got up, and Delkeg turned his back on them. He was about to head further into the mansion. But he stopped and turned back towards them.

"There is **one** thing that you should know, Roy. Knowing how you feel about Immortals. You should know that I'm one of them."

Roy didn't even hesitate. He brought out his gun in an instant, and he pointed it at Delkeg's face. "Give me one good reason that I shouldn't blow your fucking brains out."

"First off, Roy. That gun that you're holding not so steadily in your hand will never be able to kill me."

Roy looked down at his hand and saw that Delkeg was right. His hand was shaking nervously.

"Damn it."

"You should also know," he continued. "I want nothing but success for you."

"What?" Roy asked in shock.

"Immortals are like humans in a way. There are good ones as well as bad ones. I consider myself to be one of the good ones. If I had wanted to, I could have killed you before you even entered my house."

Roy knew that he was right, but he honestly didn't know what to say to any of this. After all, he had just vowed to kill all the Immortals and now this man was making him question his morals. He wasn't sure what to do in this situation.

"You will encounter good Immortals like me in your travels, Roy," Delkeg remarked. "It would be in your best interest to allow their aid when they offer it to you. If you deny them, then you're as good as dead."

Roy lowered his pistol as he contemplated everything that Delkeg had just told him. Maybe not all the Immortals were so bad after all. He really didn't know what to think.

"Another thing to consider, Roy. The good ones will willingly sacrifice their lives to ensure that all of us will perish in the end."

"But why?" Roy just couldn't understand it. Why would they sacrifice their lives just to ensure that everyone that they had known for actual centuries would die in front of them.

"Most of us are forced to do the terrible things that we do by one man. He rules over the planet that we hail from. The Demon King, Barbatos. We cannot deny him. We try to, but most who do end up dead."

"I thought you guys were hard to kill."

Delkeg chuckled. Roy had a fair point. "Barbatos wields a blade that will even kill us Immortals, and he will use it without a second thought. Similar to the holy substance, but different."

"This king of yours sounds like a tyrant."

"Come with me. I will show you the weapons that you will be using. If you don't like them, feel free to use one of them on me if you wish. It won't matter to me."

"Guess it couldn't hurt to at least see what you got."

Delkeg smiled at him. "I think you'll love the stuff that I got in store for you."

He got up and grabbed a TV remote from the drawer of an end table. He pointed it at a vacant bookshelf and clicked a button. The bookshelf slid apart, and Roy could see what looked like a staircase leading down into the depths below.

"Damn," he said, awestruck.

"This is just the beginning, kid."

Delkeg led everyone down a long, winding spiral staircase. They seemed to be walking down the circles for eternity. Finally, they reached the bottom, and Roy was impressed by what he was looking at. It was a hallway that reminded him of a spaceship or maybe even a laboratory. At the end of the hall there was a thick metal door. Sitting next to it is a keypad with the basic numbers etched onto its surface.

Delkeg stopped in front of the keypad and turned back towards the others. "Look away. I don't need any of you knowing my secrets."

Phil lifted an eyebrow. "Aren't you about to show us one of your biggest secrets?"

Delkeg sighed as he considered that. "Fair enough."

He pressed a series of numbers, and they heard locks unlatch one after the other. Then the door popped open, giving them access to the room beyond. He gestured for all of them to enter, and they made their way around him into the room.

Delkeg closed the door behind him. He didn't need anyone following them here. Just in case someone found a way to reach this place without his permission. He doubted it, but it was still possible. He heard them cry out in surprise.

"Right, forgot about that," he said, recalling what he had been doing before their unexpected arrival.

A man that they had assumed to be one of the **bad** Immortals as Delkeg would have called him was hung from the brightly lit room. A spear had impaled him, leaving his body hanging limply against the wall.

"What the fuck?!" Roy shouted.

Delkeg wandered into the room feeling like he might need to explain the unorthodox scene that they had just witnessed.

"I thought I did some fucked-up shit," Derek remarked.

The walls, floors, and even the ceiling were alight with a brilliant glow. The whiteness of the room seemingly dulled their senses. A brilliant white desk sat perched in the center of the room. A drawer was set for each edge of the desk, but beyond that were the walls themselves. Each wall held a rack that was crammed full of guns, blades, and every sort of weapon imaginable. The only wall that didn't have a rack holding weapons was where the man had been impaled. He hung from the wall with his head drooping forward. Behind him, his black blood stained the illuminated wall.

"Why do you have a dead man hanging from your wall?" Roy asked.

"Oh, he's not dead," Delkeg countered.

"Wait, what?"

The man's eyes rolled open as if to answer his question. He looked around at all the people in the room. He looked pissed as all hell. "What is this, Delkeg? A fucking party?"

"You should still be sleeping."

"Damn, I guess you're gonna have to do something about that."

"Keep talking, and I'll kill you for real."

"Doesn't matter," the man grunted. "If I get out of this shithole, then Barbatos will kill me for sure."

"If you don't tell me what I want to know, then you're dead regardless."

"So many options. All so tempting."

"Who is this guy?" Roy asked.

"He is no one. He has simply been a great source of information for what the Immortals have been doing for some time."

The man laughed. "Of course that is all I mean to you. When Barbatos finds out what you've been doing, his armies will come for you."

Delkeg gripped the shaft of the spear. "Let them come." He whispered the words rather dramatically. "I invite the opportunity."

"Fuck you, Callahan."

"I have just one question for you."

"Ask," the man grumbled.

"Who is the one in the prophecy who is to be the downfall of our glorious king, Barbatos?"

"You already know that."

"You're right," Delkeg said coldly. "I do."

He jerked the spear into the man's body, and he fell limp into a state of unconsciousness.

"What was the point of that?" Roy asked.

"Power. I give him a chance for redemption and then plucked it away before he had the chance to use it."

"You're something else."

"Don't think about it too much," he replied. "Just pick out your weapons and be on your way. I have an appointment coming up soon."

Roy walked up to a pistol and snatched it from the wall. He examined it and twirled it around in his hand.

"How is this different from the gun that I currently have?" he asked.

"They may appear to be the same to you," he answered, approaching him to better examine the gun in Roy's hand. "But the bullets are what's important. Every single bullet is coated with holy essence. The very thing that the Immortals can't stand more than anything else."

Roy shrugged and tossed his own pistol into a trash can conveniently placed near the table in the center of the room.

"Don't forget to grab a blade as well, kid," he insisted.

"Why would I need to do that when I can just shoot the bastard in the face?"

Delkeg chuckled. "What if you miss or your gun is not with you? Wouldn't it be best to have something for close combat?"

Roy pondered that for a moment. "I suppose you're right."

Delkeg nodded in agreement. "Best pick something that you know you would be able to handle."

"Yeah, yeah."

Roy grabbed what looked like a basic sword that would probably fit more if they were in medieval times.

"You expect me to carry this around all the time?" Roy asked.

"Of course not," Delkeg replied. He grabbed the sword from Roy's hand and pointed at the emblem in the center of the hilt. "This is more than just a pretty design."

He pressed down on the emblem, and the blade shot back into the hilt.

"That's cool and all, but it's still not something that I can just shove into my pocket." Delkeg sighed and shook his head. He looked over at Vince. "Is he always this needy?"

"You get used to it," Vince replied.

Roy looked over at him appalled. "Asshole."

Delkeg had wandered back to the table and slid open a drawer. There seemed to be several harnesses, but Roy wasn't sure what they would be used for.

"Use these to hold your weapons as you fight your battles. If you used your pockets, I would be a bit offended."

"Now we're talking!" Derek exclaimed. "Now we can fuck some shit up!"

At least someone was excited. Roy had to appreciate his enthusiasm, even if it was misguided. Everyone strapped their harnesses to their bodies and picked out weapons that they had thought would fit them the best. Roy couldn't help but think that some of the choices were over the top. But hey, they were their own choices after all.

Roy stuck with the pistol and sword. He strapped the pistol to his hip and the sword to his back. He saw that Vince had chosen a machine gun and a battle axe. He retracted the axe, and it now looked like nothing more than a long metal rod. He strapped both of them to his back. It seemed rather fitting for him.

Phil stuck with a pair of pistols and ignored Delkeg's advice for close combat. He planned to kill his enemies before they had the chance to reach him. If he failed, then maybe it was just meant to be. Dedalia grabbed a new rifle and a spear. The spear had been condensed to a metal pole, just as Vince's battle axe is now. Just like he did, she has both strapped to her back.

Finally, Derek took a pair of swords and a pair of pistols. He felt everyone's prying eyes on him. "What? Too much?"

"It's perfect for you," Delkeg joked.

"Is that sarcasm?"

"As much as I enjoy our time together," Delkeg said, ignoring him. "I need all of you to get out. I have an important engagement to deal with. But first, a gift for each of you."

He opened another drawer and grabbed five silver orbs with an imposing red button in its middle. The button seemed to be glaring at them. He handed one out to each person in the room. Roy grabbed his own with a look of confusion.

"What are these things?" he asked.

"These are Portoballs," Delkeg clarified. "They can take one to the place they need to be the most. You are only to use them once the General is dead. You will understand when the time presents itself. You do plan to wipe out all the Immortals, right?"

That reminded him of the General coldly murdering his wife right in front of him. The thought was still fresh on his mind. The way Delkeg explained things, he was nothing more than a pawn. This meant that if Roy truly wished to have his vengeance he would need to take out as many of the Immortals as he could. They needed to be eradicated from the world. No. The universe itself.

"I will do whatever it takes," he promised.

"How is it you even know all this?" Vince asked.

"I have my ways," Delkeg responded. "But all of you really need to leave now."

He slid his finger along a groove underneath the table, and the wall that the unconscious Immortal was hanging from slid open awkwardly. It led into an even smaller room with a metal rung ladder leading even further down into a new place entirely. There seemed to be no end to the depths of this place. Roy started to walk towards the ladder, and Delkeg stopped him.

"Wait a minute, kid. I almost forgot." He fished keys from his suit and placed them in his hand. "You're gonna need these."

"Thanks."

Then Delkeg gestured him onward. He started to go down the ladder, and everyone began following him. Derek stopped next to Delkeg.

"Don't die. Something doesn't feel right," he warned.

Delkeg chuckled and gave Derek a reassuring nod. "Don't worry about me. Worry about **them.**"

Derek let out a smirk. "Just don't go hogging all the fun."

Then he followed the others down the metal ladder. Delkeg really hoped he could back up what he had said, but he wasn't so sure. Knowing the Immortal that would be coming to his abode it would prove to be rather difficult to make it out alive.

"I only hope that all of you do what you are meant to," Delkeg muttered to himself.

He made his way back to the living room knowing full well, that is where he would meet up with his rugged opponent. He stretched his shoulders and tried his best to get himself ready for what was coming next. He knew that it wouldn't be an easy fight.

***

A few blocks away from Delkeg's manor, the Sergeant slowly opened his eyes, and everything slowly began coming into focus. He grunted as he sat up. He brushed his hand against the fresh wound that Dedalia had given him with her rifle. He knew that wasn't the best gun for her to use otherwise; he would have been dead. There was some luck in his life after all.

A passerby halted abruptly upon seeing the Sergeant in his current state, with a shocked expression. "Are you alright, man?"

The Sergeant scowled. He wasn't used to attention. He hated it. He climbed off the car he had wrecked with his fall. Then he stretched, cracking his back. "Never better."

Then he walked off into the direction of Delkeg's manor, leaving the worried man in a state of disbelief.

CHAPTER 22

DELKEG V. SERGEANT

Once everyone had completed their descent down the ladder, they noticed they were in a long, dimly lit passage. Even in the faded light, they could tell that the hall matched the room they were just in. It made Roy wonder who exactly this Delkeg guy really was. They all continued down the hall and eventually reached another door. It was a door similar to the first one. This one, however, seemed to be larger than the other one. Surely it was more important. Mounted next to the door was a similar device that they had seen by the door leading into Delkeg's armory. But the numbers on the keypad were absent. Getting a closer look at it, Roy saw that it looked like a tablet stuck to the wall complete with a touch screen.

"What **is** this thing?" Roy asked.

Suddenly the screen came to life, flashing a bright blue. Then a pleasant woman's voice echoed around them.

"State your name," the voice said.

Roy felt the woman's voice to be rather soothing. He couldn't help but think it reminded him of the popular persona used on most of today's smartphones. "Siri?"

"That is insulting. Siri wishes she could do everything that I can," the voice responded in an offended tone.

"Well, what do I call you?"

There is a loud humming noise that fills the air. It was almost as if a computer was processing his request. "You may call me Dina. I was named by Callahan Delkeg. Forgive the delay. I have not been active in some time. How can I help you?"

"We were told to come this way. Supposedly something here will help us in our battle against the Immortals."

"Of course," Dina said. "But you still never told me your name."

Roy felt stupid as she said that. Of course she was right. He never even had considered it.

"Roy Darsetts."

"Finally," she said. "We've been expecting for you some time." There was a click, and the large metal door slid open.

"Please enter."

Roy wandered into a large room and looked around in amazement. The room looked like a secret base for a super spy from the movies. The room was filled with various forms of technology that he knew he would never understand. The thing that caught his eye was the car in the middle of the room. It looked like it was ten years past any car he had ever seen on the streets. It had a certain shine to it that compelled him to approach it.

"Damn. Is this the car Delkeg wants us to take?"

"Careful," Phil joked. "Someone will see you drooling."

"Whatever, man," Roy said resentfully.

"You were indeed drooling," Dina interjected.

"Let's just get going," Roy replied.

He walked over to the car and pulled out the keys that Delkeg had so graciously given him. He felt his fingers cross the smooth surface of the car before pressing a button on the key fob to unlock the car before him. He sat in the driver's seat with Vince in the passenger's seat and everyone else in the back. He put the key into the ignition and the car sparked to life. The lights of all the gadgets in the car seemed to glow brilliantly in a powerful blue light. It was just enough not to blind him but was helpful enough that he could see all the apps that the car had installed onto its main console screen.

Then Dina's voice burst into the car after a shrill chirp. "Initializing new user."

It was rather sudden, and Roy jumped a little bit in his seat.

"Jumpy, are we?" Derek asked from behind him. "Don't worry. The car won't kill ya. As long as your nice to it."

"What kind of car is this?" Roy asked.

It seemed that Dina had finished initializing as she spoke up again. "User is recognized as Roy Darsetts. Any friends of Roy are welcome to use this car as well. This car is Callahan Delkeg's greatest creation."

"She's certainly humble," Phil said.

"I think you're just jealous," Dedalia said, rolling her eyes.

Phil couldn't help but chuckle. "I'll stick to my guns. There is too much shit going on here."

"You only think that because you don't know how to handle me," Dina said.

"The car's got jokes."

Everyone couldn't help but laugh at that.

"Roy Darsetts," Dina said. "Would you like to listen to music as you begin your journey to save the world?"

"Hell yeah!" he exclaimed. "I love this car! Put on some heavy shit!"

"Putting on some heavy shit."

Heavy metal music began blaring in the car as it swiveled towards a large hangar door. The whole room seemed more like an airport than anything else. "Opening hangar door."

The large door in front of them began sliding upwards. Roy didn't even have to push on the gas pedal, and the car seemed to shoot out of the building onto the streets of the city. It merged into the traffic and made its way to the downtown area.

***

Delkeg knew that soon he would be dealing with an unwanted visitor. He only hoped that they all had managed to get out before the Sergeant pushed him aside. Still, he would fight with everything he had to prevent his death. He just didn't feel confident as the Sergeant is quite the powerful man.

***

The Sergeant lumbered in the direction of Delkeg's abode. Delkeg saw him on his monitor from the living room. He didn't dare speak to him through the buzzer. "Looks like he's already here."

The large man stopped in front of the gate. He growled at the gate in a rather cave man like way. Then he gripped the bars of the gate tightly. The bars bent easily in his grip, and he ripped the gate free of the brick wall that had held it for so long. He tossed the gate aside as if it was nothing more than a paperweight. Then he marched towards the large house that lay in wait.

Delkeg winced as his front doors were blasted off their hinges as the Sergeant had kicked them savagely. The doors were a husk of themselves as they slid to his feet. He couldn't help but be impressed. The Sergeant's large frame entered the room. This was the part that Delkeg had been fearing the most, but now was the time to put on a show for his guest.

"You ever tried opening a door?" he asked.

The Sergeant walked towards him, ignoring his question, but had a snarl etched on his face. He stopped in front of Delkeg and glared at him. He was going for an intimidating look, and he had nailed it perfectly. Delkeg couldn't help but feel nervous staring up at his freshly burned face. He even noticed the scar beginning to form where he had assumed that Dedalia had shot him in the face.

"I'm only going to ask this once," the Sergeant said. "Where are they?"

Delkeg felt himself swallow unconsciously, but he answered confidently. "Don't know who you are talking about."

"Wrong answer," he growled.

He hurled a large fist at Delkeg's face, and Delkeg snatched his fist. "I feel like we've done this before."

He struggled against Delkeg's fierce grip. It seemed impossible. The man in front of him must be much stronger than he appeared. Then Delkeg grabbed the Sergeant's arm with his other hand and flipped him through the air. The giant man was slammed through a table that had been set up nearby.

"Look what you made me do," Delkeg said. "That table was priceless."

The Sergeant snarled as he grabbed a chair. He pressed his weight against it to help himself up. That blow hurt him more than he thought it would. Then he lifted the chair into the air and swung it at Delkeg. Delkeg lifted his arm to defend himself, and the chair shattered against his arm. Then he kicked the Sergeant in his stomach, and the large man stumbled backwards.

Delkeg rushed at him and jabbed a lightning quick punch at him. The Sergeant caught his fist, and Delkeg lobbed another fist at him with his other hand. He caught that one as well. Delkeg felt pain shoot through his arms as the large man crushed his hands. He was lifted into the air and thrown against a cupboard hung in the near vicinity. The cabinet burst apart as he crashed into it, and he clattered to the floor.

"I'm not the one who will end your life today," Delkeg said weakly. He coughed as he rose to his feet. "**They** will be the ones who will put an end to you."

The Sergeant wandered over to him with a fixed look of anger upon his ugly face. "You will die alongside your precious mortals. They are nothing more than insignificant insects."

Delkeg smiled. "Fate has already made its decision. We are all deemed to fail. Immortals will be no more."

"Fuck fate!" the Sergeant shouted.

Delkeg knew that he needed to make his move now. He tackled the Sergeant, and the large man slammed against the wall behind him. Then Delkeg quickly launched his knee up into his gut before he had the chance to react. He crumpled forward, and Delkeg grabbed the back of the large man's jacket. He hurled him through the air, and the Sergeant smashed through the sliding door leading out into the backyard.

The Sergeant had landed on a hard stone surface. It seemed to be a smooth cobblestone encircling a large structure filled with bright blue water. He had narrowly avoided falling into the structure known as a "pool" lying behind him. He saw the typical chairs one would expect at the beach on the other side of the pool. He looked up and saw Delkeg walking towards him rather casually with a cane in his hand. Delkeg had grabbed it from the wall as he made his way outside to greet him. The Sergeant wasn't sure what Delkeg thought he would be able to do with a cane but knew better than to press his luck. He got up, ignoring the pain shooting through him.

Delkeg waltzed towards the Sergeant with a slight smirk on his face. He pulled apart the cane to reveal the long, slender blade that had been concealed within. The Sergeant didn't like his sudden surge of confidence. In an instant he switched from his cool demeanor to a savage. He slashed the blade at the Sergeant's face. He stepped back just enough to avoid the attack. He grabbed Delkeg's face and smashed it against the side of the house. Blood ran down Delkeg's face, but that wouldn't deter him.

Delkeg thrust the blade at him, and the Sergeant sidestepped the attempt. He tried again in a wide swinging arc and barely missed if not for the sudden jerk of the Sergeant's head. Delkeg's hand was gripped tightly by the man in front of him. His bones cracked loudly, and he felt his blade fall clumsily from his hand. He shouted in pain. He never even had the chance to consider reaching out for his weapon. The large man headbutted him in the face, causing him to stagger back.

Rough hands gripped the front of his dirtied suit. His suit had become a bloody, stained mess from their tussle. He was lifted into the air and thrown over the pool. He landed perfectly in one of the reclining beach chairs, but it slid across the cobblestone from the impact. He lay there for a moment catching his breath and saw the worst possible outcome had come about. The Sergeant picked up his blade from the ground and approached him.

He knew if he didn't get that blade back from him, he would be finished. He wouldn't be able to meet Roy and the others on the other side. Such a depressing thought. Still, the Sergeant lumbered towards him. He got up and lifted the lounge chair like a large briefcase. It was the best chance he had in the situation. Even if it wasn't really the best option against that sword. The sword clutched in the Sergeant's hand was one of the finest he had ever made. It was designed to be unbeatable.

The Sergeant had reached him, and he smacked him in the face with the chair. The large man tripped back, and he swung the chair up into his face. The Sergeant reeled back, and Delkeg had thought that maybe he actually had a chance. At least for a moment. But then the giant man used his significant advantage in height against him. He jabbed the sword into Delkeg's chest. His mouth dropped in shock, and blood trickled down the front of his suit.

"Shit," Delkeg weakly breathed.

Delkeg knew he had lost. But the Sergeant showed no remorse. He kicked him into the pool. His blood spread out into the water around him, giving it a murky, ugly color. Delkeg managed to surface and scold the Sergeant one final time before succumbing to his inevitable fate.

"This means nothing," he said, breathing heavily. Each word became more difficult to say after the other. A sure sign that he would not be among the living for much longer. "Your fate. Has been. Deter…mine…d."

As he sunk into the pool, specks of ash rose to the surface in his place. The Sergeant stared at the disgusting look that the pool had become. "I don't give a shit about any of that."

Chapter 23

Road Rage

The Sergeant looked down into the murky water, taking in what he had done. The Immortals would be grateful to him for taking out a traitor such as him. Sadly, he didn't have time to relish the moment. He had more important things to do. If he didn't catch up to Roy and the others, he wouldn't hear the end of it from the Commander. He walked back through the destruction that he had created during his battle with Delkeg. The glass crunched under his heavy feet as he made his way through.

He had no idea how far the mortals had gone already, but he knew a way to reach them quickly no matter how far they had traveled. He just had to reach the truck. The General had left the truck in his care after all. Whether he had wanted to or not. Stepping through what remained of the front door, he could hear the revving of a motorcycle in the distance. He glanced down the road and saw it coming almost directly towards him. He smiled. His timing couldn't be any more perfect.

The Sergeant stepped in front of the motorcycle, causing the driver to try to navigate around him. He grabbed the man by the helmet and lifted him up into the air. Then he flung him against the brick wall like a ragdoll. His body forced cracks along the nicely maintained wall. The man ripped off his helmet furiously and looked down at the damage to it. Then he looked down at his over-turned bike and up at the towering man in front of him.

"What the hell is your problem, man?"

"I'm taking your ride," the Sergeant said plainly.

If he had seemed angry before, now he had reached another level entirely. His brows furrowed into a deeper rage, and he squinted up at the Sergeant.

"The fuck you are!" His words were sharp and fierce.

He ran at the Sergeant in blind fury. The Sergeant stepped aside, and the man tripped onto the ground. He felt the large man's hands hoist him onto his feet.

"You need to back off," the Sergeant warned him menacingly. "You don't know what I am capable of."

"I don't give a shit!" the man shouted furiously.

He lobbed a punch straight into the Sergeant's chest. The blow barely even phased him. The Sergeant grabbed him by the jacket and lifted him up so that the two of them could be face-to-face.

"Still feeling strong?" he asked him.

"Fuck you, dude!" he screamed.

The Sergeant had enough of this mortal. "I gave you a chance. You refused to take it."

He lifted the man well over his own shoulders and slammed him through the windshield of a car parked nearby. The man just stared up at him with a stunned gaze. He hadn't lost consciousness, but he was too sore to move.

"Please, don't take my bike," he pleaded. "It's the only thing I got going for me in this crazy world."

"Maybe the two of you will be reunited in another life," the Sergeant replied coldly.

He brought the bike up and straddled its seat, knowing full well that he was way too big for it. This, however, was a temporary solution. He would just need to reach the truck, and this pitiful man could have it back for whatever it was that he desired. He started up the bike and made his way down the road.

"Asshole!" the man shouted after him.

He sounded furious to the point of tears. He must have put a lot of love into that bike. The Sergeant left him well behind him without a care in the world. He had to admit he was enjoying the wind billowing his hair as he went.

In no time, he had reached the armored truck that he had become so fond of. He was unsure of how he would handle it if someone had taken his truck. He imagined he would react similarly to how that man had. He shook the thought out of his head and laid down the bike. He climbed into his truck and listened to it purr as it started up. Hearing the roaring engine of his truck made him smile. Now he had a job to do. Being in his truck he felt that he could do anything. "Let the hunt begin."

He veered onto the busy streets just as he had not too long ago, and he floored the gas pedal. The truck accelerated to impressive speeds for a truck so large. Without any hesitation, he plunged into the thick traffic, flinging the cars out of his way. Some even flipped through the nearby buildings. The destruction was just as bad as on the day of Roy's wedding if, not worse.

Then he saw the car he was looking for. Its shiny sheen drew his attention. It stood out like a bullseye among the sea of cars before him. Not a single one of them looked remotely close to its design. He would rather not be too obvious, though. He abruptly turned down a side street. He was sure he would be able to catch them off guard.

***

Roy was enjoying the smooth ride that Delkeg's car was able to give. He wasn't even paying attention to his surroundings. He was sure that they would be clear at this point. But then, Dina's voice interrupted his peaceful thoughts. "Initiating evasive maneuvers."

"What?" Roy asked, snapping back into reality.

A large truck burst through the building next to them and came barrelling towards them. The car sharply turned away from the truck's path of destruction and sped down the road in the opposite direction. The car seemed to anticipate the truck's arrival. It was a comforting thought that the car was designed to deal with such dangerous situations.

The Sergeant pushed the cars out of his way as he readjusted his truck. He was rather disappointed that his surprise attack didn't work. Somehow, he knew that Delkeg was responsible. He must have done something to that car to prepare for attacks like that. It was annoying, for sure, but not much he could do about it. He saw the car veering in and out of traffic as it made its escape.

He chuckled. This must be a whole new level of smart car. It didn't matter. He would just plow through the traffic and catch up with them in due time. Roy was watching as the large truck obliterated the traffic in his rearview mirror. The whole thing looked unreal. He didn't want to believe that it was. But at the same time, he knew that it was.

"Do I even want to ask who that asshole is?" he asked.

"That man is an Immortal who goes by the Sergeant," Dina chirped. "He is one of the three who came down to Earth with the sole intent of killing you and everyone in this car."

"Who is this, Sergeant?" Roy asked.

"Another time, Roy," Dedalia replied. "Just keep your eyes peeled for now. There is no telling what that madman is up to."

"Right," he agreed, as the car swerved around another car trying to escape the psycho behind them.

She was right, of course. Even if the car seemed to self-propel itself down the road, he would still need to keep his eye on the erratic driving behind him. He just needed to be sure to get far enough so that they could figure out their next move. But they needed to come up with something fast. Else they would become roadkill once the Sergeant caught up with them. But it seemed the car already had an idea of its own.

"Activating drop-off mode," Dina declared.

The door next to Derek slid upwards, and the seat he was using slowly slid sideways out of the car. It hovered over the concrete below and it began traveling up toward the speeding truck behind them. The doors slid shut once again, and the car's back end seemed to condense itself to Phil's sides, making him now barely even fit in the back.

"This car is weird," he commented, noting the lack of space available to him.

Derek glanced over and saw that Dedalia was across from him in the air. The two of them were level with one another, and they shared a look.

"Well, this is new!" Derek bellowed over the howling winds.

"Just don't lose focus!" she shouted back.

They both felt a sudden jerk as their chairs sped up and soared towards the truck. The Sergeant saw them gliding towards him. He thought he had seen it all in his time on Khais, but this was not something he had been expecting to see. His planet wasn't even close to the advancements that Earth was lucky enough to achieve. He reached over and grabbed a shotgun from the seat next to him that he kept handy for occasions such as this. In a rather crude movement, he pumped a shell into the gun and pressed the button to lower the window. The Sergeant stuck the gun out the window and leveled it with Derek's chair.

"So, that's how we're gonna play it, huh?" Derek declared.

Then he ducked as the Sergeant fired the gun. The shell whizzed over his head, and he felt his seat rock awkwardly. Now he knew that sudden movements in a floating chair were a bad idea. Good to know. The shell struck one of the rear lights on Delkeg's car.

"Sustaining damage," Dina chirped.

"No shit!" Roy shouted.

The Sergeant pumped another shell, and this is when Derek brought out his trusty pistol that he had just obtained. He shot the Sergeant's hand, causing him to drop his gun. He winced in pain as a fresh wound had protruded on the back of his hand. The gun had fallen onto the surface of a car's windshield that was passing by. The car crashed into a light pole, which toppled onto it before more cars slammed it, stopping it there helplessly.

Derek struck at this moment. He leapt off the chair and grabbed the door of the truck. Then he lifted himself up so that his face filled the window frame. "Hey there, asshat."

He reached for the steering wheel, and the Sergeant's large hands gripped his arm. He tried to pry himself free, but the Sergeant was just too strong. Next thing he knew, he was being flung from the truck. He smashed through the window of an office building next to him. He rolled against the wall of a cubicle and steadily got to his feet. Everyone just stared at him as he brushed the broken glass from his jacket. He glanced around at all the surprised faces.

"What, do I have something on my face?!" He asked lividly. "Get back to work!"

Then he ran towards a door he had hoped would be an elevator to the roof. He felt the stares piercing him as he rushed past them. Then he burst through the door. To his dismay, he was greeted by stairs. Lots of stairs that seemed to wind upwards indefinitely.

"Fucking stairs," he growled.

He sighed and hyped himself up for the stairs he would need to climb. He sprinted up the stairs as quickly as his legs would carry him.

***

The Sergeant reached over and flung open his glovebox. He grabbed a pistol and brought it out, pointing it at the passenger window. He was ready for Dedalia to do something. He knew that she would be over on the other side. He just didn't know where. She vaulted off her own levitating chair. She grabbed the door, and the Sergeant shot at the window. She turned her face away from the shattering glass, but still, she hung on.

She grabbed onto the truck's side tightly and ripped the door off its hinges. The door was sent spinning down the road. It smacked into a car down the road, and the car veered into the traffic. Several cars slammed into each other, creating a pile up that stretched across the busy street. The door was now lying dormant in front of the car that had caused the mass wreckage.

"Can we talk about this?" she asked.

The Sergeant just stared back at her. She could tell that he had no intention of backing down. She saw him starting to pull back on the trigger. "Guess not."

She scrambled into the truck, and he shot her in the shoulder before she reached him. She winced as an irritating pain bit into her arm. Then she grabbed his arm and began smacking it against the dashboard. He looked up and saw that Delkeg's car was starting to get away as it randomly drifted onto a side road.

"Nice try, bitch."

He swerved the truck towards them, battering through the cars that had been in his way. The truck scraped against a building as it pursued the car. Dedalia knew that she wasn't getting enough of his attention. She was beginning to doubt if she would be able to distract him enough.

***

Derek finally reached the top of the stairs. He kicked open the door and ran out onto the roof. He took a few deep breaths to regain his composure. He walked over to the edge of the roof. He saw that the car had brought the truck towards him. It was scary how smart that car was. He took a few steps back.

"Fuck it," he breathed.

Then he sprinted off the rooftop and soared down to the truck below. He tried to brace himself for the pain that was coming. It didn't mean a thing. The pain shot through his entire body as he slammed onto the top of the truck's trailer. His body was sent rolling across the trailer. He was thrown off the back of it, and he barely managed to grab the edge of the trailer with one hand. He grabbed the trailer with his other hand before the wind could throw him into the traffic behind him.

He pulled himself up onto the trailer and took a deep breath. "That was way too fucking close." Then he ran along the top of the trailer towards the front of the truck.

Dedalia saw the sea beginning to make itself known and knew that the trap she had in mind was coming to fruition. She just needed to keep distracting him the best that she could. The Sergeant managed to drive while Dedalia banged his arm against the dashboard. She grew tired of making no progress and twisted his wrist. He winced in pain and dropped the gun. Finally.

She put his arm into a tight lock and twisted it. He still winced, but she had seemed to annoy him just enough. He flung her off his arm and she smashed through the windshield. She rolled over the hood and grabbed the front edge before she plummeted down to the street. She clung desperately to the front of the truck.

Glancing over, she realized that Delkeg's car had taken them to just the right spot. She saw Derek running atop the trailer. Then she looked over at Delkeg's car. It was about to happen. She would have to warn Derek.

"Derek, move your ass!" she shouted.

Derek looked down at Delkeg's car and then out to the sea. He knew exactly what she had meant. Suddenly the car spun around and put itself into reverse with its headlights facing the large truck. The car fired four small discs underneath the undercarriage of the truck. They stuck themselves to its underside.

The car veered to the truck's side, and Dedalia jumped onto its hood. The car's backside had already begun to expand to its normal size. She crawled over the car's frame and slipped inside through the car's sunroof before it could do any crazy maneuvers. Then it turned towards the truck with its headlights facing it again. The Sergeant tried to turn to meet it. But then the car fired a pair of rockets from under its headlights. Derek hurled himself off the trailer and landed snugly on a floating seat.

"Well, that was convenient."

He didn't have the time to savor the moment as the rockets had crashed into the side of the truck's trailer. The explosions threw the truck onto its side, and Derek was guided safely into the vicinity of the car. Then he heard a shrill beep, and four massive explosions threw the truck into the air. The truck flipped through the air and crashed into the sea. There was an explosion of water as the truck pierced the surface of the ocean.

"Is it over?" Derek asked, worn out.

The truck sank to the seafloor rather quickly. The Sergeant drifted out a broken window. He looked down at his pride and joy sitting at the bottom of the sea, useless. Bubbles burst from his mouth as he screamed in an unfathomable rage. Then his body began shaking violently of its own accord. He began to change. It started with his hands. He held his hand in front of him as it formed into a gnarled claw. He smiled as he knew his time had come. It was time to reveal his true form. A form that would be sure to strike fear into the foolish mortals.

Dedalia had hoped that maybe Derek could be right. But something in her gut told her that was not the case. "Somehow I don't think it will be that easy."

"We can still hope, right?" Derek asked hopefully.

But then a large splash burst from the surface of the sea, and a large, gray gnarled hand appeared. It brought itself down onto the edge of the pier. Another splash, at least twenty feet away from the first, brought forth a second gray hand. It firmly grasped the edge of the pier from which it had emerged.

Then a third splash, even larger than the first two, shot forth as a large gray head drifted up through the water. The massive head had two large, curved horns that one would expect from a demon. The face was adorned with scars, cuts, and scrapes. Still, it rose even higher. The head sat atop a large, hulking body. The large monster looked down on them all with its faded yellow eyes.

"What. The fuck. Is that?" Derek asked, mesmerized.

"We should probably get out of here," Dedalia said, trembling a little bit.

She knew that he had a demonic form but had no idea it would be something so enormous. It was more of a titan than an actual demon. It was a horrific sight, to say the least.

The large demon blinked as it watched them carefully snuggled in their supposed safety within the confines of the car. Then he flashed a sinister, crooked smile. He was looking forward to this. He enjoyed the fear on their faces.

CHAPTER 24

PARALLAX

The car backed up slowly as the colossal demon gripped the edges of the pier. There was a humongous blast of water as it vaulted out of the ocean and landed heavily onto the ground in front of them. Then he let out a loud, psychotic laugh. The horrid sound echoed around them.

"I. am. Parallax," the demon said in a booming voice. The voice seemed unnatural. As if it belonged to a creature that shouldn't be in this world. "I am grateful to all of you for ridding me of that pathetic vessel. Now that I'm free, I can do whatever I want. I will enjoy destroying your entire world while all of you are powerless to stop it."

"We have to do something," Derek urged them. "We can't let that monster reach the city."

He looked up at the demon. Now that it was out of the water, it was at least as tall as a three-story building. He didn't have a clue how they were supposed to take on something like that. Not with their current firepower, at least. Based on the overwhelming presence in front of them, he doubted their weapons would do much good.

Maybe the car would know something, but he didn't think it was something for them to rely on too heavily.

"Any ideas?" Dedalia asked.

"I was hoping you would know something," Derek countered.

Then Parallax grabbed the top of a building and ripped it free of its base. He lifted the large piece of rubble and arched it back, ready to launch it at them like a baseball player at the pitch.

"That's not good," Phil remarked.

Parallax chucked the building at them. It smashed onto the ground and shattered into two different pieces. The slab of the building rolled towards the car. The car swerved around it, but Parallax kicked the other chunk, and it slammed against the car. The car was pushed through the building next to them. The battered car burst through the wall on the other side of the building. It was still sliding across the street as Parallax chased after them slowly.

Parallax knew he didn't need to rush. He was so large that he would be able to reach them in as little as a few steps. The car accelerated to get as far away from the monstrous demon as it could. It veered around the many fallen cars littering the streets. The Sergeant alone had caused a ridiculous amount of destruction with his truck. They didn't need to see what Parallax would be capable of.

Parallax smashed through the building that they had been pushed through just a moment before. Then he leaned down and picked up one of the wrecked cars off the street. He bounced it up and down in his hand in a taunting manner. Once again getting ready for the pitch. Then he hurled it at their car. The pitched car slammed onto the road next to them as Delkeg's car drifted to the side. The thrown car bounced off the concrete, sending it spinning down the road.

"Shit!" Roy shouted. "Anyone got anything before we get hit by the pitcher from hell?!"

"Initiating hover mode," Dina interjected.

"What?"

The car's tires turned inwards and slowly lifted into the air. There was a light flicker of flames shooting forth from where the tires had been. The car was now success-fully hovering in the air just as the chairs had been before. It glided through the air slightly off the ground and turned down an alley.

"This is insane!" Roy exclaimed.

He could barely hear himself over the roaring of the car's engine as it went. Phil gripped his seatbelt tightly. The car seemed to be going twice as fast now, and they were approaching the back wall of the alley at an alarming rate.

"We're all going to die," Phil said, panicked. "This metal contraption is going to be our tomb."

"You'll be fine," Dina chipped in.

The car arched upwards in front of the wall and sped upwards alongside its brick face. It raced up its surface and went barreling up into the sky as it reached the top of the structure.

"Holy shit!" Phil screamed in terror. He bunched his seatbelt in his hands as tightly as he could. He was sure they really were going to die.

"Initiating flight mode," Dina said.

A pair of wings unfurled from the sides of the car, and it glided across the sky towards Parallax.

"No way," Phil said, awestruck.

He looked around at the view and couldn't help but feel that this looked rather nice. Getting up here had been one of the most terrifying moments of his life. But he was given a quick reminder of why they were up here in the first place. Parallax clouded the view he was trying to admire. They would have to do something about that eyesore.

The sunroof slid open, and Vince knew what to do. "Guess, it's my turn."

He crawled up through the sunroof and was battered by the powerful winds. Still, he unstrapped his machine gun and began opening fire on the massive demon in front of them. The never-ending mash of bullets seemed to do nothing more than crack the demon's rough skin.

"Pathetic," Parallax declared in his booming voice. "That barely feels like more than a tickle. Just give up while you have the chance."

"That's the thing about us humans!" Vince shouted over the howling winds. "We don't ever quit when something we care about is on the line."

Parallax growled in disapproval and lifted his arm to protect his face from the onslaught of bullets. He seemed to have gotten his attention at least, but he hadn't anticipated the rage that would follow. The demon swung his arm at them savagely.

"Hold on," Dina suggested.

Vince strapped his gun and gripped the car as best he could. Then the car barrel-rolled out of the range of Parallax's attack. Then it fired a rocket into the demon's face. He howled in pain as an explosion tore through the flesh of his face. A fresh burn had formed on his face. The new burn had somehow matched the one that the Sergeant had worn near the end of his life.

"Don't do that again!" Vince demanded. He was still breathing heavily from the shock.

If he had fallen out, he didn't want to imagine what could have happened.

"Hold that thought," she said.

"What?" he asked, crawling back into the comfort of his seat.

"Dedalia, I'm dropping you in," she said.

"There's something wrong with this psycho car," Vince said as he got back into his seat with the others.

He slumped in his seat and took a few deep breaths. The car tilted onto its side so that her window faced down towards Parallax.

"Got it," she said, ready for her descent.

The door slid open as she unfastened her seatbelt. Then she slid out of the car and fell to the demon below. Then the car went back to its normal state and sealed up her door.

Dedalia collided with Parallax's left horn and clutched it in a tight bear hug. "Guess, I'm the trump card."

Hearing her words infuriated the demon that she clung to, and he shrieked in a piercing rage. "Get off me!"

She pushed against the horn and gave it a mighty kick. He stumbled forward, and his face crashed through the building in front of him. He gripped the edge of the building in a powerful grip so that he wouldn't fall all the way through.

"Damn it!" he snarled.

Dedalia punched the demon's horn again and again. Each blow seemed to do more damage than the last. Parallax screamed in fury. He swung his head back, and Dedalia smashed through the wall that had remained intact. Unflinching, she clung to his horn. Her legs dangled in the air, but she held tight to the horn with one hand and continued to bash it in with her other.

Parallax flailed around awkwardly as he did everything, he could to get her off his horn. "Get the hell off!" His loud echoing voice seemed to pierce the air itself.

The others watched in amusement as the large demon seemed to be throwing a tantrum below them.

"She really is making him her bitch," Derek replied, rather amused.

"Do we even need to do anything?" Phil asked, with an eyebrow raised.

"She probably could handle him all by herself," Vince remarked. "But we should probably still help her. There's only so much that she can do to that behemoth."

But still, everyone in the car couldn't help but watch in a trance as Dedalia held tight to Parallax's horn and continuously destroyed it bit by bit. It was impressive. Dedalia's next punch smashed through the hard surface of Parallax's horn. She had successfully snapped the horn in two. She grabbed the top half of it in her hand.

"Damned parasite," Parallax shouted.

Just then, Dedalia leaped off his head. He was oblivious to what she had done. It was bound to be a delayed reaction. He hadn't realized what had happened but later would have felt tremendous pain. It dawned on him when he saw half of his horn in her hands.

"What have you done?!" he screamed.

Then she thrust the broken horn through the demon's chest. He howled in pain as the blood trickled down his chest. He fell to one knee as Dedalia fell onto the top of a car nearby. Looked like her time was up. The next attack was already lined up. Parallax coughed up blood. The blow appeared to have severely weakened him. Derek shifted in his seat, itching to get himself into the fight.

"Derek," Dina said. "I'm sending you in."

"About fucking time," he said, anticipating his next moment.

He had his seatbelt unfastened before she had even swung the car onto his side. The door slid open and he fell towards Parallax. He freed the hilts from their straps and pressed the emblems with a wide grin on his face.

The blades shot free, and he slid them down Parallax's back. Blood sprayed into his eyes, but he beared it and kept going. He went all the way down until he slid off the bottom of Parallax's back. He spiraled through the air and crashed on the top of a dumpster. He lay there groaning in pain.

"Damn, hope that was as cool as it felt," he grimaced.

The sunroof slid open, and Vince knew that he was next. He crawled out of the sunroof and unholstered his trusty rod. At least that was all that it seemed to be. Then he pressed the button along the handle, and the axe blades shot out of the end. He balanced himself on the roof of the car before vaulting himself off the car and soared down towards Parallax.

The pain must have gotten to the large demon as he had fallen onto his other knee. He just stayed there coughing up his own blood.

"Parallax!" Vince shouted.

He didn't bother looking up. He knew what was coming. He still couldn't believe it had come to this. After all that he had been through, maybe now is the opportune time. He had a good run after all. Time for the next generation of demons to take his place. His thoughts ran dry as the blade of Vince's axe sunk into the back of his head.

Parallax was still in disbelief. This outcome should not have been possible. Humans are weak and feeble creatures. The mere notion that they were able to bring down such a powerful creature such as himself is unthinkable.

"Impossible," he muttered weakly. Even his booming voice had failed him.

Then he collapsed onto the road in front of him. Cars flipped aside as the large demon's body crashed into them.

Vince's axe retracted from Parallax's skull, propelling him through the air. He rolled across the pavement and slammed into a car. Weakly, he crawled over to where his axe had landed. He grabbed it off the ground and put it back in its place on his holster. The city around him was an absolute mess. Crumpled cars lay alongside burning automobiles everywhere he looked. Almost looked like the end of the world had happened already, but he knew that the rest of the city was at least safe. That mattered more than anything else.

Then he walked over to the car where Dedalia was lying and offered his hand. She clasped his in her own. He pulled her off the car and placed her on her feet.

"I don't care what anyone says," he said, beaming at her. "You're badass."

Derek limped over to where the two of them were standing. He looked to be rather upset. "Don't mind me. I mean I thought what I did back there was pretty badass too."

"It was alright," Vince replied humbly.

"Jackass!" Derek shot back.

Vince and Dedalia laughed while Derek scowled at the two of them. It was times like these that they needed to see a little bit of laughter in their lives. The car pulled up next to them. In the background, they all watched as the large demon that had given them so much trouble was slowly decomposing into nothing more than a large pile of ashes. It was hard to imagine what had gone down here today. They had managed to do the impossible.

The dissipating demon behind them made it feel like maybe they would be able to accomplish what they had set out to do. They would be able to beat the Immortals and rid the universe of them in due time. The doors leading back into the car slid open as if inviting them back inside.

"Looks like our ride's here," Dedalia said.

"I'm not giving them five stars," Derek groaned.

They resumed their seats in the car, and it started up again, ready to continue onward. Then the car sped on by the large pile of ash that was once Parallax. One demon down. Only two more to go.

CHAPTER 25

ROAD THROUGH THE VOID

The car raced past the destruction that Parallax had left in his wake. Roy couldn't help but glance back at the city lying in ruins behind them. Everyone just went on with their daily commute, unaware of the destruction that had ensued behind them. They just went on with their everyday lives as if nothing had happened. They were completely oblivious to what had transpired no less than a minute ago.

"So now what?" Roy asked.

"Well, we track down the Lieutenant and kill him," Phil said.

"At least we know that not just any Immortal will be following us," Derek replied. "Not after witnessing what we just did to Parallax. He was a high-ranking demon, after all."

"That just means the strong ones will be after us," Dedalia stated. "That's not much of a comfort."

"Still, we don't know how to reach the Lieutenant or if we should even be going after him in the first place," Roy noted.

"The General is far more dangerous than the Lieutenant," Phil assured him. "It just makes sense to go after the Lieutenant first."

"How do you even know that?"

"Trust me. I have witnessed him before. The Lieutenant is nothing compared to him."

Then the screen in the center console came to life. Everyone stopped what they were doing and focused on the screen as the apps all dissipated. A large icon replaced the apps, bringing to their attention that a call was coming in. The screen really was like an advanced computer integrated into the car itself.

"Incoming message," Dina chirped.

"Might as well answer it," Roy said.

"Transmitting message."

A man's face appeared on the screen, and they all recognized him at once. This was the Lieutenant. He was the one that they were going after next. He smiled at the tense faces staring back at him.

"Why hello, heroes," he said excitedly.

"What do you want?" Roy asked in an annoyed manner.

"I know you killed my friend, and I'm gonna do all of you a favor. Don't get me wrong, I can't let you idiots get away with that. But I'm gonna send you the coordinates to my location so I don't have to come to you."

"Why should we believe you?" Vince scowled.

He laughed at them through the screen. He didn't even seem to care about Vince's interjection. "You don't have to if you don't want to. But know that if you don't find me, then I will find you, and I will not be nearly as friendly."

"We're feeling the motivation here," Derek replied in a sarcastic tone.

"Motivation?" the Lieutenant asked. "You should be careful what you ask for."

He seemed to have been waiting for them to ask that. Dedalia looked at the screen quizzically. Something about how he said that made him seem to be overly confident. She didn't like it.

"You realize we will kill you, right?" Roy responded grimly.

The Lieutenant laughed again. It seemed even louder this time. "You can try. Just leave me Derek and I can deal with the rest of you later."

"Is this over those stupid sunglasses?" Derek asked.

"Stupid?!" the Lieutenant asked, clearly offended. "Those completed my outfit, you dick!"

Derek rolled his eyes. This guy clearly had a few screws loose. "Grow the fuck up, man."

"The real reason I want you to find me is simple. I have something. Or, should I say, **someone** that Dedalia may want to see. I want to see that pretty face of hers distort as she sees him."

That got her immediate attention. She stared at the screen, her face tense with curiosity. Seeing her narrowed expression, the Lieutenant laughed yet again. He jerked a man into the center of the camera. His face was bloodied, and his hair was disheveled. He glanced up at them all with weary eyes, but he locked onto Dedalia.

"Dedalia," he said quietly. He appeared to have suffered brutal beatings, his face covered in wounds. His eyes seemed to glaze over, as if he could barely hold them open.

225

"Darkus?!" she exclaimed. "What the hell has that bastard done to you?!"

Before he could respond, he was pushed off-screen and the Lieutenant's smug face filled the screen again. He was still laughing at the whole situation.

"Don't worry about what I've done to him," he said, smiling widely. "Worry about what I'll do if you don't show up for your predetermined deaths. All the things I could do to this damned gorilla."

"Don't you fucking touch him!" Dedalia screamed in a rage.

"Scary," the Lieutenant said mockingly. "What are you going to do, girl? You don't even know where I am."

The coordinates appeared on the bottom of the screen as he said this.

"Whoops. I guess you do now, huh? Nothing personal, kiddos. The Commander was quite clear in making sure that all of you die in horrific fashion. Personally, I don't give a shit about any of this. But orders are orders after all. I'll be waiting. Just remember. The longer you take, the more I make poor little Darkus here suffer."

"I'll fucking kill you!" Dedalia shouted.

"Oh, I know you will try," he chuckled, and the screen quickly returned to its default as the message ends. Dedalia tightly clenched her hands into fists.

"You know he was just trying to rile you up," Phil said, sounding disappointed in her. Normally, things like this wouldn't bother her in the slightest. However, this time it was different.

"Yeah," she gritted through her teeth. "It worked."

Phil had never seen her look so angry, so he figured it would be best to drop it.

"Initiating auto pilot," Dina said blankly.

Derek looked over at her with a serious demeanor on his face. "You alright, Dedalia?" He sounded rather genuine. It seemed so unnatural from his normal self.

"I'll be fine. I just need some time."

She plucked some headphones from her pocket and stuck them in her ears. Then she sank back into her seat and let the music wash over her.

"Fair enough."

The car continued onward to the place marked on the map in the center of the console. They all went quiet as the car propelled itself to its destination. Everyone seemed relaxed, but they were all anxious about what they were really going to do. The air was tense as the car closed in on its destination.

"So, anybody got an idea on how we beat this guy?" Roy asked, breaking the silence. The only one who even reacted was Derek.

"You should probably take away his stick," he replied, staring out the window.

"That's helpful. Thanks."

The car suddenly jerked down an alleyway. Then the car seemed to accelerate even more.

"What the hell?!" Roy exclaimed. He couldn't seem to regain control of the car. At the rate that they were going they would crash into the wall, and it would be game over for everyone.

Vince seemed to be waking up from a nap, and he blinked the scene into focus. Yep. They were sure to crash. "What did you do?"

"I didn't do shit!"

"Why are we shouting?" Derek asked.

It seemed that everyone in the car had been trying to get a quick snooze in. It made sense, considering all the stuff that they had been through today.

The car was about to hit the wall, but it wasn't activating hover mode like it had before. Instead, something else happened. The wall spread apart, brick by brick out of their way.

"Wait, what?" Roy asked, stunned.

They were taken into a place that was unmistakably not Earth, but they weren't sure what it was either. As the car entered unfamiliar territory, Roy was astounded by his surroundings. They were on a long bridge of stone, leading towards a looming tower in the distance. The most unsettling aspect of the bridge was its suspension over a black nothingness. Rocks and rubble floated into the air as if gravity didn't exist in this place.

Roy didn't know what to think of the place that they had entered. He glanced over the edge of the bridge and saw that the way down seemed to truly never end. Rubble swirled around them in a menacing way, but the car kept advancing towards the tower.

The tower stood tall in front of them. A bleak cloak of darkness coated the tower. A singular red window sat at its peak, making it seem like a creepy eye was looking down on them as they approached. Roy gripped the steering wheel nervously. He couldn't help but feel nervous as they inched ever closer. But he couldn't do anything to stop it, because the car just kept going. There was nothing he could do.

Roy looked up and thought that he saw a man standing at the window looking down at them. He was sure it was the Lieutenant himself. Then his overwhelming anxiousness began slipping away as he remembered why they had come here. He was one of the ones that had brought about the fate of his now dead wife. His nervousness switched to that of anger. Once they took care of him, then they would be one step closer to tracking down the **true** man responsible. The General.

The car stopped in front of a pair of large, ornate doors that led into the tower. They all got out and approached the door. The doors seemed to have ancient glyphs etched onto them. The most prominent was that of a demon's face blaring in the center of each one. There was no telling if the demon's face was that of the Lieutenant or something else entirely.

"Let's kill this son of a bitch," Roy growled.

***

Roy was right. The Lieutenant had indeed been looking down on them from the window. He even watched as they entered the tower. He sneered down at them even though he knew they wouldn't be able to see him. He didn't think they would show. Pity.

"Looks like they made it," a man said from behind him.

This man was Darkus. The one that the Lieutenant had spent time beating the crap out of for nothing more than a convincing video. Darkus had scrapes and bruises still drawing attention to his face. His hair was still a tattered mess. He wore a tight T-shirt showing off his bulging muscles and a pair of jeans.

"So, it would seem," the Lieutenant responded. He sounded to be rather disappointed by this update. It didn't bother Darkus in the slightest. He wasn't much of a fan of the Lieutenant anyway. He just had to tolerate him for now.

"Will you meet them at the door?"

The Lieutenant finally turned away from the window. "Why would I do that? I should send you down there to fight in my stead."

"Do you really want to do that, though?"

"Of course not," the Lieutenant snapped. "I need you to remain here. I will show your bitch of a sister true despair."

"Why do you hate her so much?" Darkus asked.

The Lieutenant took a long and elated sigh. "She is the only Immortal who ever made a fool of me. In front of our great king, no less. So, I will make sure she is proved the fool in the end."

"Good luck with that," Darkus muttered.

"What was that?"

"Nothing. Nothing at all."

"Don't worry that group of pawns downstairs are eager to throw away their lives so that we don't have to."

"If you're so eager to kill them, why don't you just do it yourself?"

"I am no longer being forced to fight them," he said, relaxed. "I will fight them when I'm ready to. So now let's just enjoy the show."

"You really are a lazy bastard," Darkus shot back coldly.

"Silence!" the Lieutenant ordered. "Remember. You are my prisoner. Handed to me by the Demon King himself. Disobey me, and I may have to test the limits of your immortality."

"That'd be better than being stuck in this room with you."

"You will help me, or I will send you down into the depths of the Void. Got it?"

"I got it," Darkus replied, annoyed. "You don't gotta remind me."

"I let you roam free in this place," the Lieutenant snarled. "The least I expect is obedience." Darkus could feel his irritation peaking, but instead of furrowing his brows, he responded to the Lieutenant with a smile.

"You better hope Dedalia doesn't reach you," he warned. "Especially once she finds out you lied about what we got going on here. You will wish you were dead. I promise you."

CHAPTER 26

AN UNPLEASANT WELCOME

Everyone wandered into the tower after Vince gave the doors a mighty push. The room that greeted them was massive and open. The inner décor matched the dark demeanor of the building. Dedalia freed her headphones from the confines of her ears and put them back into the folds of her jacket.

"Let's do this," she said quietly.

She began traveling to the other side of the room. Everyone followed her, but then they noticed that they were not alone. Five other people were waiting for them on the other side of the room. Roy figured that they were probably Immortals, under the Lieutenant's employ. They were probably weaker Immortals like Elliot from his wedding. Their shoes seemed to squeak as they approached the people waiting for them.

Seeing them seemed to anger Dedalia even further. Surely, they were just in her way, and she didn't have the time to deal with them. They noticed the heroes approaching them and began to advance towards them. The man in the center of the group towered over the others. A short mohawk protruded from the top of his head. He was wearing a black vest over a gray T-shirt. He looked to be the strongest of the bunch. Perhaps, even the one in charge. He exuded confidence as he approached them.

The man opposite Roy looked like a normal guy. He wore a leather jacket over a basic shirt and jeans. Even his hair seemed simplistic. He looked at Roy with no emotion on his face. He seemed to be a rather soulless individual.

A short Asian man dressed in leather was wandering towards Vince. He should be terrified going against a man as big as Vince is, but he didn't appear to be scared in the slightest. It was written all over his face. He was ready to put the hurt on the large man in front of him.

A woman was standing in front of Phil. She had long brown hair bound into a bun. She was wearing a neatly pressed jumpsuit. She looked as if she should be manning someone's desk somewhere. She looked well out of place here. However, the look on her face was one of harshness.

Finally, a bald man approached Derek. He had a crazy squint in his eyes. Like the others, he was wearing dark, leather clothes. A scar resembling claw marks draped over his right eye. He looked ready to brawl any moment.

Dedalia glared at the person standing in the center. If fire could blaze in her eyes, it would be at this moment. "Where the fuck is he?!"

He looked down at her unimpressed and smirked. "Don't know what you're talkin 'bout."

"Don't give me that shit!" She shouted up at him. "I know you know where Darkus is!"

Roy wasn't sure who Darkus was or why Dedalia hadn't bothered to mention him before now. He had so many questions, but now wasn't the time. All he had gathered is that Darkus is her brother. Everything else about him is still shrouded in mystery.

"Darkus is chillin' with da' boss," he said, calmly.

"Chilling? I saw what he did to him. Get the hell out of my way!"

He just chuckled at her. "You think I give a shit what da boss has done? It's his business. Not mine."

"Get the fuck out of the way! I swear if you don't move, I'll shove your head through your ass!"

Roy knew now that getting on Dedalia's bad side is the equivalent of asking for death. Still the man in front of her was unflinching. He kept his face calm with a slight smirk, guarding any real emotion he might have.

"Feisty!" he exclaimed. "But I'm still not scared of ya, little girl."

Dedalia clenched her hands into fists so tight that her knuckles popped loudly in the air. "You should be."

He laughed loudly and then turned to his cohorts as if to ask them their opinion. They all laughed nervously. They didn't seem to share his calm demeanor. Then he turned back towards her. "You sure are full of yourself, little girl."

He randomly launched a fist at her face, but she ducked underneath his arm and flung a flurry of punches into his torso. She pushed him back, and she kicked him in his left knee. He collapsed onto his knees, and she spun a foot into the side of his face. He was knocked onto his side and looked up at his allies. His face had contorted into disbelief. Black blood ran down the side of his face. He spit more of his dark blood onto the floor before turning to his comrades.

"Kill them all!" he commanded. "Bunch of imbeciles!"

Everyone fought against their designated adversary all at once. The man across from Roy hurled a fist at him, and he dodged under the attack. He countered by punching him several times in the stomach. The man stumbled back, and Roy let loose a kick that connected with his gut. He was pushed further back, and he reeled forward as he tried to regain his balance.

Roy ran at him and flung his fist up into his face. His black blood sprayed up into the air as he staggered backwards. Then Roy leapt into the air and kicked him in the chest with as much force as he could. The man was thrown onto his back, but so was he. He wasn't built for crazy stunts like that. He was hoping that all his efforts would keep him down for a while. He scrambled to his feet and saw that the man was doing the same thing.

"C'mon!" Roy declared, clearly frustrated. "Just stay the hell down!"

The man smiled through the wounds streaking across his face. "I don't think so."

Derek dodged the bald man's attacks continuously. It seemed that no matter how hard he tried to hit Derek, it was just to no avail. Derek could tell it was pissing him off. Good. He was relying on it. The man's rage would lead him to make a mistake, and Derek could finally go on the offensive.

"Hold still would ya," the bald man taunted.

Derek shook his head in disbelief. He was just incredibly annoying. He wasn't even sure if the man was really all that dangerous. The man lunged at him, and Derek stepped out of his way. He grabbed the man's arm and twisted it behind his back. The man howled in pain, and Derek smashed his elbow to the back of his head.

The bald man tripped forward, and Derek grabbed the back of his jacket. He noticed that the fight between Phil and the woman was getting rather close to where they were. He could use that to his advantage. The man tried to break free of his grip, but before he could, Derek tossed him into the woman next to them.

Derek had knocked both Phil and the woman onto the floor.

"Thanks for the assist," Phil said scornfully.

"No problem," Derek said obliviously. Then he went back to his fight with the bald man. He didn't seem to notice any issue with what had happened.

"Asshole," Phil grunted.

He got to his feet and the woman was doing the same thing in front of him. Before that inconvenience, Phil had been dodging her attacks quite well. Not much he could do about it now, though. He would just have to keep it up until he could find some kind of opening.

"If that dumbass messed up my hair," she said irately.

"I really don't care," Phil said coldly. He could feel himself breathing heavily. He wasn't used to actual fighting. It was already wearing him out.

"Never underestimate your enemy," she said quietly. "You may just find me to be more than you bargained for."

She ran at him, and he sidestepped her. He brought his knee up into her stomach, causing her to stumble forward. Then he grabbed her bun and dug his fingernails into her scalp as a desperate attempt to distract her. Tears welled up in her eyes from the pain.

"Motherfucker!" she screamed.

Then, before she could get out of his grip, he kicked her in the back. She fell onto the floor face first. She quickly turned onto her back with a look of hatred blazing in her eyes.

"I really hate fighting," Phil sighed.

He wasn't sure how much longer he would be able to keep this up. She sprang back up on her feet and lashed out at Phil viciously, giving him a much harder time than he had before. All the moving around was making Phil feel rather fatigued. But he powered through it all the same.

The man that Vince was fighting should have been the easiest of all, but somehow, he was the most challenging. He moved quickly, almost fast enough he couldn't even see him move. He effortlessly deflected Vince's punches without even breaking a sweat. He jabbed his palm into Vince's throat, and he was worried for a second that he was going to die. The blow was painful for sure, but it was not to the extreme that it should have been for an Immortal.

This is when Vince figured out his trick. He sacrificed overwhelming power for speed. He would be able to get many more hits in, but the damage is severely weakened. As Vince had come to this realization, the man had vaulted himself up into the air. Then he roundhouse kicked Vince in the face. He planted his feet onto the floor to prevent himself from toppling over.

Vince managed to grab one of his flailing legs as the man fell back down to the floor and flung him through the air. He smashed through the front doors and rolled down the bridge outside. Vince looked around at the others, and it seemed that they were doing quite well in their own personal battles. This gave him a sliver of hope. Maybe they would be successful in Roy's suicide mission after all.

Dedalia freed her rod from the straps on her back and pressed the button along the handle to free the spear from within. She glared at the man in front of her. She pointed it at him as he lay there helplessly. "You're finished."

Then she got the response that she had not been expecting. He started to laugh loudly. He grunted as he got to his feet. She was so dumbstruck by him that she let him do so.

"Why the hell are you laughing?" she asked in disbelief.

"Why?" he asked, still laughing like a maniac. "You really think you've won. You may know what we can do. But the same thing can't be said about your precious friends."

"What are you talking about?"

"This whole time we've been toying with you. We were letting you think that you were winning. Then once your guard is down, we will crush you all at once."

"You won't stop us. We will get through you, and we will reach the Lieutenant."

He grinned and shook his head. "Keep living in that fantasy, little girl. You've already lost. The mortals have rubbed off on you. They gave you a feeling of hope. A feeling that will soon be taken from you."

"Shut the hell up!" she demanded. Then she leveled her spear with his neck, as it was easier for her to reach.

Still, he chuckled. "It's time you are shown your place in all of this."

The Asian man rushed back into the tower and flipped into the air. He wrapped his legs around Vince's neck as Vince gazed upon all the different battles. The man sent Vince spinning onto the floor before he had even realized what was happening. He groaned as he felt tremendous pain shoot through him.

He rolled across the floor trying to rid himself of the man who had latched onto him. Vince turned onto his back, and the man had pushed himself up onto his chest. Then he brought a knife down towards Vince's throat. He stopped just short of piercing his throat. Vince couldn't help but gulp. He was terrified. He knew the man could finish him in an instant. Yet he knew he didn't for the simple reason that the man in the mohawk was trying to set an example.

Roy finally understood what Vince had meant so long ago when he told him that he would have to be better than him. He turned back towards the man he had been fighting before. This was his moment. The moment to show him what he could do.

Roy sent a fist at the man in front of him, aiming for his face and the man grabbed him by the wrist with ease. He crushed Roy's hand, and he heard his bones crunching under the pressure. He winced in pain, and the man sucker-punched him in the face. The blow dazed him, and he slid back a couple of steps. Then the man clobbered him in the face with another punch, and Roy sprawled out onto the floor unconscious.

While Phil was distracted by all the craziness that was occurring around him, the woman that he was facing bashed him in the stomach with a strong punch. He reeled forward, and she quickly sent her fist soaring into his face. She sent him spinning through the air, and he slammed onto the floor face first. He was knocked out cold.

Derek knew that he would have to somehow pull this off as his friends were being beaten one after the other. He was getting less confident in his fight against the bald man. He knew he would have to go on the offensive, and he would have to do it now. He hurled a fist at him, and the man caught it easily. He tried to do the same with his other fist. The bald man grabbed that one as well, and he began crushing Derek's hands. The reverberating sound of his bones cracking echoed throughout the room.

Derek cringed as the searing pain traveled through his arms. Then the man headbutted his face. He staggered back in a daze. Then the bald man swung a punch into Derek's face. He fell unconscious onto the floor. The bald man stood over his unconscious body with a satisfied smile on his face.

Dedalia didn't want to believe that what was happening could possibly be real. They were winning. How could everything have changed so quickly?

"Do you see now?" the man in front of her asked. "You have lost, little girl."

She fell to her knees and tears began to well up in her eyes. Maybe all of this was for nothing. They would all perish before they even reached the Lieutenant. He wasn't even the true target that they needed to reach. All of Roy's determination would be for nothing. Then tears streamed down her face as she came to this realization. He smiled at the woman's suffering. He was going to relish relieving this woman, who was groveling at his feet, out of her agony.

CHAPTER 27

DARKUS

While the heroes were dealing with their adversaries, the Lieutenant was getting his own sense of pleasure in tormenting Darkus even further. He walked over to his desk and slid open a drawer.

"Let's watch as the fated heroes are brought about to a grisly end," he said in a provoking manner.

He pulled a remote free from the drawer and pointed it at the large window that overlooked the chaotic void outside. He pressed the singular button on the remote, and the window became a giant TV screen. It showed what the heroes were dealing with at the base of the tower.

Darkus clenched his jaw at the sight of his sister. Dedalia had effortlessly beaten her enemy and was going in for the kill. But he didn't trust it. He could see that she wasn't thinking rationally. The whole thing seemed far too easy. It didn't look good for her or the people that she brought with her.

"If anything happens to my sister," Darkus grimaced.

"You know it's gotta be convincing."

Darkus took a deep breath. He needed to remain calm. He had to find the right moment. The moment that would bring the Lieutenant to his knees. Still, he felt the sweat dripping from his brow as he worried about Dedalia's well-being. He knew that they were up to something; he just couldn't figure out what it was.

But then he saw Dedalia fall onto her knees, shedding tears as her friends were knocked unconscious one after the other. This was when he lost it. He turned his back on the screen and began walking towards the way out.

"I can't watch this shit anymore," he said quietly, pained.

The Lieutenant turned to face him as he was walking away and pointed at him profusely. "Are you disobeying me again? I will report you to Barbatos himself if you don't get your shit together!"

Darkus stopped abruptly, clenching his hands into fists. His jaw tightened as he did his best to suppress his anger. He knew that the Lieutenant could, in fact, have the Demon King summoned to this place. If Barbatos came here, he would be dead for sure.

He may be terrified of Barbatos, but the man behind him didn't scare him in the slightest. He would have to feign helplessness to get close enough to deal with him regardless. He turned back towards the Lieutenant with a pained look on his face. "Let's talk about this."

The Lieutenant smiled as Darkus walked towards him. "That's right. Come back to me and resume your place."

Darkus felt his rage burn with the intensity of an inferno but held it back and stopped in front of the

Lieutenant. "So, you want me to watch as your pawns brutally murder my dear sister?"

"That's right," the Lieutenant smiled.

"Fuck you," Darkus snarled.

Before the Lieutenant could scold him anymore, Darkus grabbed his head and smashed his face on the desk. His black blood smeared on the clean surface, and he threw the Lieutenant against a cabinet situated nearby. The wooden doors shattered, and the random trinkets contained within rained down on him. He seemed surprised that Darkus retaliated.

Darkus wandered over to where the Lieutenant lay helplessly on the floor. He stopped next to him. "You talk too much."

Then he stomped on his face, causing him to lose consciousness He stepped over the Lieutenant's body, and he reached into the cabinet, grabbing a long metal rod. This is the weapon that his oppressor had kept from him for so long. He had been forced to do the Lieutenant's bidding for a long while, as his weapon had been stowed away from him. But now with the mortals here, he felt that the Lieutenant's days were numbered, and he finally had the chance to make him suffer as he had. He pressed a button at the edge of the handle and a pair of large axe blades sprung out from the end.

He wandered over to the doorway and made his way down the twisting stairs. He looked down at the struggling heroes below. "It's time to take out the trash."

He could see a glimpse of the man who was taunting his sister cruelly. His anger was quickly reignited, and he leapt down towards him, ready to finish the bastard.

Dedalia gazed up at the man in front of her through her tears, feeling hopeless. This would be their graves.

"So, any last words before I snuff the last remaining shred of hope you have left?" he asked her with a sinister look on his face.

She looked down at the floor. She couldn't believe it had come to this. He smiled at her moping despair. Suddenly, a loud crash echoed through the room. She looked up in disbelief. Darkus had slammed the man into the floor. His axe had smashed into his back and plowed him against the floor. It was **red** blood, though. The axe he had used seemed to be one of Delkeg's. A good thing too. She opened her mouth to say something, but nothing would come out.

The man fell to ashes in a splattered pool of his own blood. Then everything began to make sense. Darkus was never really a prisoner. He simply pretended to be one. She didn't really understand it, but she was still grateful.

"Darkus?" Dedalia exclaimed in disbelief.

Darkus reached down and pried the axe free of his victim's back. Even though she saw him in front of her, she still couldn't believe it. He was the last person that she had been expecting to be their savior. But she wasn't opposed either.

"Looks like it's my turn to save your ass," he said, his eyes ablaze. He stared intensely at the other Immortals gathered in the room.

"Are you going to help Roy as well?" she asked wearily.

"If that's what you want."

Vince pushed the Asian man off him, and the two of them continued their brawl from before. He had grown accustomed to the small man's swift, vicious attacks and had a much easier time countering him.

The bald Immortal turned towards Darkus, and ran towards him shouting a battle cry. Darkus whirled the axe in his hand eagerly.

"No one makes my sister cry!" Darkus shouted.

The bald man had reached him, and he tried to bring a fist to Darkus' face. He failed and Darkus lopped off his head with a vicious swing of his axe. Blood sprayed into the air as the headless man collapsed onto the floor, staining the clean floor tiles. The man and woman who had each defeated their own foes approached him with hatred written all over their faces.

This didn't bother Darkus even for a moment. He waited for them to come close before swinging at both of them. They both ducked under the axe. Then he brought the handle of the axe into the woman's face. She flipped roughly onto the floor. The man tried to retaliate, but Darkus spun the axe around, and the blades sunk into his side. He was thrown aside and slid across the floor.

The woman had flipped onto her back and was trying to get back up. Unfortunately, her hands slipped on the surface of the bloodied tile. Darkus swung the axe into her chest, and she fell back limp to the floor. The man who had been at her side had gotten back to his feet. Emotion clouded his face. He was furious. Darkus was surprised that he was capable of such a thing. In the end, it didn't even matter.

"Die, asshole!" The man screamed in anger.

Darkus was under the impression that the woman had meant something to him. Now she was nothing more than a pile of ash on the clean floor. If he wasn't the enemy, he may have even felt bad.

The man ran at him, and Darkus swung the axe towards him. The man lifted his arm up to protect himself as he ran. The axe sank into his arm, and he hollered in pain. Darkus jerked the axe free of his arm, and the man stumbled back. Then he swung the axe violently into the man's chest as the man tried to regain his balance. He coughed up his blood all over himself and looked up at Darkus with empty eyes. Darkus yanked the axe free of his body, and he fell forward, landing at Darkus' feet.

Darkus turned around and saw that Vince was still fighting the Asian man. The man navigated around Vince's massive frame, and Darkus chucked the axe through the air. The axe sunk into the Asian man's back, and he fell to the floor instantly. Vince looked down at the now dead man and then back up at Darkus. Disbelief danced in his eyes.

"You could have killed me, jackass!" he shouted.

"But I didn't," Darkus replied nonchalantly.

Darkus waded towards him and stopped at the man who was slowly turning into a small pile of ash. He reached into the pile laying at Vince's feet and pulled his axe free. Then he strapped it to his back just as the others would have done.

"Who are you?" Vince asked.

"I'm Darkus," he replied. "The one who just saved all your asses."

"Where did you get that axe?"

"Let's just say the Lieutenant unwillingly gave it to me."

"Is he dead?"

"No, just unconscious. By the time you reach him, he should be waking up from his nap."

"Why didn't you kill him?" Vince sounded disappointed.

"It won't look good if I kill him," Darkus explained. "I'm supposed to be his lackey. If the Demon King finds out that I was the one to kill him, he would storm down here and kill us all."

"How's that different from any of us killing him?"

"If I do it, he will be enraged. If one of you, does it, he will be scared. After all mortals shouldn't be capable of killing an Immortal. Especially not one as powerful as the Lieutenant."

"How do you know all this?"

The others regained consciousness and began wandering towards them. Dedalia joined them before the others. Darkus looked at Vince with the utmost seriousness.

"Just trust me," Darkus assured him.

"Trust you?" Vince scoffed. "I don't even know you."

"I will vouch for him," Dedalia responded.

"Quite the warm welcome, sister," Darkus said.

"Sister?" Roy asked. "You never mentioned you even had a brother."

"It was for the best," she sighed. "The less you all knew about him, the less danger he would be in."

"Danger?" Derek asked, looking around at all the ash and blood scattered onto the once clean floor. "You see this crime scene he just made in mere seconds?"

"There was a reason for that," Darkus replied.

"And? What was the reason?"

"They made my sister cry."

"You gotta do something about that temper, man," Derek said in disbelief.

"On that note, I will take you all to where the Lieutenant is currently taking his power nap."

"Why are you helping us?" Roy asked.

247

"I would do anything to help my dear sister," he insisted.

Roy couldn't help but think of the man behind all his suffering, as Darkus had said that. The General. He may not be in this damned tower, but he was still one of the ones responsible for her death. He knew that Darkus must have been one of the good Immortals that Delkeg had mentioned not so long ago. He felt that he understood Darkus just a little bit more. He even respected the man for all that he did to help them.

Roy's hands balled into fists at his side without him even realizing it. Darkus had to admire his newfound courage. Maybe he was exactly the kind of person that they needed.

"Take us to the son of a bitch," Roy demanded, returning to the grim reality after the cold embrace of his thoughts.

Darkus smiled. Roy was the person they needed right now. "You got it."

Darkus stepped away from them and stopped next to a wall nearby. He placed his hand against the wall, and the floor seemed to tremble violently.

"What the hell is going on?" Roy asked. "Are you going to kill us too?"

"Just give it a moment," Darkus replied calmly.

The floor they were standing on began to slowly ascend towards the top of the tower. Roy couldn't believe it. Something like this shouldn't exist. Yet here he was riding a giant elevator to the top of the tower straight out of some fantasy.

"How is this happening?" he asked.

"This place isn't even Earth," Darkus explained.

248

"When you went through that wall, you were all teleported to a small pocket of my planet. A place that is called Khais."

"What are you saying?"

"The wall was a portal through time and space. And now you're in **my** domain."

"He's right, Roy," Vince stated. "This kind of thing would be impossible if it was really Earth."

The whole thing just seemed unreal. Surely it wouldn't be so easy to go to another world.

"This is just the beginning, Roy," Darkus said, interrupting his thoughts. "If you truly wish to vanquish the Immortals, you will see far stranger things than what this tower has to offer."

Roy remembered his oath to vanquish the Immortals, no matter what. He felt he was obligated to do so. He had to do this. The Immortal perched atop this tower merely served as another steppingstone. So, he knew he was bound to see many more bizarre things than what this tower could offer.

"I'll bring down every last motherfucker who gets in my way."

"Good," Darkus said, smiling. "That's the kind of spirit you are going to need. Don't know if you will live to make it a reality, but it's good to have dreams."

"Did you ever believe in him in the first place?" Dedalia asked.

"No. I just wanted to see how far he could go."

"That's low, man," Derek said.

"You're an asshole," Dedalia growled.

Their giant makeshift elevator came to a stop. On the opposite side of them is a staircase seemingly inviting them in.

"This is our stop, kids," Darkus replied, unfazed by Dedalia's comment. "Let's give em hell."

"Just another being ready to be shown its place," Roy replied.

"The world could use more people like you, Roy. Scratch that. The universe."

"The universe will remember you too, Darkus."

Darkus chuckled. "You sure know how to make someone feel important. I sure hope that you're right."

He guided everyone to the stairs. They climbed the winding stairs with Darkus in the front. If he had to, he would take the brunt of the Lieutenant's fury. He planned to make it as easy as possible for Roy and his friends.

It may not be the General up here, but less competition would make things all the easier. It was time. Another powerful Immortal was going to bite the dust.

CHAPTER 28

THE LIEUTENANT

Darkus stopped at the top of the stairs and turned towards the others. "Follow my lead."

Then he led them into the room where the Lieutenant was currently awaiting them. The room was spacious, but it was nothing compared to the room they had seen at the base of the tower. A layer of comfortable carpet draped the floor underneath their feet. Cabinets and bookshelves lined the walls alongside the carpeted floor.

Across from them, a smooth-looking desk stared back at them. A rather nice chair was placed against the desk. Still, there was no computer or even a laptop. It conveyed an impression of simpler times. Something that Roy realized now that he took for granted in the technological age that he was accustomed to. Maybe this really was another planet after all. They may have technology completely different from ours. Roy couldn't help but wonder if they even had internet. What a dreadful thought if they didn't.

Darkus was surprised to see that the Lieutenant had recovered so quickly. He had gone to the stained window that the others had seen from outside and seemed to be lost in thought. Blood would still be covering his face, Darkus was sure of it.

"I have brought them, Lieutenant," Darkus declared.

"I can see that, Darkus," he replied quietly. "What I wish to understand is who's side you are truly on here."

"I think you already know that, Lieutenant."

He turned to face them, and his blood-splattered face became rather noticeable. The others gasped in surprise.

"What the hell happened to your face?" Roy asked.

The Lieutenant scowled at him. "Your good friend here decided to give me a parting gift. He was supposed to be my prisoner, but it would appear it was some sort of ruse."

"I was **never** your prisoner," Darkus said bluntly. "I just tolerated you."

"Well played, Darkus. Well played. But it doesn't matter. Today, you and all your precious friends will die."

"Is that right?"

"I knew you would turn on me one day," the Lieutenant stated. "I just didn't realize it would be so soon. Over something so trivial, I might add."

"What?" Darkus asked. His emotions were starting to spiral out of his control. He could feel that he was getting close to the point of breaking. This man needed to be taken care of.

"If I had known that's all it would take to send you over the edge, I would have done so sooner," he said, grinning.

"Fuck this!" he snarled.

He ran to the Lieutenant, blinded by his rage. Then he jabbed a swift punch at his face. The Lieutenant dodged him with minimal effort and grabbed his throat. Then he hoisted Darkus into the air and smashed him through the desk. Darkus lay there in the pile of scraps, seemingly unconscious. This was the true ruse that he had planned. Pretending to be his prisoner had been nothing more than a distraction.

Vince felt that he had to do something. So, he took things into his hands. He ran towards the Lieutenant and tackled him. The Lieutenant slid across the floor and grabbed his shirt. The Lieutenant stopped just short of the imposing window. Then he flung Vince into the bookshelf nearby, the books raining down on him as he fell to the floor.

"Idiot!" Dedalia shouted. "We need to work together!"

"Time to kill this son of a bitch!" Derek declared.

Derek, Roy, and Dedalia ran at the Lieutenant, while Phil hung back to rummage through his jacket to find the proper gun for the situation. The Lieutenant wasn't impressed by all the people rushing him. He lazily took out his staff and expanded it to its full size. Then he began whirling it in the air in front of him.

"Go ahead and gimme your best shot," he taunted, smiling.

He swung the staff at the three of them. Roy and Dedalia ducked underneath it, while Derek lifted his arm to guard the blow. He hadn't ducked his head fast enough, the impact knocking him onto the floor. Then the Lieutenant jabbed Roy in the foot, causing him to stumble forward. Then he swung the staff up into his face before Roy could regain his bearings. The staff smacked him in the face, flipping him onto the floor.

The Lieutenant swung the staff at Dedalia's face, and she caught it in her hand. She grinned at him. "Surely, you can do better than that."

He flung her off the staff, and she slammed against the ceiling. As she fell back to the floor, he swung the staff into her, and she was thrown across the room. She smashed against a wall and slid to the floor. As she fell unconscious to the floor, a crater had formed on the surface of the wall.

Phil had freed a shotgun from the confines of his jacket and pumped a shell into it. "Hey, fuckface!"

The Lieutenant turned towards him with an unamused look on his face. Phil shot the Lieutenant in the chest, he staggered back as Phil pumped another shell into his gun. The Lieutenant began twirling his staff at a rapid rate as Phil shot shell after shell into the spinning staff. Still, the vortex of air he created deflected each shell. Phil began inching towards the Lieutenant spinning his staff, hoping getting closer to him would somehow help.

But he made the wrong move. He got too close, and the Lieutenant knocked the gun out of his hand in a quick motion with his staff. Then he spun the staff around and smacked Phil in the face. The Lieutenant onto the floor, making him slide into a wall.

Derek was now on his feet and was wandering over to the Lieutenant. "You'll have to hit harder than that, Asshat," he said.

"You people just don't stay down, do you?" the Lieutenant inquired.

"Not when something important is on the line," Derek responded. He ran to the Lieutenant and the staff thrust into his chest with a swift strike. He was flung into the bookcase next to Vince.

Vince had crawled out of the books and had gotten to his feet. He freed the rod from his back and pressed the button to release the blades of his axe from the end. "You have caused enough suffering."

Then he ran toward the Lieutenant and brought his axe down at him. The Lieutenant lifted his staff up to meet the axe. Vince pressed down on the staff with as much strength as he could.

"Are you so eager to throw your life away?" the Lieutenant asked.

"I will do whatever it takes," Vince strained. "I will never stop."

He struggled as the Lieutenant began pushing back against his axe. He wouldn't be able to keep him distracted much longer. He felt that Darkus had something in mind, but he wasn't sure what it was. Hopefully he made his move soon.

"I made a promise to his brother," Vince declared. "The very man you should fear. The legendary Demon Slayer, Michael Darsetts."

"Family," the Lieutenant ridiculed. "Disgusting. His brother may be the bane of our existence, but now it means nothing. Michael Darsetts is dead."

"Is that really what you think?"

"What do you mean?"

"You really think that Michael Darsetts is dead?" Vince asked him

"Of course he is," the Lieutenant assured him confidently.

"Last I heard, he was captured."

"Being captured by that demon means he is as good as dead."

255

"But what if he escapes and finds you?" Vince disputed.

"Enough!" the Lieutenant ordered.

He broke through Vince's defenses, sending his axe spinning onto the floor. The staff slapped Vince in the face and threw him onto the floor. He rolled towards the window but stopped right next to it. He seemed to be luckier than he had realized.

The Lieutenant advanced towards Dedalia as she slowly was regaining consciousness. He whirled the staff lazily as he approached her and stopped in front of her. He bent down so that she could see his face more clearly.

"All of you have lost," he said, with a sinister grin. "Any message you would like to give before I blot out all that you hold dear? I will start with your weak and feeble friends."

Darkus had finally gotten to his feet. He nodded at her and was making his way over to the Lieutenant from behind. She was in a daze as she regained consciousness. But she noticed Darkus' nod as soon as he gave it. This was when she knew that everything was about to be turned around. She smiled at him.

"Enjoy your trip, asshole," she said, smiling.

"What?" he asked, surprised.

He stood up and shook the thought out of his mind. Then he reared the staff back. He was ready to finish her by thrusting his staff through her chest. But then something happened that he hadn't expected. Darkus grabbed the end of the staff. He tried to jab her and felt a powerful force stopping him. He glanced behind him and saw Darkus standing there with a smile on his face.

"Have a nice flight," he said with a smirk.

He hurled the Lieutenant off the staff, and the Immortal smashed through the crimson window overlooking the Void below. There was a clatter as Darkus dropped the staff onto the floor and the Lieutenant tumbled down towards the bridge below.

"Get him, Dedalia!" Darkus shouted. "While you still have the chance!"

She didn't need to be told twice. She stood up and unstrapped the rod from her back, pressing the button to release the tip of her spear. Then she ran out of the tower and vaulted herself into the air. She soared down towards the Lieutenant still falling. She lined up the spear with his body as they descended. Anger flooded her eyes as she got closer and closer to him.

The Lieutenant knew there wasn't anything he could do to escape her. So, he just braced himself for what was to come. Her spear pierced through his chest just before they crashed onto the stone bridge. The bridge shook vehemently as they slammed against it and the spear pierced through his back. He coughed up black blood all over himself.

Dedalia had thought that he was finished, and they could move on. They would finally be able to begin the hunt for the one who had put them all through this. However, the sight of him smiling through his bloodied face shook her newly found confidence. At first, she didn't understand, but then she saw his skin turn pale grey. Then she understood clearly. He was doing the same thing that the Sergeant did before he had become the towering demon, Parallax.

She pried her spear free of his chest and began slowly stepping backward. He rose to his feet, and the Lieutenant slowly began to change into something else entirely.

CHAPTER 29

ALIOTH

The Lieutenant mutated into a rather horrific-looking creature. His skin became gray and scaly. Spikes sprouted all over his body and two jagged horns formed on top of his head. He stood a foot taller than Vince. He was rather small compared to a demon like Parallax. He looked down at Dedalia with eyes of crimson.

"That feels so much better!" he exclaimed. "I must thank you, Dedalia. Without your help, I would have never been freed from that pathetic vessel!"

"No problem," she said with a tinge of sarcasm.

She wasn't sure what to do in this situation. She could have probably taken him, but there were still many things to consider. For one, she was all alone. Furthermore, they were standing on a bridge over the never-ending Void. One wrong step and she would not just be dead; she would be erased from existence.

The demon looked deeply into her eyes. It made her feel rather uncomfortable.

"So, who exactly are you?" she asked him. "I know you are not the Lieutenant. I'm sure he is dead, and you are the monster that was within."

"Very good, Dedalia. I am the monster within. I am Alioth. One of three of the Commander's most respected demons."

"The Commander? Is he the one behind all of this?"

"Perhaps I have said too much. Not that it will matter. You and your friends will die in this place."

Darkus had witnessed everything down below in horror. He had urged her to chase him down there. He had no idea a demon had been hiding within him. Now she was there facing the demon completely by herself, and he had told her to do so. He needed to get himself down there.

He walked over to the statue head of a demon nearby. It was sitting peacefully on a pedestal. He pressed his hand in between the horns and activated a secret button. A voice echoed through the room.

"Preparing for descent," a man's pleasant voice announced.

He would join Dedalia in the fight, and if he failed at least the others would join to finish it. He ran towards the broken window. He leaped out of the tower as the floor began to tremble. Darkus lined himself up with the demon. This would be one way to make an entrance, but at least he would know that Dedalia would have the backup she needs.

"Descending," the man's pleasant voice said, reverberating through the tower.

The floor jerked as it began descending to the bottom of the tower. Roy slowly opened his eyes as the floor seemed to slowly dip down to the bottom of the tower. He didn't see the Lieutenant anywhere at least, so that may be a good sign. Maybe they got him? Somehow that didn't feel right. Parallax didn't go down that easily. He was sure that it would be similar for whatever demon hid away within the Lieutenant.

"You're nothing more than another demon to be put in his place," Dedalia said glaring up at Alioth. She wasn't scared of him as the demon wished, but she still needed to be careful in a place like this.

"Your overbearing confidence is misplaced," Alioth said. "No matter, I will strike you down before you have the chance to use your feeble little stick."

Dedalia assumed a stance ready to stab him at any given moment. He confidently moved towards her. Then Darkus crashed into him, and the two of them slid down the surface of the shabby stone bridge. They stopped at the edge of the bridge. The spikes on the demon had scratched Darkus' body, and he felt a searing pain emanating through his body. He stared down into the emptiness of the Void below him. He knew full well that the Void was eagerly awaiting his descent. The darkness longed for him, but he needed to stay afloat and live another day. However, he hadn't expected to get that close to the Void in the first place. The bridge seemed narrower than he had anticipated. He couldn't help but wonder if this was really a good idea after all.

"Darkus?!" Dedalia shouted. "Are you fucking insane?!"

"Maybe just a little," he said, holding his fingers up in the air to match it.

"An impressive entrance," Alioth applauded. "But the Void calls for you."

He pushed Darkus into the air in a rather impressive display of power. Darkus smashed through a large, jagged piece of rubble and went tumbling down towards the Void.

"Darkus!" Dedalia screamed.

Alioth got up and cracked his neck. "Well, that was something. Now where were we?"

Dedalia became blinded by her overwhelming rage and ran at him.

"How predictable," he said indifferently. "Will you offer your life to the Void as well? After such a noble sacrifice from your dear and precious brother?"

"Shut the fuck up!"

"My silence won't change a thing. Your fate will remain the same."

She screamed in frustration as she lunged the spear at the demon's face. He jerked his head out of the way and grabbed the handle of the spear. He yanked the weapon out of her hands and tossed it into the Void.

"You bastard!" she screamed.

He jabbed his claws into her shoulders and lifted her up so that her face was level with his own. She winced in pain as she was held aloft, the blood trailing down her arms.

"Do you wish to join your brother in the Void?" he asked. "Or will you help your precious friends? This is the choice I will leave you."

"Get your fucking claws off me!" she screamed.

"That is your choice then."

He ripped his claws out of her flesh, and she was thrown into the Void. He began making his way back towards the tower.

"Now how shall I destroy the others?" he wondered.

Alioth saw the front door burst open as the heroes charged through it. Phil was leading them out onto the bridge with the others behind him. He was cradling a bazooka on his shoulder.

"Why do they never quit?" Alioth sighed.

Phil fired the rocket towards him. Alioth didn't even try to dodge it. He didn't have as much space to navigate with the thin structure of the bridge. He knew it was inevitable. He let the rocket slam into his chest, and the explosion threw him off his feet. He fell over the edge and sunk his claws into the side of the bridge. He also knew the explosion wouldn't be enough to kill him due to his status as a high-ranking demon. However, the blast sure did pack more of a punch than he would have liked.

He would give them a moment of hope before he climbed back up. Still, the pain he endured was more severe than he had imagined. He slowly climbed back up to the top of the bridge. He felt a large burn on his chest where the blast had struck him.

They analyzed the wreckage in front of them. There was burning rubble in place where Alioth had been standing. He was nowhere to be seen. They cautiously made their way over to where the fire was flickering. They needed to make sure that he was in fact dead.

They didn't reach the fire before Alioth finished climbing back onto the bridge. He stood up and straightened his back. A large burn had already scarred in the center of his chest from the blow the rocket had caused.

"That's definitely gonna scar," he groaned.

They all looked at him in disbelief. He should have died, but somehow, he survived. Demons of his caliber were much harder to kill than a regular demon, it seemed.

"Shoot the son of a bitch!" Derek shouted. "Don't just stare at him!"

Nobody needed to be told a second time. They brought out their guns and opened fire on the spiky demon. Most of the bullets seemed to whizz right past him, while some managed to dig into his rough, scaly skin. Still other shots simply ricocheted off the spikes lining his body. Roy fired off his pistol, Vince shot his machine gun, while Derek fired upon him with a pistol in each hand.

Phil hung back while they all kept Alioth busy. Alioth endured the biting of the bullets, but still he continued towards them. Phil got what he had wanted. He produced a rifle and took a deep breath as he aimed it up at Alioth's face. He fired the rifle, and the bullet zipped through his right horn. It shattered instantly, and the demon's calm demeanor changed at once.

It seemed a switch went off in Alioth's brain. Demons are very attached to their horns after all. "Enough games! I will tear all of you fuckers apart!"

"He's fucking lost it," Roy observed. "Hope you got a plan, Phil."

"Working on it," he promised.

They would need to do something fast. Alioth appeared to be getting angrier by the second. Phil didn't have a plan, but he hoped that Roy would have at least some form of comfort in knowing that he did. He had really been banking on the horn exploding, causing more damage to the demon than it did. It looked like they would have to wing it. Phil stepped in front of the others to get a better vantage point on the encroaching demon.

***

Darkus had crashed into a large floating platform after his fall toward the Void. He was surprised it hadn't shattered from the impact. He got up and saw that it had cracked, but not much else. He heard Dedalia screaming above him, and he was reminded of what had happened. He had been forced to abandon her. Maybe his plan wasn't as good as he had anticipated, as now she was fighting the demon on her lonesome once again. He was starting to feel rather useless in this battle.

Her spear tumbled down toward him. It was at that moment he knew that the fight wasn't going well. He caught the spear in his hand. He strapped it alongside his axe just to make sure it was safe until he was able to return it to her. Then he saw her falling towards him.

"Shit!" he exclaimed.

It was just as he had feared. He ran towards to meet her at the edge of the platform. She crashed into him, and the two were knocked into the center of the platform. He heard the platform crack even further beneath him and knew that it wouldn't be able to withstand much more abuse. He would have to do something soon, or they both would fall into the Void. No more lucky moments. Just embracing the nothingness that only the Void could offer. He had an idea of what to do but knew she wouldn't like it. However, there was little choice. Not if she wanted to help her friends.

"Darkus?" she asked woozily. "We gotta stop running into each other like this."

He chuckled at her and wished he had more time with her. But it seemed this is not what fate had in store for them. He wasn't sure what would happen to him. He may even be erased from existence. Dedalia crawled off

Darkus and got back to her feet. She clasped his hand, and they helped each other onto their feet.

"Are we dead?" she asked.

"Not yet," Darkus replied.

"How are we alive?"

"Dumb luck," he remarked. "If not for this platform that just happened to be here, the Void would have devoured us, ceasing our very existence."

"What now?" she asked.

"You're going to rejoin your friends and kill that bastard."

Dedalia could tell that something was wrong. It was in Darkus' eyes. There was something that he wasn't telling her.

"What about you, Darkus?" she asked.

"Don't worry about me," he said quietly.

She could tell that this was painful for him, but he was doing his best to hide it. Still, she saw right through him just as she always did.

"If everything goes to shit, you won't remember me anyway," he said sadly. His voice strained as he said this, but he continued to put on his façade of everything being fine.

She jabbed him in the chest and the platform that they were standing on shook rather violently. More cracks appeared beneath their feet.

"You're not sacrificing yourself!" she shouted, feeling her emotions spiraling out of control.

"I am," he said plainly. "You and I both know you're more important. So, I will take the fall for the both of us, and you will live."

"Asshole," she shot at him angrily.

The platform was already starting to fall apart all around them.

"It's now or never, Dedalia," he told her.

"I know," she said through her teary eyes. "It just feels like I just got you back in my life, and I already have to leave you behind."

"You know it'll be better to have you up there than me."

"You're right. Just do it."

He handed her spear with the tip still protruded out, ready to pierce its next foe. Then she grabbed the shaft of her spear shakily. She took a deep breath as Darkus grabbed the back of her jacket and lifted her into the air. He reared her back and got ready to launch her back up onto the bridge. He tried to ignore the tears welling up in his eyes. This was harder than he thought it would be. But it still had to be done.

***

Alioth had reached Phil, and the bullets ricocheted off the spikes on his body. Phil knew that shooting him this close would be foolish, so he decided to smack him with the rifle he was holding. The gun stuck to a spike on the demon's arm.

"Well shit," he said, disappointed.

Alioth curled his hand around Phil's throat and brought him into the air. The constant flurry of bullets from his friends did little to the demon. The demon's grip tightened, forcing him to gasp for air. He was sure he was about to die here. His friends couldn't do much to help either. Their guns were the most effective weapon they had against a demon such as him. But the bullets just bounced his spikes.

"You will pay dearly for demolishing my horn!" he shouted in his face. Phil was disgusted by the spit from the demon now trailing down his face.

"You say you're different from the Lieutenant," Phil said straining. "But I don't see much of a difference."

***

Darkus found the right angle to launch Dedalia at the demon above them.

"Give the bastard hell, sister," he ordered.

"You know I will," she said determined.

Then he hurled her up towards the bridge. The platform crumbled beneath Darkus' feet. He fell deeper into the Void, sure that this would be his end. Dedalia heard the demon shrieking in rage. She couldn't help but wonder what irritating squeal he would release when she made her presence known.

"Alioth!" she screamed.

He turned towards the sudden sound, and Dedalia crashed into him. Her spear burst through his chest. They stumbled backwards and the demon was thrown onto his back. She watched as Phil was freed from the demon's grip and rolled off the edge of the bridge. She vaulted herself off the demon and ran to help him. She clasped his hand but began sliding off the bridge herself.

Vince tossed his gun aside and ran after her. He grabbed her ankles before she had fallen off the bridge completely. He struggled to bring them both back up. Roy put down his gun and lay down next to Vince to help him pull the two of them up. After the two of them strained to bring them both up, they took a moment to catch their breath. They were panting heavily.

"You're all insane," Vince panted.

"You're the one who signed up for this shit," Dedalia remarked.

They heard laughing from behind them. Derek stood next to the decomposing demon, pointing his pistols at him. The demon was laughing maniacally as his body crumbled into a pathetic pile of ash.

"You're all dead," the demon cackled. "Once the General. Finds out."

At that, the rest of his body fell into the pile of ash. Dedalia gripped the handle of her spear now sticking out of the pile of ash and pulled it free. The flakes of ash whisked around them. She retracted the tip of the spear and slipped it back into the holster on her back.

"Another demon down," she said.

"Are all the Immortals hiding demons like this?" Roy asked.

"No," Vince explained. "Just the really powerful ones."

"How many should we expect?" he asked.

"Even I don't know that," Vince replied.

"Well, then I guess we're just getting started."

"It's going to be a long road ahead," Vince told him.

"That's alright. I'll keep walking it well after I kill the bastard who murdered my wife."

"That's good."

"So, you guys done trying to fall into the Void now or what?" Derek chipped in.

"Wasn't exactly on my bucket list," Phil groaned.

"I found something good in this pile of shit," he said, looking down into the ashy remains of Alioth.

Roy and the others wandered over to him. They looked closely at the small object in his hand.

"What is it?" Roy asked.

"Dunno but take a good look at it," Derek replied, skimming it over in his hand.

Roy grabbed it from Derek's hand and saw that it looked like a flash drive. But written on it was a single word. General. They have finally found something that would lead them to who they had been looking for all this time. They would at last reach the monster they had been searching for this whole time. Roy would finally have his chance at vengeance. Just the thought seemed to put his mind at ease.

"Let's go put this motherfucker in his place," he declared.

"Couldn't agree more," Derek said, smiling.

They returned to the car with Roy and Vince in front. This was it. He finally had the chance to bring his fight to the son of a bitch who stole his better life away from him. Roy plugged the flash drive into the slot beneath the console's screen. The General's face flooded onto the screen. At least they knew that they were on the right track.

"Calculating location of the General," Dina's voice said.

This really was it. They will be coming for the General. The only thing they would have to worry about now would be the repercussions of their actions.

"Who's ready to kill this bastard?" Roy asked.

He tapped the General's face on the screen, and the image changed. It now had become a GPS showing the General's location. His days are numbered. They were coming. The car turned around and went back to the wall they had used to enter this freaky place. It slid apart for them just as it had when they entered, and they continued down the streets of New York as they made their way to where the General was hidden.

CHAPTER 30

THE PORTAL

Darkus fell towards the nothingness beneath, knowing full well that once darkness embraced him, he would no longer exist in anyone's world. He inched closer and felt his nervousness crawl forth as the Void seemed to reach up for him. He crashed through a chunk of rubble which matched his own size. Then, he tumbled downwards, gaining speed as he plummeted to his doom.

He smashed through the debris seemingly without end. He was desperate to reach the bottom and end his misery. But then he saw something he hadn't expected in the dreary darkness that came ever closer. It appeared to be a glowing light below him. Then a platform appeared beneath him. He slammed against it with his back facing the sky above.

Groggily, he looked over at the thing producing the brilliant light and saw it seemed to be a swirling circle with a room visible in its center. The platform must have emerged from this thing. He was sure it had to be some sort of portal, but he couldn't be sure. Among all the weird things he had encountered in his life, this didn't seem too crazy. The platform glided him back towards the portal he was staring at.

"In we go, then," he said still unsure of the glowing circle.

He hoped it would take him someplace where the never-ending dangers of the Void couldn't reach him. He had enough punishment physically and mentally for one lifetime.

The platform docked itself alongside a cavern floor. It seemed like a boat docking at a pier. He looked around the cave and had to admire its setup. It was an open cave, but it had been set up so that someone could live here comfortably. He looked up and saw that this could have been a very accurate assumption.

A couch was floating in the center of the cave, and sitting on it, reclined comfortably, was a man with long, brown hair. His long brown, wavy hair seemed to flow behind him, and his face was clean shaven. He was wearing a bathrobe tinted in an azure shade.

Darkus was in disbelief. He didn't even know what to say. "Who the hell are you? What is this place?"

That's all he could manage in his own confusion. The man perched on his floating couch, gazed down upon him. He snapped his fingers, and the couch brought him back to the ground.

"My apologies," he apologized. "I forget most people aren't accustomed to seeing such things."

Darkus climbed off the platform and saw he hadn't even attempted to sit up. The whole situation was just bizarre. "You didn't answer my questions."

"You're right," he replied, unconcerned. "I'm the Portalkeeper. And I have just saved your life. You should be a little more grateful."

"Sorry, I don't know you."

"I would imagine not. There's a select few even among the Immortals who know of me."

The Portalkeeper stood up off the couch rather awkwardly and he staggered towards Darkus in a drunken stance. He regained his composure and shook the weird feeling off.

"Are you alright?" Darkus asked, lifting an eyebrow suspiciously.

"I know this may seem strange, but I assure you that I am fine. I haven't been on my actual feet in quite some time. I just need to make a slight adjustment."

"Why did you even save me?"

"It's simple. The prince, Alciel, wishes for you to live. You have yet to serve your purpose."

Darkus didn't want to believe what he was hearing. The only reason that he hadn't been devoured by the Void is because someone else had banked on his survival.

"How do you know the prince?" he asked, surprised.

"That's not important," the Portalkeeper said rather blatantly.

He stepped towards Darkus and nearly fell against him. He gripped Darkus' shirt to regain his balance.

"It's been too long since I've gotten off that couch," he said, sounding fatigued. "Feels weird."

"Get to the point."

"Right, right. So pushy. We need you to go back up to that bridge and die."

Darkus pushed him away, nearly knocking him over.

"What?!" he asked in shock.

"I never was good at explaining things," the Portalkeeper replied. "You see, the Maker will be on his way here soon, and we need you to die by his hand."

"I'm not following," Darkus replied. "You saved me just so I could be killed by someone else?"

"Not **dead**, dead. You just need to be convincing."

"You want me to play dead?"

"We need both the Immortals and Roy to think you're dead," the Portalkeeper said, sounding rather serious. "Everything is riding on this."

"They should already think I am dead," Darkus assured him.

"We need to make sure. When the time comes, it will make sense. I imagine right now it does not."

"I have never been more confused."

"Excellent."

Darkus glared at him quizzically. Something was off with this guy. But he had no choice but to trust him.

"So, if I go back up to this bridge, what then?" Darkus asked.

"The Maker will arrive and stab you," he said clearly.

"That sounds fun."

"Don't worry. You'll be fine."

The more this man spoke, the less sense that everything made. He seemed to sense Darkus' skepticism. He placed a hand on his shoulder. "I know that this may seem to be a bit much, but you need to trust me. If you can trust in me, then you can trust in your prince."

Darkus sighed. All the times that he had met Alciel, he had never given him a reason not to trust him. The prince is a stand-up guy. But with everything going on, he was a little uneasy. There was a chance that the Maker **actually** kills him.

"How do you know all this?" Darkus asked.

"In due time, Darkus, everything will be explained," he said mysteriously. "But for now, you need to ask where your loyalties lie. Are they with Barbatos or Alciel? That will decide the outcome of your fate in this moment."

Darkus pondered what he was telling him. The Portalkeeper went from laid-back to deadly serious as he studied Darkus' expression. Darkus didn't know how to fathom it. The way it sounded, the king and prince were preparing to go against each other. He would have to choose which side to support. Roy and the mortals or Barbatos and the Immortals. He knew full well that Dedalia would be on the side of the mortals. If he wished for her success, he would have to side with Alciel.

He knew his choice before he even said it. "I'll side with Alciel."

"Good," the Portalkeeper smiled at him. His odd demeanor seemed to come back into play. "Step onto the platform that brought you here."

Darkus did as he was bid. Then the platform slid back out through the portal and slowly began to ascend back to the bridge. The ascent back to the bridge felt much shorter than his painful descent down. He reached the bridge in no time at all. Then he stepped onto the bridge. The platform next to him crumbled and fell into the depths of the Void.

He felt a chill, and the hair on the back of his neck stood up on edge. Something or **someone** was coming, and they were filled with rage. It was probably the Maker that the Portalkeeper had warned him about. If he wished to please Alciel, he would have to pull this off just right.

CHAPTER 31

A NEW FOE

In the midst of a desert far from the tower where Roy and his friends had been triumphant in their battle against the Lieutenant sat an arena. The arena was a massive structure that brought demons from across the planet to enjoy spectacles that could only happen here.

The Chaosbringer trudged through the desert towards the arena. He could teleport, but it was easier when he could see where it was that he needed to go. The walls of the structure made it difficult to reach the place where the Maker sat comfortably. Still, the heat in this place was more intense than he had anticipated. He pulled back his hood and wiped the sweat from his brow. This was just another small step in his grand plan.

He entered through one of the open archways and made his way down the curved hallways. Small, scrawny demons wandered past him constantly. They were rather squeamish in nature. They looked up at him with small, beady eyes. Upon seeing him, they would quicken their pace. Their scaly skin was filthy, but that would be expected of them in a place like this. These smaller demons are known as Imps. They are the lowest form of demon. Nothing more than scapegoats among the army.

In a pair of cells down the hall from where the Chaosbringer is walking lay two cages side by side. Each cell held two prisoners. They were lying opposite from one another. The one on the right, held a large muscular man and a more average-looking man.

The large man had spiked red hair and a goatee encircling his mouth, matching the crimson color of the hair on his head. He wasn't wearing a shirt, showing off his bulging muscles. He wore short armor that reached for his knees. He looked like he must be some kind of barbarian. Didn't really fit in a modern setting. A large battle hammer was leaning against the wall next to him. He lay back on an uncomfortable bed with his arms folded across his chest.

The other man wore a long jacket and seemed to be prim and proper in comparison to the one he shared the cell with. He wore an eyepatch over his right eye and his brown hair is spiked in the front. A scar stretched across the same eye and reached for his cheek. A spear sat against the wall next to him, the tips curled into what looked like a pair of horns.

In the other cell across the hall, there was a woman in a hooded robe. The robe seemed to be frayed, barely still intact. However, the hood did a bad job at hiding the pointed ears of an elf. She sat against the wall with her face concealed by the shadow of her hood. A bow sat next to her. It was ancient in appearance with strange glyphs etched onto it. Even the bowstring seemed to glow in a radiant light.

A man sat across from her, leaning against the wall with his head hung low. His long, blonde hair was disheveled, and his thick beard was unkempt. He appeared to be lost in thought. He was wearing a brown, dusty jacket and torn jeans. A sword lay next to him. It seemed to glow with a brightly lit blue aura.

The Chaosbringer made his way in between their cells, catching the muscular man's desperate attention. The red-haired man practically vaulted off the bed and gripped the bars. His eyes looked at the Chaosbringer pleadingly as he passed.

"C'mon, man," the muscular man pleaded. "Get us out of here."

The Chaosbringer stopped for a moment and turned towards him. He seemed to look him up and down. "You're lucky you're behind those bars. If it had been up to me, you all would have been executed on the spot."

Then he continued onward, and the red-haired man slunk back onto the bed. He looked defeated. There seemed to be no way out of this place. "What a dick."

"You are too trusting, Vulcan," the man sitting across from him said.

He seemed to have accepted the fact that they weren't getting out of here anytime soon. He was just waiting for their imprisoners to let them out. He knew that was the only way they would be leaving their cell.

"I try not to judge people by how they present themselves, Dragos," Vulcan replied.

He sighed. His optimistic nature often led him to his own personal turmoil. He felt as if people often walked all over him. He is just a big man with an even bigger heart.

The hooded woman lifted her head and faced the other cell. She had been listening to the whole thing, but she didn't agree with Vulcan's desperation.

"You really should," she said coldly. "That man looked like one of the least trustworthy people that have ever come through here."

"I know," he sighed. "But I can't stand being trapped in this tiny room, Aeolia. I need to get the hell outta here."

"Have you noticed just how many demons are in this forsaken place?" she asked, frustratedly. "The whole fucking army is here! Even if you somehow get out of here, you will have to get through every single one of them!"

"It's alright, Aeolia," the man opposite her said. "At least this place has yet to break his spirit. Unlike the rest of us."

"You are too kind, Arthur."

"I know," Arthur replied. "It's one of my best qualities."

"Ha," Dragos grunted. "Your kindness will be your downfall."

"You may very well be right," he agreed.

***

The Chaosbringer had left the four prisoners behind him and marched towards a staircase that was protected by a pair of Archdemons. They stood as tall as him and nearly matched him in muscle.

"Chaosbringer," the demon on the right said. "To what do we owe the pleasure?"

He seemed to be as scared as the Imps had been before. He did have quite a reputation, so he wasn't overly surprised by this.

"I need to speak with the Maker," he told him.

279

"Go on ahead," the demon beckoned.

Then the two demons stepped aside, and he began climbing the twisting stairway.

It seemed he had been walking up the stairs for some time before he finally reached the top. Then he had to make his way down to the small enclosure that held the seats for the most influential figures in the arena. There were stone seats placed in the center of the enclosed area. The purpose of this place was to give the best view of the arena. It did live up to that expectation. Any fighters would appear to be directly in front of them.

A hunched and decrepit-looking demon approached him. He had a strange-looking sword wrapped in bandages strapped to his back. His horns curved back, resembling a ram. The demon appeared to be quite old. His gray beard sagged off his chin. He seemed to squint at the Chaosbringer as he walked towards him.

"We weren't told you were coming," he wheezed.

"That's because I didn't say that I was coming," he replied.

"You know my master doesn't like surprises."

"I know. But this time it is necessary, Pazuzu."

Pazuzu scowled in disapproval but stepped out of his way. The Chaosbringer noticed two men nestled in two chairs in the center of the room. One of them was bald and had the tattoo of a music note on the side of his head. He wore a long leather jacket that reached his ankles. He glanced over at the Chaosbringer and smirked to himself. He didn't know why he was here, but he was sure to enjoy the show.

The man sitting next to him was big and powerful. His long hair was grizzled and out of control. He has a scar in the shape of a Z etched on the front of his face. He is wearing a vest over a T-shirt with ragged jeans. He didn't seem to notice him, but that was fine.

The Chaosbringer wandered over to the two of them. The two of them were brothers. They were not a part of the Maker's employ but acted as mercenaries. However, being Immortal made their work a lot easier. They even preferred work given to them by the Maker.

"What brings you here, Kryptone?" he asked the bald man.

Kryptone turned and looked up at him, seemingly to study him. "What else?" he asked. "Waiting ever so patiently for more work."

The big man next to him whispered in his ear. "Do we know him?"

"Of course we do, Zigrone," Kryptone said, better to draw attention to him. "This is the Chaosbringer. Show some respect, bro."

"My bad," Zigrone apologized pathetically, looking up at the Chaosbringer.

The two of them were strange to say the least. "Don't worry about it," the Chaosbringer assured them. "As long as the two of you do good work, you have nothing to worry about."

Zigrone nodded at him, while Kryptone just smiled and shook his head.

"You're way too serious, man," Kryptone chuckled.

The Chaosbringer continued to the front of the space to see a man lying sprawled on a large chair. He slumped lazily onto the back of the chair. He has long hair that seemed to willow in the breeze. Or rather what little breeze there would be in the tiny area. He wore a loose, black robe. He looked up at the armored man approaching him. He rolled his eyes upon seeing him, knowing that soon he would be annoyed.

"Here we fucking go," he said, springing up on his feet.

He knew that he would be on his feet soon anyway. He usually was when talking to the Chaosbringer.

"I bring news, Maker," the Chaosbringer said.

"Yeah, what the hell is it?" he asked.

"You will need your army ready sooner than you thought."

"Is that right? Why is that?"

"Parallax and Alioth are dead," the Chaosbringer informed him. "It will only be a matter of time before Baelor is dead as well and the mortals will be marching on your doorstep."

"I'm not worried about that," the Maker said, unconcerned. "I have my monsters to protect me."

"That foolish notion is what will get you killed."

The Maker's brow furrowed. He seemed to be getting irritated. This was good. It was what the Chaosbringer had been hoping for. Now he just needed a little push.

"I don't remember asking your opinion, Chaosbringer!" he shot back.

"Just know that if you underestimate them, you're as good as dead."

"You seem to think rather highly of them. Should I be worried that this whole time you have been helping them?"

The Chaosbringer's face twisted into anger in an instant. He roughly grabbed the Maker's throat and lifted him up.

"You dare to insinuate that I would help the lowly mortals?!" he shouted furiously. "You ever make such an accusation such as that in my presence again and I will rip off your fucking head and make sure you never find it again!"

The Maker looked down at him with the color vanishing from his face. He was gasping for air. The Chaosbringer tossed him back into his chair. The Maker panted heavily as he stared at him. He had forgotten just how powerful he truly is.

"I only came here to help you," the Chaosbringer snarled. "If you would spit on my aid, I will instead make you wish for death. I'm very good at death, you know."

"Yeah, I get it," the Maker gasped.

"I have information on Darkus," he said, regaining his composure.

It was like a switch went off in the Maker's mind. He quickly sat up in his chair.

"Tell me more," he replied seriously. "I would gladly strike that asshole down."

A sinister smile stretched across the Chaosbringer's face. "He is currently wandering through Alioth's domain. If you leave now, you may even catch him before he joins Roy and his friends."

The Maker leapt onto his feet instantaneously. "You don't have to tell me twice. Be back in a second."

He bent down, and the wind swirled around him. Then he shot up into the sky like a rocket. Any stone that got in his way rained down in his place, and the Chaosbringer smiled even wider. The Maker rose up into the sky and scanned the horizon. There was a cliffside in the distance that hid Alioth's tower from onlookers of his desert. But he knew it was there. He would just have to fly over the cliff to reach the tower.

The Maker stretched his hands out in front of him and, like a jet, launched himself at the cliff. He soared through the sky with a murderous speed. He even outmatched the speed a jet would have been travelling at. Darkus wouldn't even see him coming.

***

Darkus had just stepped off his platform, and it had returned to the Void. The Maker descended in front of him. He slammed onto the bridge in front of him. His fist slammed into the stone face of the bridge, and he looked up at Darkus with blazing anger in his eyes.

Understanding dawned on Darkus's eyes. Everything that the Portalkeeper had told him is coming true. He wondered how he knew that this was going to happen, but he didn't have time to ponder it. The Maker was walking towards him, piercing his soul with an intense gaze. He remembered what the Portalkeeper had told him. He needed to die, and he had to make it convincing.

"Shit, it's you," he said, doing his best to sound surprised.

"Darkus," the Maker snarled. "Now that you aren't protected by Alioth, I finally have the chance to take you out once and for all. You will no longer be the pain in the ass you have always been."

"Just curious, why do you hate me so much?"

"You had the audacity to kill my pets during the battle against Chaos. You are lucky that I have been lenient all this time. Due to the meddling of Alioth, but now I can guarantee you will die and not come back to this world. I only hope the Void will be as cruel as I wish for it to be."

284

"You have so much hate. Try molding it into some-thing more productive."

"Stop treating me like your better than me!" the Maker shouted in his fury. "You are beneath me! And you always will be!"

The Maker stretched out his hand, and a dark energy swirled in front of him. It stretched out into a long shape, and he gripped the darkness. The energy dissipated, and in his hand was a sword. Darkus recognized that the sword was similar to those used by the mortals to defeat his kind. This didn't look good for him.

The Maker reared the sword back and readied to rush at his foe. Darkus couldn't help but feel nervous. The Portalkeeper said he wouldn't die, but he wasn't so sure. Still, he knew he needed to act.

"If you wish to reach the mortals, then you go through me, asshole," he taunted. He even lifted his hand in a bring it on gesture. This seemed to infuriate the Maker.

"Enough!" he screamed.

Then he ran at Darkus, ready to finish him. Darkus let him come. He needed to give him the impression that he would be dead. The Maker reached him, and he dodged a swing of the sword. But then the Maker plunged the sword into his chest. Darkus gasped and coughed up blood all over himself. The sword may have looked like one meant for slaying Immortals, but it was nothing more than a cheap copy. The one thing that the Maker was best at. Maybe this is what the Portalkeeper meant by the fact that he would live.

"Damn," Darkus gasped.

Then the Maker ripped the sword free of his body, causing him to stumble back. While Darkus was still woozy, the Maker launched a kick into his chest. The force knocked him off the edge of the bridge. He went tumbling down into the depths of the Void.

"Good riddance," the Maker said, gazing down at his falling body. "May the Void devour your soul."

The Maker flew back up into the sky and soared back to the comfy confines of his arena. He landed next to the Chaosbringer.

"It is done," he assured him. "Darkus won't be bothering us anymore."

"Good," the Chaosbringer grinned. "Then the next part of the plan will be simple. The mortals won't even see it coming."

They both smiled, savoring the fun that they were sure to have next. Roy had no idea, but the General he hunted so mercilessly was just the beginning. The beginning of his plunge into the unsettling darkness that only the Immortals could provide.

END